An Improper Courtship

Lords & Ladies of Mayfair

Laura Beers

Chapter One

England, 1813

Mr. Greydon Campden held a secret; a secret that could ruin him and his family. By night, he took his rightful place as the dutiful second son of an earl but, by day, he worked as a Bow Street Runner. He hadn't intended to lower himself to work, but it gave him a purpose. And heaven knows that he needed one.

He had always played second fiddle to his older brother, Phineas, the Viscount Rushcliffe, from the moment he was born. He was the spare, the afterthought. His birth was planned to ensure that their precious family legacy would continue for another generation. But as he grew older, he realized that he needed to carve out his own path, much to his family's chagrin.

The hackney jostled back and forth as Greydon returned from the docks. His plain brown clothing reeked, his boots were caked in mud, or at least what he hoped was mud, and he was looking forward to taking a nice, long bath. He had met with an informant by the River Thames, but he did not linger afterwards. No good came from visiting the docks. It was a lawless place and no one responded well to outsiders.

As the hackney came to a stop in front of his whitewashed townhouse, he reached his hand out of the window and opened the door. He stepped onto the pavement and went to pay the driver.

With a look of uncertainty on his face, the driver asked, "You sure this is where you want to be, Bloke?"

"I am sure," Greydon said as he stepped back.

The driver shrugged. "Suit yourself," he responded as he flicked the reins.

Greydon took no offense since he did not look the part of a gentleman, making him appear deucedly out of place in Mayfair. He would need to hurry inside before any of his prying neighbors might notice his unfashionable clothing.

He approached the main door and it was promptly opened by Davy. The heavy-set butler had been with his family ever since he was a child, and he had a pleasant disposition about him.

"Good evening, sir," Davy greeted as he opened the door wide. "I trust your errand was met with your satisfaction."

"It was, but I find that I am in desperate need of a bath."

Davy tipped his head. "I shall see to it." He paused as he knitted his brow. "Lord Pendle has been asking about you."

"That is surprising," Greydon muttered. His father seemed to care less and less about him now that his brother had gotten married. Which was fine by him.

"He is in the study," Davy shared.

Greydon knew it was best to get this over with. He had been at odds with his father since he started working as a Bow Street Runner nearly five years ago. His father thought it was beneath him and demanded that he find a more respectable profession. When he refused, his father threatened to disown him but had yet to make good on his promise.

He stepped into the study and saw his father was sitting at

2

his desk, as he usually was at this time of day. If he wasn't at the House of Lords, he was in this study working on the accounts. He did little else with his time, at least since his wife died a few years ago.

Time had been kind to his father. His full head of hair was mostly black with some white around the temples and the wrinkles on his face had not begun to deepen, making him appear much younger than he was. The earl had a commanding presence about him, but over time, it affected Greydon less. As he grew, his father's capacity to control him diminished.

"Father," Greydon said in the most cordial tone that he could muster up. They had stopped with the pleasantries long ago. It was easier that way. Trying to pretend that you have a relationship is exhausting and neither of them had time for that.

His father leaned back in his seat and pursed his lips. The earl's eyes held the usual contempt for him, but something was different about them. They appeared sad- almost. Was it even possible for his father to show such emotion?

"Good, you are finally home," his father hesitated, "and you look awful."

"Thank you for that." Not that he disagreed with his father. He knew he looked and smelled unpleasant, but being a Bow Street Runner meant that you went into rather unsavory conditions.

"Close the door," his father ordered. "I have something I need to discuss with you before word gets out."

Greydon did as he was instructed before he approached the desk.

His father held his gaze. "Your brother is dead. You are now my heir," he said in his usual no-nonsense voice. "I will need you to start becoming familiar with our accounts so you can do your duty to this family."

Greydon's mind spun at what his father had just revealed.

How had he said it so calmly, as if he were spouting one of his useless facts? Greydon had so many questions and he wasn't quite sure where to even begin.

He felt his legs grow weak and he went to sit down in an upholstered armchair. The ticking of the long clock timed the silence. "How did Phineas die?"

His father grimaced before saying, "You may as well know the truth since it will no doubt get out soon enough." He paused. "Phineas was murdered."

Greydon reared back. "*Murdered?!*" he asked in disbelief. He knew his brother had a terrible reputation, but he didn't think anyone wished him dead. "By whom?"

"His mistress, Lady Eugenie."

An image of a thin, lanky girl that he had known from his youth came to his mind. How had she managed to murder his brother? "I hadn't realized Phineas had taken Lady Eugenie as a mistress."

"Apparently so. I think we both know that he was rather fond of the ladies," his father said. "I thought marriage would rein him in, but I was wrong."

Greydon needed to know more details about the murder. "How did she kill him?"

"A knife was plunged into his heart," his father replied. "The coroner said that Lady Eugenie was found over the body with blood on her hands."

"A crime of passion," Greydon said. "Did she say why she did it?"

His father shook his head. "No, the coroner did not reveal that information."

Greydon's thoughts strayed towards Phineas' widow and what she must be going through right now. "I assume Harriet knows."

His father nodded. "She was notified earlier this morning, and I already had a doctor confirm that she is not increasing."

Greydon stared at his father in disbelief. He couldn't

believe that his father was so insensitive that he would subject his own daughter-in-law to such an invasive procedure after only learning of the death of her husband.

"That was a rather cruel thing for you to do, Father," he remarked.

His father looked uninterested or unconcerned by his remark. "It had to be done straightaway. I wouldn't wish for her to get pregnant with another man's child."

"Harriet wouldn't do something so despicable," Greydon said. "She has always acted with the epitome of grace."

"Women are emotional creatures and she might seek out another to comfort her during this difficult time," his father said.

"That is unfair of you to say."

His father shrugged one shoulder. "I am being pragmatic with our given situation."

Greydon rose from his seat and walked over to the window. He shouldn't be surprised by his father's distant demeanor when it came to Phineas' murder. When Greydon's mother died, his father reacted in a similar fashion, carrying on in a resolute manner. He had long suspected his father's heart had been irrevocably broken when his mother died, making him even more ornery over the years.

He had so many questions that he needed answered and he would start with the coroner. He wanted to ensure the case was strong so Lady Eugenie would pay for what she had done. A noose around her neck was no less than what she deserved.

Placing his hand on the window frame, he let out a sigh. He wasn't particularly close with his brother, but he never wished ill-will to fall upon him. He led his life and Phineas had led his, knowing they both had a different path. Phineas was the heir, the chosen one. Their father tended to have a soft spot towards Phineas and often overlooked his unruly behavior. Whereas nothing Greydon had ever done in life was good enough for his father.

His brother was a known rake. He generally spent his time in gambling halls and with his mistresses. His reputation was one of ill-repute, but he didn't care. He did what he wanted, when he wanted, and he was more concerned with himself than others. It had always been that way, though.

His father leaned forward in his chair. "I know this is sudden, but we must accept Phineas is dead and move on. You are my heir and are now known as the Viscount Rushcliffe. I will expect you to stop working as a Bow Street Runner since you have much to learn."

Greydon pushed off from the window and turned to face his father. He knew the man was callous in his approach, but did he not love his son enough to grieve him, even for a day?

His father continued. "I sent word to Helena, but I do hope she won't fall apart upon hearing the news."

"You sent a messenger to inform my sister that Phineas is dead?" Greydon asked. Did he care so little of his daughter? Helena was the spitting image of their mother and he often wondered if it was too painful for his father to look upon her.

"What would you have me do?" his father asked defiantly. "I am a busy man and I do not have time to run across Town."

"There are some things that are more important than work."

His father gave him a blank stare, as if he had never considered that possibility. "This 'work' has allowed you to live in the lap of luxury and I am proud of the fact that you will inherit a thriving estate."

"I am most grateful for that."

"Are you?" his father asked. "Because you have spent your time running around London looking like a commoner." His voice was gruff.

Greydon glanced down at his soiled clothes and hoped that this discussion wouldn't turn into an argument about his duty to this family. He didn't think he had the energy to fight with his father. He just wanted to step away and attempt to process what had happened to Phineas.

His father pushed back his chair and rose. "No doubt, the morning newssheets have caught wind of Phineas' death and we need to prepare ourselves for the scandal that will ensue."

"I care little about that," Greydon said.

"I'm afraid you have little choice in the matter now," his father responded. "We must be above reproach if we want this scandal to be short-lived."

When he didn't respond, his father pressed, "You must think about Helena. You don't want her name to be dragged through the mud during this difficult time."

Now his father wasn't playing fair. He knew that Greydon and Helena shared a special bond and he would do whatever it took to protect his younger sister. She was many years younger than him and he had always been fiercely protective of her.

Greydon clenched his jaw. "I do not want Helena's name to suffer."

"Of course you don't," his father said, pleased with himself. "Go rid yourself of those clothes and take a bath. Then the work shall begin."

"I would prefer to start tomorrow," Greydon said.

"For what purpose?" His father waved his hand over his desk. "We have so much that we need to see to."

Greydon frowned. "It can wait."

His father went to sit down at his desk. "I'm afraid it can't," he said. "Phineas was many things, but he knew his duty. Do you?" His words were demanding, which was coupled with his habitual expression of an arched and haughty lip.

He was a smart enough man to know what his father was trying to do. He was attempting to manipulate him into doing his will. But his father made a crucial error. Greydon had stopped caring what his father thought about him long ago. He was his own man, and he made his own decisions.

In a calm and collected voice, Greydon said, "I will begin after breakfast tomorrow."

His father huffed. "I hadn't taken you for someone that would shirk his responsibilities."

"No, Father, but I am going to take some time to grieve properly for Phineas," Greydon informed him. "At the least, he was my brother."

His father looked at him with a sort of contemptuous disfavor. "Suit yourself, but I will be here if you change your mind."

"I won't be changing my mind," Greydon said before turning to leave.

As he walked out of the study, his mind reeled with the fact that his brother had been murdered. He wanted answers-*no, he needed answers*- and he wouldn't rest until Lady Eugenie paid for what she had done.

It had been nearly three weeks and Lady Enid Longbourn could scarcely believe that she was back in her old bedchamber. It was just as she remembered. The purple-papered walls, the silk spring curtains that were fastened at the bottom, and the wardrobe that was made of a light rosewood. A settee sat at the edge of her bed and faced the hearth. In the gardens, just outside of her window, were lilac trees and their sweet fragrance drifted up to the open window on the morning wind.

This had been her bedchamber since she had outgrown the nursery. It held so many memories for her, good and bad, and she felt such happiness at being home, despite her father going out of his way to make her feel uncomfortable.

It was entirely her fault, though. She had eloped with John Longbourn, causing her father to disown her. But it wasn't long before she realized that she had made a terrible mistake. John was not who he claimed to be, and she was trapped in a cage of her own making. Only upon his death was she finally free of the abuse at his hand.

The bruises may be gone but not the memories of how she had gotten them. She didn't think that those would ever fade. She had endured much at his heavy hand but she had only fled when he started hitting their daughter, Marigold. That was something she could never abide.

A knock sounded at the door.

"Enter," Lady Enid said as she moved to sit up in bed.

The door opened and Alice stepped into the room. "Good morning, my lady," she greeted with her usual easy smile.

Enid returned her smile. "Good morning."

Alice had been her lady's maid before Enid had eloped with John, and she was more than happy to return to assist her now that she was home. She had red hair, freckles that dotted her cheeks and a smile that was infectious. Despite being near the same age, Enid felt much older than Alice due to her life experiences.

"You best hurry if you want to visit Marigold before breakfast," Alice said. "You know how your father is about you being late."

Enid tossed off the covers and put her legs over the side of the bed. "With any luck, my father has already left for the House of Lords."

"That is highly improbable."

Alice had a point. Father had decided that breakfast was to be a family affair. Everyone was required to attend, including Malcolm and Rosamond, who only recently got married. The meal was pleasant enough, but the conversation was usually stifled by her cantankerous father.

Enid rose and walked over to the wardrobe. She opened

the door and started thumbing through her pale-colored gowns. These were gowns for a debutante, not a widow. Perhaps she would use some of the inheritance she received from her great-aunt to commission new gowns.

Society dictated that she should mourn her husband by wearing black for a whole year, but she refused to do so. Her whole marriage had been a lie, and she didn't want to spend one more day pretending to be someone she wasn't.

She pulled out a blue gown and held it up. "This will do for today," she said before handing it off to Alice.

"Yes, my lady," Alice responded.

Enid walked over to the dressing table and picked up a brush. After she ran it through her brown tresses, she placed it down and went to twist her hair back into a tight chignon at the base of her neck.

Alice walked over and picked up the pins off the dressing table. As she handed them to Enid to secure the chignon in place, she said, "I wish you would let me style your hair."

"There is no need since I am perfectly capable of doing it on my own," Enid responded.

"Yes, but you are a lady."

Enid felt a need to correct her and rushed to say, "We both know that I am ruined." It was important for her that everyone knew she didn't have the grand illusions that things would go back to the way they were before she had eloped. She was different now, and she wasn't entirely sure it was for the better.

The only saving grace for her was that she had Marigold. She adored her one-year-old daughter and that was the only reason she never stopped fighting.

As Alice assisted her in dressing, she said, "You are still the daughter of an earl."

"Who disowned me."

"Yes, but he let you return home."

"Reluctantly," Enid reminded her.

Alice gave her a knowing look. "He could have said no, but he didn't."

"That was only because my brother threatened to take my mother and me and retire to our country estate," Enid said. "I daresay it was more about my mother leaving than me."

"You do have his grandchild."

Enid blew out a puff of air. "Yes, I do. But I don't think my father has visited Marigold once since we moved in a month ago."

"These things take time," Alice encouraged.

"I doubt it," Enid responded. She didn't want to be a naysayer, but she was trying to be realistic. Her father no more wanted her here than he wanted a rock in his boot. It meant little to him that Marigold was here.

Alice fastened the last button on her gown and took a step back. "I am of the mind that Lord Everton will come around."

"I do appreciate your optimism but I fear that it is in vain."

"We shall see," Alice responded, "but you must hurry if you want to stop by the nursery."

Enid didn't need to be told again. She departed from her bedchamber and walked down the corridor towards the nursery. She was almost there when the door opened and her mother slipped out. When she saw Enid, her mother put her finger up to her lips, indicating she should remain silent.

Her mother waved her forward as she stepped away from the door. "Marigold just went down for a nap," she informed her in a hushed voice.

"At this hour?"

"Yes, Marie said that she woke early when a bird hit the window," her mother replied.

Enid gave her mother a baffled look. "A bird hit the window?"

"Apparently so, and it woke Marigold up."

"That is odd."

Her mother nodded. "I won't disagree with you there."

With a longing glance at the nursery, Enid said, "I had been hoping to see Marigold before breakfast."

"Well, you will have to wait until after breakfast," her mother responded. "Shall we adjourn to the dining room?"

"I suppose so."

As they started walking towards the stairs, her mother said, "You don't seem too excited for breakfast."

"I'm not," she admitted. "Father does not want me here."

Her mother gave her an encouraging look. "It doesn't matter what your father wants because I want you here. And Marigold. She might be my favorite thing about you living here."

Enid smiled. "I am well aware by the amount of time you spend with Marigold."

"She is my granddaughter and I just adore her."

"Marigold is lucky to have you as a grandmother," Enid remarked, knowing she spoke true. Her mother doted on Marigold something fierce and it warmed her heart to see the affection between them.

They descended the stairs and she saw Osborne standing ever so vigilant in the entry hall. He tipped his head at them as they proceeded on to the dining room.

Once they arrived at the dining room, Enid let out a sigh of relief that her father had not yet arrived. She had only a few moments of reprieve before her father soundly insulted her. Or he ignored her. He rotated between the two, depending on his mood. She preferred the latter.

Enid sat down and murmured her thanks as a footman placed a plate of food in front of her.

She had just reached for her fork when her white-haired father stepped into the room and claimed his seat at the head of the table.

With the briefest of smiles, her father said, "Good morning, Diane."

"Good morning," her mother replied.

Any hint of emotion vanished from his expression as his eyes flickered towards her. "Enid," he said.

At least he acknowledged her today, she thought. "Good morning, Father."

A footman stepped forward and handed her father the newssheets. They all started eating in silence and Enid felt no need to force a conversation.

Her father glanced at the door and huffed. "Where are Malcolm and Rosamond?"

"I am sure they will be down soon," her mother replied. "You must be patient since they have only been married for a week now."

"They should have gone on a wedding tour and saved us from their obnoxious displays of love," her father grumbled.

"I think it is sweet," her mother said.

Enid took a bite of her eggs, knowing that her opinion would not be welcomed by her father. But she also found it sweet to be around a couple that was so obviously in love with one another. She had thought she had found that in John, but he had done a good job of hiding his true nature until they were married.

She had every right to be resentful about her past experiences with John, but she knew if she didn't leave her bitterness and hatred behind, he would still control a part of her from beyond the grave. And she didn't want to give him that power.

Malcolm stepped into the room with Rosamond on his arm. "Good morning, family," he said cheerfully.

They all replied in kind as Malcolm assisted Rosamond into her seat before he claimed the chair next to her. He reached for his napkin and draped it onto his lap.

"It is good of you to join us," her father said sardonically.

Malcolm exchanged a smile with his wife. "We both had a hard time getting out of bed this morning."

Her father did not appear amused by Malcolm's admission. "Spare us the details," he muttered as he brought the newssheets up in front of him.

Turning his attention towards Enid, Malcolm asked, "Would you care to join us for a ride through Hyde Park after breakfast?"

Her father interjected, "Absolutely not!"

No one appeared perturbed by her father's outburst and Malcolm continued. "It is still early so it shouldn't be terribly crowded."

Her father slammed his fist on the table. "Enid is not allowed to leave the townhouse, for any reason. I forbid it," he stated. "If anyone saw her, just think of the repercussions."

"George, it has been a month. Surely, you do not expect Enid to remain in the townhouse forever," her mother calmly said.

"I do," came his prompt reply.

"That would be terribly unfair to her," her mother remarked. "People will eventually discover that Enid has returned home."

Malcolm reached for his cup of tea as he asked, "Will you join us, Enid?"

Her father's nose flared slightly, a sure sign that he was growing more agitated by the moment. "Are you not hearing what I am saying?" he demanded. "No good will come out of Enid leaving this townhouse."

Placing his teacup back onto the saucer, Malcolm said, "I hear what you are saying, but I disagree with you. Enid needs to be free to live her life as she sees fit."

"Need I remind you that Enid is ruined?" her father asked.

"A ride through Hyde Park would hardly change that," Malcolm responded, "and the decision resides solely with Enid."

Enid knew what her brother was about. He was trying to help her by easing her back into high Society, but she had burned that bridge long ago. However, it would be nice to take a ride on her horse again, assuming her father hadn't gotten rid of her gelding.

Bringing a smile to her face, Enid said, "I think a ride sounds nice."

As her father scowled, Malcolm clasped his hands together. "Wonderful." He reached for Rosamond's hand. "Isn't that wonderful, dear?"

Rosamond nodded. "It is," she replied.

Her father muttered a few curse words under his breath as he brought the newssheets up. Enid had been worried about how Rosamond would respond to her father's disagreeable persona, but she had taken it in stride. Fortunately, Enid's father did not dare speak harshly to his daughter-in-law because it was her dowry that had saved their family from ruination.

"Is my horse still in the stables?" Enid inquired.

Malcolm bobbed his head. "Yes, it is right next to Rosamond's ugly horse."

Enid arched her eyebrow, surprised by her brother's callous remark. "That was rather an insensitive thing to say, Malcolm."

Rosamond laughed. "No, it is true. Bella is rather ugly, but I love her."

Her father lowered the newssheets and announced, "Lord Rushcliffe was murdered last night."

"Murdered?" Malcolm repeated back.

"Yes, Lady Eugenie Lancaster killed him," her father said.

Enid shifted towards her father. "Lady Eugenie?" she asked, hoping she had misheard. "That can't be. She wouldn't hurt anyone."

Rather than dismiss her, her father engaged her by saying, "Apparently, she was Lord Rushcliffe's mistress."

Stunned, Enid lowered her gaze to the table. Lady Eugenie had been her dear friend when they first came out together and she was beautiful and clever. Why would she ever lower herself to become a mistress to a known rakehell? It just didn't make sense to her. And for her to commit murder seemed even more far-fetched.

Her mother's concerned voice broke through her musings. "Are you all right, Enid?"

"I am," she replied, bringing her gaze up. "I just can't believe Lady Eugenie would do such a terrible thing. It goes against everything I thought I knew about her."

Her father scoffed. "People may hide their true natures for a time, but eventually the truth always comes out."

"I am well aware of people hiding their true natures, but I do not believe that is the case with Lady Eugenie," Enid said.

Shoving back his chair, her father stated, "I don't have time for a philosophical debate. I am needed at the House of Lords."

Enid watched her father walk out of the dining room as her mind reeled with what she had been told. She still couldn't believe that Lady Eugenie was a murderer, and, frankly, she refused to believe it.

"I hadn't realized you were so close with Lady Eugenie," Malcolm said, eyeing her closely.

"Yes, we came out together, but she was my only friend that didn't turn her back on me after I eloped with John," Enid shared. "I wasn't welcome in her townhouse since her guardian forbade it, mind you, but we wrote to one another. I always looked forward to receiving her letters."

Rosamond's eyes held compassion as she said, "Some people never know what they are capable of until they are put into a terrible position."

"I understand, but Lady Eugenie wouldn't have murdered Lord Rushcliffe. I am sure of it," Enid pressed.

Malcolm pushed back his chair and rose. "If that is the

case, she will be exonerated in a court of law," he said with a glance at the window. "We should depart for our ride before it gets too late."

Enid removed her napkin from her lap and placed it on the table before rising. She refused to turn her back on Lady Eugenie, but what could she do to help her?

Chapter Two

Greydon reined in his horse in Hyde Park and stared out at the Serpentine River. His heart was heavy, and he suspected it would be that way for some time. He had been up most of the evening, dwelling on Phineas, and wondering what he could have done differently with his brother.

He did not condone his brother's way of life, and it was a great source of tension between them. It had just made sense for them to avoid one another, but now he regretted taking the easy path. He should have tried to make peace with Phineas. Now he would never have the chance to make amends. His brother was gone, and so many things were left unsaid between them.

His pride had won out and it had cost him greatly. It was just one of the many regrets that he would be forced to live with.

With a heavy sigh, Greydon knew his future looked bleak. He was the second son, the one who was free to carve his own path, but everything changed the moment his brother died, making him an heir to an earldom. Him. A man that worked as a Bow Street Runner to satisfy the gnawing guilt that he felt every single day for the loss of his friend at the hands of ruffians. His friend who he had failed to help. It was only because of him that Matthew was dead. If he hadn't fought with the ruffians, his friend would still be alive. His blasted pride had gotten in the way... again.

As he tightened the reins in his hand, he knew he didn't want to be confined to a desk, looking over the accounts, and dealing with the mundane tasks that came with the title. He wanted to solve crimes and help others during their times of need. It filled him with a sense of purpose.

But that life was over.

He saw three riders approaching in the distance. He immediately recognized Lady Enid Longbourn as she rode alongside her brother, Lord Brentwood, and his wife. He would recognize Lady Enid anywhere. She haunted his thoughts and invaded his dreams, but she had no idea of the effect she had on him. How could she? They had only just been introduced a month prior, but he had known of her for years.

Lady Enid had saved his sister from the gossips' sharp tongues when his sister had spilled a drink on her own ball-gown. Rather than turn up her nose at Helena, Lady Enid had sprung into action and helped mitigate the repercussions of her actions, at a great risk to herself at the time.

How silly it was for a young woman's reputation to be ruined over a spilled drink, but members of the *ton* demanded nothing less than perfection. It was hypocrisy at its finest, and it was precisely why he didn't want to be a member of the peerage.

As the riders drew closer, he took a moment to admire Lady Enid. She was a beautiful young woman with her brown hair, narrow chin, and broad cheeks. The way the sunlight danced on her fair skin, and the twinkle that lived in her eyes, he knew he'd never want to look away. But he must. There could be no future between him and Lady Enid. Her decision to elope with Mr. Longbourn had determined that.

The memory of Lady Enid standing up to her husband came to his mind and he had to admit that he had never met a lady who was so brave. She stared at Mr. Longbourn in the eyes and never blinked, even when he attempted to shoot her. No wonder he found her so intriguing.

He noticed that Lady Enid was not wearing black, which was customary during the mourning period. He was pleased that she was choosing not to mourn her late husband. He was a blackguard and didn't deserve her respect.

Lady Enid reined in her horse and offered him a brief smile. "Good morning, my lord," she said softly. "I wish to offer my condolences for your loss." Her words were genuine, just as he expected her heart to be.

Greydon tipped his head. "Thank you." He wasn't quite sure what else he could say on the matter. He hadn't gotten used to people calling him "my lord", and he thought it would be some time before he grew accustomed to it.

Lord Brentwood spoke up. "I am sure it was a terrible blow to lose Phineas so young."

"It was," Greydon said. "Frankly, it seems rather surreal right now."

Lady Brentwood's eyes held sympathy. "If I may offer some advice, I would encourage you to take time for yourself during this difficult time. The grief will be there whether you want it to be or not."

Greydon knew Lady Brentwood was speaking from experience. He had grown to greatly admire her strength and determination. Because of her heroic actions, she had become the ward of Lord Ashington and eventually made an advantageous marriage to Lord Brentwood. She had done well for herself, considering she was the daughter of a seaman. But that was a secret he would take to the grave with him.

As he went to respond, Lady Brentwood's horse whinnied, drawing his attention towards the unusual-looking animal. It looked as if the horse's eyes were bulging out from its face and the neck was abnormally large. "You have rather a unique-looking horse," he attempted.

Lady Brentwood laughed. "Bella is terribly ugly, but I adore her."

"You know that your horse is ugly?" Greydon asked.

"I have eyes, don't I?" Lady Brentwood joked. "But Bella and I are as thick as thieves and I know that she rather despises Shakespeare."

Greydon gave her a baffled look. "How would you know such a thing?"

Lord Brentwood interjected, "Rosamond used to read to Bella in the stables."

"You used to read to a horse?" Greydon asked.

Lady Brentwood shrugged. "I wanted my horse to be cultured and reading to Bella seemed like a good idea at the time."

To his surprise, a laugh escaped his lips. "That is the stupidest thing I have ever heard, but thank you for making me laugh," Greydon said.

Leaning closer to her horse, Lady Brentwood whispered, "Do not listen to him, Bella. You are the most cultured horse here."

In response, Bella snorted and shook her head.

Lady Brentwood leaned back in her saddle with a satisfied look on her face. "Bella has taken no offense to your comments."

Lord Brentwood smiled lovingly at his wife. "We have a stable full of beautiful stallions, but Rosamond is insistent on riding Bella."

"You knew I would never part with Bella," Lady Brentwood said.

"Yes, and I would expect no different from you," Lord Brentwood responded, his words filled with pride. "You are an immensely loyal person."

Greydon felt a twinge of jealousy at the love that was so

evident between Lord and Lady Brentwood. When they spoke to one another, they seemed to exude happiness. If he didn't count them both as friends, then he would find it rather obnoxious.

Turning his gaze towards Lady Enid, he asked, "How are you faring?"

"I am well," came her quick reply. But her eyes didn't match her words. They held a sadness to them that he found disconcerting. He suspected she was trying to hide her feelings but had forgotten that people's eyes speak, giving far too much away.

As much as he wanted to press Lady Enid, he knew it wasn't his place to do so. He was just her friend, at least he hoped she considered him as one.

Lord Brentwood's voice drew back his attention. "I must pose the same question to you," he stated. "How are you faring?"

"I am well," Greydon said, using Lady Enid's words. With any luck, Lord Brentwood wouldn't press him on the issue.

But he was not so lucky.

"That wasn't very convincing," Lord Brentwood responded. "It is all right if you are not. It is not every day that one's brother is murdered."

Greydon knew that Lord Brentwood was just offering encouragement, but he found it to be rather vexing. What right did he have to tell him how he should feel? He wasn't even sure how he felt at the moment. "I assure you that I will feel better once Lady Eugenie has been brought to justice for my brother's murder."

Lady Enid grew rigid in the saddle. "What do you know of your brother's murder?"

"Nothing more than what was reported in the newssheets, but I intend to speak to the coroner," Greydon replied. "I want to ensure the case is strong against Lady Eugenie."

"Is it possible that the coroner made a mistake when he arrested Lady Eugenie?" Lady Enid asked.

Greydon furrowed his brow. Where was Lady Enid going with this? "It is not. She was found standing over my brother's body with blood on her hands."

"Yes, but there could have been another reason why she was there," Lady Enid said. "Couldn't there be?"

"It has been my experience that innocent people do not have blood of the deceased on their hands," he replied.

"Perhaps there was a perfectly rational explanation for the blood being on her hands," Lady Enid pressed.

Greydon frowned. "I doubt it," he said. "May I ask where this is coming from?"

"I just feel that maybe, just maybe, Lady Eugenie didn't murder your brother," Lady Enid said in a hesitant voice.

"Based upon what?" Greydon asked in a voice that was much harsher than he intended.

"I do not believe Lady Eugenie is capable of such a thing," Lady Enid replied. "She is too kindhearted."

Greydon waved his hand in front of him. "Well, by all means, I will inform the coroner of this new information and I have no doubt that they will release her at once," he mocked. "Had we known Lady Eugenie was so kindhearted then she would have never been arrested."

Lady Enid tilted her chin. "I know I must sound ridiculous to you right now, but Lady Eugenie is my friend."

"Anyone is capable of murder, given the right circumstances," Greydon said. "Even you proved that with your late husband."

Lord Brentwood cleared his throat. "You are out of line," he warned in a firm voice.

"No, he is right," Lady Enid said, rushing to his defense. "I did shoot John but only because he intended to kill me, and I do not regret my choice."

"But you wanted to kill him before he even reached for a

pistol," Greydon urged. "That is why you brought a pistol with you."

Lady Enid nodded. "It is true. I knew that John would never leave me alone as long as he was alive. I needed to protect my daughter."

"There is a fine line between murder and protecting oneself," Greydon said. "But that is not what we have here. Lady Eugenie stabbed my brother."

"I just feel——"

Greydon cut her off. "No, you don't have the right to feel anything. Lady Eugenie may be a kindhearted person, a saint, even, but in that moment, she was nothing more than a cold-blooded murderer."

Lady Enid held his gaze, and he could see the questions in her eyes. He had never spoken so harshly to her before, but he was angry. How dare she try to say that Lady Eugenie was innocent based upon her social interactions with her? Besides, it didn't matter what Lady Enid thought. This case was based on facts, not feelings.

It was a long moment before Lady Enid spoke and she seemed overwhelmed by emotion. "My apologies, my lord. I didn't mean to upset you." The sincerity in her voice was his undoing and he was beginning to wonder if he should also apologize for his stern words.

But why should he? He'd done nothing wrong. Lady Enid was trying to defend the person that murdered his brother. She was out of line, not him. So why did he feel so guilty?

While he wrestled with his thoughts, Lady Enid urged her horse forward and headed down the path.

Lord Brentwood eyed him disapprovingly. "That was in bad form, Rushcliffe."

Greydon glanced at Lady Enid's retreating figure before asking, "You don't honestly believe that Lady Enid has a valid point?"

"It doesn't matter what I believe; it matters what *she* believes," Lord Brentwood replied.

"What she believes is wrong," Greydon muttered.

"Then prove it to her, but don't dismiss her out of hand," Lord Brentwood counseled. "That isn't fair to you, or her."

Greydon hated to admit that Lord Brentwood wasn't entirely wrong, and that irked him greatly. He was a man that dealt in facts, and he would prove to Lady Enid- through facts- that Lady Eugenie had murdered his brother.

With her back up against the wall, Enid sat on the ground in the nursery as Marigold busily went about the room. She was pleased that her daughter had not only embraced her new life but was thriving. It warmed her heart to see how happy Marigold was.

Her mother had taken it upon herself to stock the nursery with toys and Marigold did not lack for anything, including love. Her mother was constantly visiting the nursery, doting on Marigold, and she was grateful for that. Children could never have too many people in their lives that loved and encouraged them.

Marigold was babbling as she sat down next to her with a doll in her hand. Enid leaned her head against the wall as she smiled. How she adored her daughter. If it hadn't been for her, she would never have found the strength to leave her husband. She refused to stand by and let John abuse Marigold. Her daughter was her everything.

Enid's eyes roamed over the nursery, and she felt a little nostalgic. She had spent so much time in this room as a child that she had memorized everything. The ivory-papered walls that were lined with small flowers, the thick, faded carpet, and a window where birds would often perch themselves on the sill. If she closed her eyes, she could almost hear the sound of her laughter as her nursemaid played with her.

The door opened and her mother let out an exasperated sigh. "I should have known this is where you were," she said. "We have guests."

"No, *you* have guests," Enid corrected. "No one wishes to see me."

"That is not true," her mother said. "Lady Oxley and her daughter, Miss Bolingbroke, have come to call and I have no doubt they would be delighted to see you."

"I hardly know either of them."

"More the reason to speak to them," her mother encouraged. "I do believe you might have more in common with Miss Bolingbroke than you realize."

"I do not believe that to be true."

Her mother's eyes left hers as they focused on Marigold. "You must make an attempt to re-enter Society, for Marigold's sake."

"No one will accept me. I am ruined, Mother," Enid said. "I have made peace with that. Why can't you?"

"Because I will never give up on you, and do not ask me to do so."

Enid could hear the determination in her mother's words and knew she would not back down on this. She had to admit that it felt good to have an ally. "If it means so much to you, I will go, but you will see that it is a mistake."

As she stood up, her mother cast her a chiding look. "I do not understand why you choose to sit on the ground in a gown. There is a perfectly good chair right next to you."

"I prefer to be closer to Marigold."

"But your gown is terribly wrinkled and you do not have time to change," her mother said. "We shall have to make do."

"What horror that I am wearing a wrinkled gown," Enid

teased, bringing a hand to her chest. "How can you possibly be seen with me?"

Her mother did not look amused. "You are impossible, Child." Her words were light.

The nursemaid stepped out of an adjoining room. "It is time for Miss Marigold's nap," Marie announced.

Enid picked up Marigold and hugged the little girl tightly against her. "Sleep well, my love," she murmured before she handed Marigold off to Marie.

Her mother stepped out of the nursery and Enid followed. As they started walking down the hall, her mother glanced over at her and asked, "How was your ride through Hyde Park?"

An image of Lord Rushcliffe came to her mind. He was large- commanding- and exceedingly handsome. His brown hair was longer than what some would consider fashionable, but she thought it suited him quite nicely. Despite his size, he had never given her a reason to fear him. Quite the opposite, in fact. His words were usually gentle when he spoke to her.

But not today. He had spoken harshly to her and she didn't fault him for that. She should never have brought up Lady Eugenie. After all, his brother had just been murdered and she hadn't meant to upset him.

Knowing that her mother was still waiting for a response, she replied, "It was uneventful." With any luck, her mother wouldn't press her.

"Interesting, because Malcolm mentioned you spoke to Lord Rushcliffe," her mother said in a prying tone.

"We did," she responded, hoping there was no need to elaborate on what they had spoken about. She didn't wish to go into details.

"I hadn't realized you were acquainted with Lord Rushcliffe."

"We have met, on multiple occasions, in fact," Enid said. "He is a kind man."

Her mother eyed her curiously. "I think it is promising that a man of his station didn't dismiss you, considering your reputation."

"Lord Rushcliffe is too much of a gentleman to ever do such a thing," Enid said, knowing her words were true. He knew much of her past, but he never once made her feel less because of it.

While they descended the stairs, her mother remarked, "I was acquainted with his mother, Lady Pendle, and I was saddened by her untimely death."

"I never had the privilege of meeting Lady Pendle."

"She was a good woman, with an even better heart," her mother shared. "I know she did not approve of her eldest son's sullied reputation, and she tried to curtail his wild ways."

"Everyone was well aware of the late Lord Rushcliffe's reputation but, fortunately, he did not hanker after debutantes."

As they stepped into the drawing room, she saw Lady Oxley and her daughter, Miss Bolingbroke, sitting on the blue camelback settee. Lady Oxley had a frown on her face that disappeared the moment she saw them.

Lady Oxley rose. "Diane," she greeted.

Her mother walked over and kissed Lady Oxley's cheek. "Elizabeth," she greeted warmly. "I do thank you for coming to call."

"It is my pleasure," Lady Oxley said as she turned her gaze towards Enid. "When you told me that Enid had returned, I wanted to see her for myself."

Enid dropped into a curtsy. "My lady," she murmured.

Lady Oxley smiled, her kind eyes radiating warmth. "You are looking well, my dear," she acknowledged. "I daresay that motherhood agrees with you."

She could feel herself relax in the viscountess' presence. "Thank you," she said.

Gesturing towards her dark-haired daughter, Lady Oxley asked, "Are you acquainted with Anette?"

"I am not," Enid admitted.

"We must rectify that at once," Lady Oxley said, glancing down at her daughter. "Anette loves nothing more than making new friends. Don't you, dear?"

Miss Bolingbroke nodded. "I do. I just sit around all day and make lists of qualities that I want in friends."

Lady Oxley pressed her lips together. "You must excuse my daughter's dry sense of humor."

"There is nothing to forgive," Enid said.

"You are too kind," Lady Oxley murmured as she returned to her seat.

Her mother went to sit across from Lady Oxley and her daughter and Enid claimed the seat next to her. A maid brought in a tea service and placed it on the table before departing from the room.

"Would you care to pour, Enid?" her mother asked.

Enid moved to sit on the edge of her seat and poured four cups of tea. Then she handed one to each of the women.

While they sipped their tea, Lady Oxley turned her attention towards the portrait above the fireplace. "I just adore that portrait of you," she acknowledged.

"That was painted on my wedding day," her mother said, growing nostalgic. "It was the best of days."

"My husband and I are commissioning portraits of us and it is an exhausting task to plan for," Lady Oxley revealed.

"I just had a portrait commissioned and it is hanging in the parlor. Would you care to see it?" her mother asked as she placed her teacup down on the table.

"I would," Lady Oxley replied, rising. "Would you care to join us, Anette?"

"No, thank you," Miss Bolingbroke replied.

Enid spoke up. "I shall remain here and keep her company."

Lady Oxley nodded approvingly. "That is kind of you," she said.

After the ladies departed, Enid took a sip of her tea and listened to the gentle ticking of the long clock in the corner. She thought it would be best if she made an effort to get to know Miss Bolingbroke. It was far preferable than sitting here and staring awkwardly at one another.

As she thought on what she should ask, Miss Bolingbroke surprised her by asking, "Do you regret eloping?"

Enid choked on her tea. "I beg your pardon?"

Miss Bolingbroke held her gaze and repeated the question. "Do you regret eloping?"

"I do not wish to speak of that," Enid replied.

"That is a shame," Miss Bolingbroke replied as she sat back. "I am writing a book and I thought one of my characters could elope."

"You are writing a book?" Enid asked.

"I am," Miss Bolingbroke said. "Or at least I am trying to, but my brain is befuddled with so many ideas."

With a glance at the doorway, Enid inquired, "Does your mother know you are writing a book?"

"She does, and it is a great source of contention in our family." Miss Bolingbroke put her hand up. "I know what you are going to say."

"I doubt that."

"Women do not write books and I am just wasting my time," Miss Bolingbroke said with an exasperated voice.

Enid placed her teacup down and admitted, "I think it is brilliant."

Miss Bolingbroke looked at her, baffled. "You do?"

"Why can't more women write books?" Enid asked. "To answer your earlier question, I feel shame at eloping, but I do not regret my actions because it gave me my daughter."

Miss Bolingbroke perked up. "It was rather convenient that your husband died, was it not?" she asked.

Enid didn't want to reveal that she had played a hand in his death so she replied, "It was."

"Do you want to tell me how he died?" Miss Bolingbroke pressed. "The newssheets were rather vague on that detail, reporting only that he died."

"No, I do not wish to elaborate."

Miss Bolingbroke bobbed her head. "I would imagine it was a great relief when he did die, though."

"That it was," Enid admitted.

Rosamond stepped into the room and a bright smile came to her lips. "Anette," she said. "What a pleasant surprise."

"Hello, Rosamond," Miss Bolingbroke greeted. "I see that married life suits you rather nicely."

"That it does." Rosamond sat down next to Enid. "What brings you by today?"

Miss Bolingbroke waved her hand towards the door. "My mother is looking at a portrait with Lady Everton so I was just asking Lady Enid some questions."

"For your book?" Rosamond asked knowingly.

"Yes, for research," Miss Bolingbroke confirmed.

Rosamond shifted to face Enid. "What questions did she ask of you?"

"Whether or not I regret eloping," Enid replied.

Her sister-in-law laughed. "You must excuse Anette but she means no ill-will with her questions. She is just curious."

"That I am," Miss Bolingbroke agreed. "What I wouldn't give to interview Lady Eugenie and ask her why she killed her lover."

Enid stiffened. "I do not believe that Lady Eugenie killed the late Lord Rushcliffe."

"But wasn't she caught in the act?" Miss Bolingbroke asked.

"I know that is what was reported in the newssheets, but Lady Eugenie is my friend. I just can't believe she would do such a thing."

"She is your friend?" Miss Bolingbroke asked.

"She is."

Miss Bolingbroke bit her lower lip before saying, "You should visit her and speak to her. Perhaps she could shed some light on what has happened."

"I don't even know where Lady Eugenie is being held," Enid said.

With a glance at the empty doorway, Miss Bolingbroke lowered her voice. "It was reported she was being held at The Brown Bear, a public house, until the coroner does the inquest. It is across the street from the Bow Street station."

"I couldn't possibly go there..." Her voice trailed off. Why couldn't she? She was already ruined so she didn't risk jeopardizing her reputation. Besides, it would be a chance to prove to Lady Eugenie that she wasn't alone at a time like this.

While she mulled over her thoughts, Rosamond shared, "A public house is no place for a lady. I have heard they are terribly dirty and there are more rats than occupants."

"That may be true, but I think it would be best if I went," Enid said. "I could hear what happened directly out of Lady Eugenie's mouth and not rely on what is reported in the newssheets."

"And if she does admit to killing her lover?" Rosamond asked.

"Then I will know the truth," Enid replied.

Rosamond glanced at Enid with pursed lips. "Is there any way I can talk you out of this madness?"

"I need to do this," Enid said.

Miss Bolingbroke interjected, "Would you care for me to accompany you?"

"I do not think that is wise," Enid responded. "You would be risking your reputation if you set foot near a public house."

"Who will accompany you, then?" Miss Bolingbroke asked.

"I am a widow and there are some perks to being one," Enid said.

Miss Bolingbroke's eyes grew wide. "Please say that you don't intend to go by yourself?"

Before she could answer, her mother and Lady Oxley stepped into the room, effectively ending their conversation.

Enid knew it was intolerably stupid of her to even consider going to visit Lady Eugenie in a public house but she had to do something to help her friend- even if that meant she went into the most vile of places.

Chapter Three

Greydon sat in the comfortable upholstered armchair at White's as he stared at the fire in the hearth. He was biding his time until he could speak to the coroner who was over Lady Eugenie's case. He needed answers, and Sir David Abbott was the only one that could help him.

He had worked with Sir David before on multiple cases, and he considered him to be competent at his job. Sir David was direct in his questions when he interviewed the witnesses, and their names were properly recorded in the coroner's rolls.

Greydon's drink remained untouched in front of him as he attempted to appear unaffected by the attention he was garnering. Men would glance his way, some with pity in their eyes, but no one dared to approach him. Which was fine by him. He wasn't in the mood to converse. He was only at the club until he could get the answers he so desperately sought.

He knew that his time as a Bow Street Runner was coming to a close now that he was an heir to an earldom, but he wouldn't hang up his red waistcoat until he was sure that Lady Eugenie would pay with her life for killing his brother.

Lord Brentwood's voice came from behind him. "There

you are," he said as he came to stand by him. "I have been looking for you."

"For what purpose?" Greydon asked. He had no business with Lord Brentwood so why was he here? And couldn't the man see that he wanted to be alone?

Lord Brentwood sat in the chair next to him and lowered his voice. "I need to speak to you about a delicate matter."

"Can we not speak of this later?" Greydon asked.

"Why? Are you busy?" Lord Brentwood asked with a knowing look at his full glass.

Greydon frowned. "What is it that you want, Brentwood?" The faster he got this over with, the sooner he could be alone again.

With a glance over his shoulder, Brentwood said, "I need your help with something."

"And you naturally thought of me?" he asked gruffly.

"I did, because it has to do with my sister," Brentwood said.

Now he had Greydon's attention. "What is it that you want?"

"I intend to re-enter my sister into Society, and I was hoping that you would consider helping her."

"That is foolhardy," Greydon said. "Enid is ruined and the *ton* will never accept her."

"I don't believe that to be true."

"Then you are a bigger idiot than I thought."

Brentwood leaned forward in his seat. "With your elevation in status, your acceptance of Enid would go a long way with changing the *ton*'s minds."

"The only person that could help Enid now would be the Prince Regent."

"I thought of that, but I doubt I could get an audience with him," Brentwood said. "And even if I was successful, I am not sure if he would help us."

Greydon's eyes were drawn to the fire as it crackled. "Why does Enid even want to rejoin high Society?"

"She doesn't, but I believe it would be for the best."

"Enid is a clever woman," Greydon said. "If she is content staying away from high Society, I would not press it."

"But I think she is capable of so much more than what she has settled for."

Greydon shifted in his seat to face Brentwood. "Perhaps, but who are we to judge?" he asked.

"Enid has been to hell and back at the hands of her late husband and I want her to be happy."

"Has she said that she is unhappy?" Greydon asked.

"No, but I can only imagine how lonely it is just spending all of her time at the townhouse, never venturing out, and never experiencing things that we take for granted."

Greydon didn't want Enid to feel an ounce of unhappiness, but what could he do? Enid was ruined the moment she eloped and there was no coming back from that. She had made her bed and now she had to lie in it. On the other hand, if there was the slightest chance that the *ton* might accept her once more, should she take it?

A server placed a drink in front of Brentwood and asked, "Will there be anything else, my lord?"

"Not at this time," Brentwood replied.

After the server walked off, Greydon let out a sigh. "I do believe what you are asking is a fool's errand."

Lord Roswell Westlake appeared next to Brentwood and asked, "What is a fool's errand?"

"I want to re-enter Enid back into Society," Brentwood replied.

"That would be a tough feat," Lord Roswell said as he reached for a chair to sit down. "It was just reported in the Society page that Enid is back in Town and the article wasn't particularly kind to her."

"More the reason to act," Brentwood pressed. "Besides, I

know my father. He will try to pressure her to wed the first person that asks so she won't be a drain on our finances."

Lord Roswell nodded. "I could see a member of the gentry trying to arrange a marriage with Enid. She is, after all, the daughter of an earl, despite being disgraced and all."

"Would Enid enter into a marriage of convenience?" Greydon asked. That thought did not sit well with him.

"No, but that won't stop my father from trying to force her hand," Brentwood said. "He wants to wash his hands of her and be done with her."

"I daresay that he won't win any parenting accolades with his approach," Lord Roswell joked.

Brentwood grinned. "No, he most assuredly would not, but my father is set in his ways."

Greydon went to reach for his drink but thought better of it. He needed a clear head when he spoke to the coroner. "I just would leave things the way they are, especially since Enid has not asked for your help."

"When has that stopped me before?" Brentwood asked. "I would like to see my sister happily settled with a man that loves her above all else."

"She only lost her husband a month ago," Greydon pointed out.

"Yes, but he was a blackguard," Brentwood grumbled.

Turning towards Lord Roswell, Greydon asked, "Do you intend to go along with this madness?"

Lord Roswell shrugged. "I do not have any qualms about it," he replied. "A few well-timed words to the right people wouldn't hurt anything."

Greydon cared more for Enid than he dared to admit and he did want her to have the happiest of futures. But that didn't mean he wanted to open her up to the criticism that would obviously come from her returning to Society. The *ton* was full of vipers and they would strike at the first sign of weakness.

Brentwood continued. "Before you say no…"

"How did you know I was going to say no?" Greydon asked, speaking over him.

"Lucky guess," Brentwood replied. "Regardless, before you say no, all I am asking is for you to call on my sister on a few occasions. That shouldn't be too difficult a task for you."

"Pray tell, how will that help her?"

"Once the *ton* sees that you have embraced her return home, the gossipmongers might not be as cruel," Brentwood said.

"I doubt that," Greydon muttered.

Lord Roswell interjected. "I disagree. After all, a lot of people are intimidated by you and I doubt they would want to cross you."

"That is because I purposely keep people at arm's length," Greydon said. "It is a strategy that has worked well for me."

Brentwood stretched out his legs. "I have come to realize that your bark is much worse than your bite."

"That would be a mistake on your part," Greydon said.

Lord Roswell pointed towards the black armband on his sleeve. "My condolences on the loss of your brother."

"You don't need to pretend to mourn him. I know what a despicable cad he was," Greydon asserted.

"Phineas may have had a terrible reputation but he was still your brother," Lord Roswell said. "That should mean something."

"It does, and I will ensure that Lady Eugenie pays for what she did," Greydon asserted with a clenched jaw.

"Vengeance won't help you mourn your brother," Lord Roswell counseled.

"It will help," Greydon said as he abruptly rose. "If you will excuse me, I have somewhere I need to be."

"Greydon..." Lord Roswell attempted.

He put his hand up, stilling his friend's words. "I do not need your pity."

"Good, because you don't have it," Lord Roswell said. "I

have no reason to pity you but I do wish you would take some time to mourn your brother."

"What good would that do?" Greydon demanded. "The newssheets reported that the mothers of London can breathe a sigh of relief now that my brother is dead. No one else is mourning him. Why should I?"

Brentwood gave him a pointed look. "Because you are better than that."

"Apparently not," Greydon said. "I hadn't spoken to my brother in quite some time before his death. We have been at odds with one another for as long as I can remember."

"Yes, but that doesn't mean you don't feel his loss," Brentwood pressed.

"To do so would imply that my brother meant something to me," Greydon said. "And he didn't. Not anymore."

Rising, Lord Roswell's eyes held compassion. "I think he meant more to you than you are letting on."

"Don't presume to know me," Greydon said, his voice taking on an edge. He may have recently become friends with Lord Roswell, but that didn't give him the right to encroach into his personal life. He was a man that preferred to be alone. It was much simpler that way. But Roswell and Brentwood had impressed him, on multiple occasions, and he determined that he could trust these men. Which was not something that happened very often.

Lord Roswell offered him a sad smile. "I know better than you are letting on, and I am worried about you."

Greydon scoffed. "Worried about me?" he asked in disbelief. "Whyever for?"

"A man that is grieving deeply doesn't always think clearly," Lord Roswell replied. "Just promise me that you won't go off half-cocked on us."

"You have no say in my life," Greydon challenged.

Lord Roswell stepped back and put his hands up in

surrender. "Very well, but if you do require my assistance, for anything, let me know."

Greydon knew that Lord Roswell was only trying to help, but he didn't need, or want, his help. Or anyone's help, for that matter. He was just fine the way he was. Yes, his brother had died. But that didn't mean everything stopped for him. If anything, he was busier now that he was his father's heir. He had to become acquainted with their accounts and help his father run the estate.

Why couldn't everyone just leave him alone?

As he turned to leave, Brentwood's voice stopped him. "Will you help Enid, then?"

It was on the tip of his tongue to refuse him, but he knew that he would always regret it if he didn't help Enid find the happiness she deserved. He wanted to see her smile again- truly smile- as if she had never experienced pain.

"I will call upon her three times," Greydon conceded. "No more, no less."

Brentwood tipped his head. "Thank you."

"Don't thank me yet," Greydon said before he walked away from his friends. He hated to admit it, but he was already looking forward to seeing Enid again.

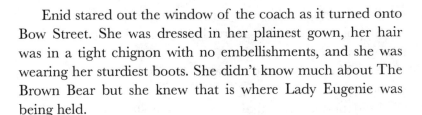

Enid stared out the window of the coach as it turned onto Bow Street. She was dressed in her plainest gown, her hair was in a tight chignon with no embellishments, and she was wearing her sturdiest boots. She didn't know much about The Brown Bear but she knew that is where Lady Eugenie was being held.

The coach came to a stop outside of an unassuming, two-level, brown-brick building and a plaque near the main door read *The Brown Bear*. The pavement in front of the public house was relatively clean and there was a guard out front.

A footman opened the door and assisted her out of the coach. "Would you care for me to accompany you, my lady?"

"No, thank you," she replied. This was something that she had to do herself. "But wait here. I shouldn't be long."

The footman tipped his head before he stepped back.

Enid walked towards the door and the guard eyed her with a critical look. "Are you lost, Miss?" he asked in a harsh voice.

"No, I am here to see a prisoner," Enid said.

The guard harrumphed. "Are you now?" he mocked as he stepped in front of the door. "I suggest you run along."

Enid squared her shoulders. "I demand to see Lady Eugenie."

"You demand?" the man asked with a lifted brow. "Well, little lady, I don't take kindly to people demanding anything."

As her confidence wavered, a male voice came from behind her. "She is with me," he said.

Enid turned her head to see a tall, black-haired man behind her. He had brown, astute eyes and tanned skin. His fine clothing marked him as a gentleman, and he was holding a satchel over his shoulder.

The guard glanced hesitantly between them. "Are you sure, Mr. Moore?"

"I am," Mr. Moore replied. "Now, will you kindly let us enter the building so I can see my client?" His words were cordial enough, but his tone was anything but.

Stepping aside, the guard held open the door without saying a word.

Mr. Moore gestured towards the door. "After you," he encouraged.

Enid nodded her thanks before she stepped inside. She stopped in the entry hall and waited for Mr. Moore. A rounded-faced guard sat at a desk in the center of the room and he had a frown marring his features. It went away when Mr. Moore appeared by her side.

The guard rose. "Good afternoon, Mr. Moore," he greeted. "Are you here to see Lady Eugenie?"

"I am, Allen," Mr. Moore confirmed. "And this lady will be accompanying me."

The frown returned to Allen's features. "Sir David said Lady Eugenie was to have no visitors."

"This lady is not a visitor but, rather, she works for me."

Allen's eyes perused the length of her with disbelief in his voice. "Since when did you hire women?"

"That is none of your concern," Mr. Moore replied. "Will you go retrieve Lady Eugenie or do I need to speak to Sir David about this?"

"And what is this lady's name that you so graciously hired?" Allen asked with his thick eyebrows raised up.

Enid closed her eyes, knowing her luck had run out. How would this stranger know her name?

To her surprise, Mr. Moore did not hesitate as he revealed, "Her name is Lady Enid Longbourn."

Allen glared at her for a long moment before he came around his desk with keys in his hand. "I will bring Lady Eugenie to Room A, but I will remain outside of the door."

"I would expect no less of you," Mr. Moore said.

As the guard walked away, Mr. Moore pointed towards a corridor and asked, "Shall we?"

"Thank you, sir," Enid replied, feeling conflicted. How did he know her name? She was quite certain that they hadn't been introduced before. But perhaps she was wrong. It had been over two years since she had been in Society.

Mr. Moore matched her stride and they walked in silence down the dimly lit corridor. Once they arrived at Room A, he opened the door and allowed her to enter first.

Enid stepped into the small room and saw a table with two

chairs that faced one another. The lone window had bars over it and offered little in the way of light.

Mr. Moore pulled out a chair and reached into his pocket for a handkerchief. He dusted off the chair before he asked, "Would you care to sit?"

Enid murmured her thanks as she sat down. She wasn't quite sure what she should do in this situation. Should she just ask how he was acquainted with her? But would he think of her as brazen for asking such a thing? Although, what did it matter what he thought? She was already alone with him in a room, and she didn't even know his name.

Mr. Moore smiled as he placed his satchel down onto the table. "It is evident that you don't remember me, my lady, but I am a friend of your brother's."

"I am afraid I am at a disadvantage, sir," Enid said. "I don't recall being introduced to you."

"We were never properly introduced, but we attended the same social events," Mr. Moore shared. "Since we have no one to introduce us, allow me the privilege." He bowed. "My name is Samuel Moore and I am the eldest son of Lord Harrogate. I also happen to be Lady Eugenie's barrister."

"It is a pleasure to meet you," Enid said with a polite tip of her head.

Mr. Moore gave her a pointed look that was no doubt meant to intimidate her. But it failed to do so. She had seen too many things, done too many things, for her to be affected in such a way.

"Does Malcolm know that you are here?" he asked.

"No, he doesn't," she replied, "and I would prefer to keep it that way."

"You want me to lie to Malcolm?"

"No, I would just like you to keep this conversation private," Enid replied. "I assume you know how to keep a secret, Mr. Moore."

"More than you know, but I have no intention of keeping

a secret from my friend. He has a right to know what his sister is up to."

"Then I shall hire you as my barrister."

Mr. Moore crossed his arms over his chest. "Do you require the services of a barrister?"

"I do not, but it would be for the sole purpose of keeping my visit a secret."

"Do you know what a conflict of interest is, my lady?"

"I do."

"Then you must know why you can't hire me."

Enid tilted her chin. "Even if you tattle on me to my brother, it will make little difference. I am a widow, and I can do as I please."

"Yet you are not dressed like a widow."

She ran a hand down her green gown. "Well, if you must know, I am in the process of acquiring new gowns."

"Are you not mourning your husband?"

She pressed her lips together before admitting, "I am not."

The silence between them stretched to several minutes before Mr. Moore dropped his arms to his sides. "Lady Enid," he said, "this is no place for a lady. You should go home before your reputation is tarnished even more."

"I do not think it would make a difference."

His eyes seemed to take in every detail as they roamed her face in what she assumed was a quick assessment. "Tell me, my lady, why are you here?" he asked.

"To see Lady Eugenie, of course."

"But, why?" he pressed.

Enid appreciated his direct approach and found it quite refreshing. "I want to speak to her and confirm my suspicions."

"Which are?"

She knew that Mr. Moore wouldn't stand by and let her tell him half-truths so she might as well be honest with him. "I don't believe she killed Lord Rushcliffe and I want to offer my support to her."

Mr. Moore bobbed his head in approval. "You and I have something in common, because I don't believe Lady Eugenie killed Lord Rushcliffe either."

The door opened and Lady Eugenie stepped into the room. Enid resisted the urge to gasp as she took in her friend's haggard appearance. Her blonde hair was disheveled, there were brown streaks down her fair skin and her ill-fitting, tan gown was terribly soiled. But Eugenie's eyes caused Enid the greatest alarm. They had a distance to them, as though she were lost in her suffering.

Allen stuck his head in and said, "You have ten minutes."

After the door was slammed shut, Enid rose and rushed over to embrace her friend. "I am so sorry this is happening to you."

Lady Eugenie dropped her arms and took a step back. "How are you here?" she asked in disbelief. "The guards won't even let me see my sister."

"Mr. Moore was gracious enough to allow me to accompany him," Enid said with a grateful glance over her shoulder at the barrister.

Mr. Moore gestured towards the table. "Why don't you both have a seat so we can get started?"

Enid returned to her seat as Lady Eugenie sat on the other side of the table.

Leaning his shoulder against the wall, Mr. Moore asked, "How are you being treated?"

Lady Eugenie's shoulders slumped. "It gets cold at night with the threadbare blanket that I was given, but at least it protects me from the rats that crawl over me while I sleep."

Mr. Moore grimaced. "Don't give up hope. We will get you out of here."

"Sometimes, the guards taunt me by telling me what I

should expect at Newgate," Lady Eugenie said. "I truly hope I don't end up there."

Enid leaned forward in her chair and rested her arms on the table. "How did you end up here?"

Lady Eugenie glanced at Mr. Moore before saying, "I went to visit Lord Rushcliffe and his main door was open. I thought that was odd so I went inside. I found him on the bed with a knife sticking out of his chest. I tried to save him, but it was in vain. Then, not a moment later, I was surrounded by people and I was arrested. I have been here ever since."

"Where were the servants?" Enid asked.

Glancing down at her hands in her lap, Lady Eugenie replied, "Lord Rushcliffe kept an apartment for his... um... discretions. It was a place that his wife knew nothing about."

"When did you become Lord Rushcliffe's mistress?" Enid asked.

Lady Eugenie's eyes shot up. "I was not his mistress," she asserted.

"Why were you there, then?" Enid inquired.

"I would rather not say," Lady Eugenie replied.

Mr. Moore shoved off from the wall. "You will need to eventually tell us why you went to Lord Rushcliffe's apartment."

"It has nothing to do with his murder," Lady Eugenie said.

"How can you be so sure?" Enid asked.

Lady Eugenie rose and walked to the window. As she stared out, she replied, "I can never reveal why I was there. I am willing to take that secret to my grave."

Mr. Moore rubbed his hand on the back of his neck. "It might come to that if you aren't completely honest with me."

"I can't give you what you seek," Lady Eugenie said in a resigned voice.

"Quite frankly, I was hoping you would confide in Lady Enid," Mr. Moore remarked. "What is so terrible that you would be willing to die for?"

Lady Eugenie offered him a sad smile but remained silent, causing Enid to say, "Please let us help you. You were the only one that was there for me when I was married to John and I want to return the favor."

"I'm sorry, but I can't…" Lady Eugenie started.

The door flew open, and Allen stepped into the room with a smug smile on his lips. "This meeting is over. The coroner wants to speak to Lady Eugenie."

"This is unacceptable!" Mr. Moore declared. "I am her barrister and she has a right to counsel."

Allen crossed the room and grabbed Lady Eugenie's arm. "Tell that to Sir David," he said before he forcefully led her out of the room.

Mr. Moore picked up his satchel and said, "If you will excuse me, I need to go have a word with Sir David and I can promise you that it won't be a conversation a lady should be present for."

"I understand."

"May I walk you to your coach first?" Mr. Moore asked. "It would make me feel better to know you are safely away from this place."

"As you wish."

Chapter Four

The hackney jerked to a creaking stop in front of The Brown Bear. Greydon reached his hand through the broken window and opened the door. As he stepped onto the pavement, he adjusted the black top hat on his head and approached the main door of the public house.

The guard out front acknowledged him with a tip of his head. "Good afternoon, Mr. Campden," he said as he went to open the door.

He was relieved that the guard hadn't made the connection of who he truly was. The fewer people knew that he was a viscount, the better. "Good afternoon," Greydon responded. "Is Sir David Abbott in his office?"

"He is," the guard confirmed.

"Very good," Greydon said as he stepped through the door. It took his eyes only a moment to adjust to the dimly lit hall.

Allen rose from his desk in the main hall. "What brings you by, Campden?" he asked.

"I need to speak to Sir David," Greydon replied. Greydon had discovered that with the notoriety of the case that Sir David had opened an office in the public house. While his usual office was with the authorities, Sir David had decided he needed to be available for any unforeseen problems at The Brown Bear.

"He is rather busy at the moment, but I will go ask if he will see you," Allen said, coming around his desk. "Wait here."

Greydon remained rooted where he was as Allen walked down a darkened corridor. He hoped that Sir David would take the time to speak to him, even if it was for only a few questions. He wanted to get all the facts about his brother's murder so he could prove to Lady Enid that Lady Eugenie was guilty, ending any doubt that she may have about the woman's innocence.

He wasn't entirely sure why it was so important that Lady Enid came to the same conclusion as he did, but it was. He didn't want Lady Enid to be deceived by anyone.

Allen stepped back into the hall. "Sir David will see you now," the guard informed him.

"Thank you," Greydon said. He didn't need to be shown to Sir David's office since he knew there was only one room Sir David would have taken. As his work as a Bow Street Runner had dictated, he had been in this particular establishment several times.

Once he arrived at the door, he knocked and waited until he heard Sir David's gruff reply, "Enter."

Greydon turned the handle and stepped into the office. A desk was situated in the middle and two chairs sat in front of it. There was a window, providing little light since it opened to the alley. No pictures hung on the walls but there were a few knickknacks on the mantel that hung over the hearth.

Sir David glanced up from the piles of papers on his desk. "What is it that you want, my lord?" he asked, skipping the need for any pleasantries.

He closed the door, hoping to keep the conversation private. "When did you discover the truth?"

The tall, lanky man with a long face made a tsking noise.

"You underestimate me. I have known for some time now, but I did not think it was my place to reveal such a thing," he said. "But it is only a matter of time before everyone else finds out. Your brother was murdered and you have assumed his title."

"Perhaps, but I would prefer to keep it quiet as long as possible."

"I can respect that," Sir David said, giving him an expectant look. "Now, what is it that you want?"

Greydon sat down. "I wanted to ensure that Lady Eugenie will pay for what she has done to my brother."

"She will," Sir David replied. "There is no doubt in my mind that she killed him, and I am preparing to call a formal inquest. With the witness statements and all of the evidence we recovered from the scene, I am confident the jury will reach a verdict rather quickly."

"Good, good," Greydon muttered. "With any luck, Lady Eugenie will plead guilty before this case even goes to trial."

"It does not look good for her. She was caught standing over the body with blood on her hands. We believe that she stabbed him while he slept."

"You mentioned witnesses. Did they see her stab my brother?" Greydon asked.

"No, but they heard Lady Eugenie screaming and they came off the street to see what the commotion was."

"She was screaming?" Greydon asked. "Whatever for?"

Sir David shrugged. "I do not claim to understand the complex minds of women, but the witnesses claimed she was hysterical."

"That seems rather odd, does it not?" he asked.

"I do not believe so," Sir David replied. "She shoved a knife through your brother's heart and, upon realizing what she had done, she grew hysterical. It isn't the first time a woman has done such a thing."

"I suppose not," he replied, not fully convinced of Sir David's words.

Sir David picked up a piece of paper. "She claims that she just happened upon the scene and saw Lord Rushcliffe lying in bed with a knife already in his chest. She went to render aid as she screamed for help."

"She claimed she happened upon the scene?"

"Precisely, I was immediately skeptical of her response," Sir David said. "Everyone knows what type of women go into that apartment."

"Did she admit to being my brother's mistress?"

"No, but it was not hard to put those two together," Sir David said. "Women have always thrown themselves at Lord Rushcliffe."

Greydon leaned forward in his seat. "What of motive?"

"Jealous lover," Sir David replied, placing the paper back down onto the pile. "Your brother was not one to keep just one lover."

"And the murder weapon?"

Sir David opened a drawer and pulled out a cloth that held a long-bladed dagger with a plain wood hilt. "It is a dirk dagger," he replied, placing it down onto the table for Greydon's inspection.

"That is an odd weapon of choice for an English lady," Greydon pointed out. "How did she get her hands on a Scottish dagger?"

"She hasn't been forthcoming with that information."

Sir David scooped up the dagger and cloth and returned it to his drawer. "As you can see, we have a strong case and you do not need to worry. It shouldn't be long before Lady Eugenie will have a noose around her neck."

"Has she retained a barrister?"

Sir David bobbed his head. "Her guardian immediately hired Mr. Samuel Moore upon hearing the news."

"Mr. Moore is a highly competent barrister. I would not discount him or his connections," Greydon advised.

"Even he won't be able to save Lady Eugenie," Sir David asserted. "The evidence is stacked up against her."

Rising, Greydon said, "That is good to hear."

Sir David looked up at him with pursed lips. "By chance, are you acquainted with Lady Enid Longbourn?"

He gave the coroner an odd look. "I am."

Leaning back in his chair, Sir David asked, "Will you kindly inform her that she is not welcome here?"

"I am sure she is aware that a public house is no place for a lady."

Sir David huffed. "You would think, but she accompanied Mr. Moore to see Lady Eugenie. He claimed that he had hired her to assist him on the case."

"Why would she do such a thing?"

"Again, women are such complex creatures. No one can seem to follow their trains of thought, but I suppose she wanted to see her friend," Sir David remarked.

"How long did she speak to Lady Eugenie?"

"Only for a few minutes," Sir David replied. "I had a few questions I had to ask Lady Eugenie so I broke up their meeting."

Greydon frowned. "I shall speak to Lady Enid at once."

"Thank you." Sir David paused and his face grew solemn. "Do you wish to see your brother? His body is just down the hall in the makeshift morgue."

Did he want to see his brother's corpse? He was conflicted. He had seen many dead bodies over the years as he worked cases as a Bow Street Runner, but he had never had a personal connection to any of them. But this was entirely different.

He wanted to see Phineas one more time, but he also didn't want his last memory to be of his brother's lifeless body.

Sir David's eyes held compassion. "I can see you are not ready but I would not wait for too long. I am preparing the body for burial."

"I would like to see my brother," Greydon said.

"Follow me, then," Sir David ordered as he headed down the corridor. He came to a stop at the last door and opened it.

Greydon followed him inside, ignoring the putrid smell that hung in the air, and saw Phineas' body was laid out on a table in the center of the room. A dried bloodstain was on his white shirt, and he still wore a pair of tan trousers. Greydon walked closer and saw his face was bloated and discolored.

Sir David pointed at the bloodstain and said, "That is where the dirk entered. It punctured his heart, making his death rather quick."

Greydon lifted his brother's stiff arm and asked, "Were there any defensive wounds?"

"None," Sir David said. "I doubt that he even saw the attack coming."

As his eyes roamed over the hand, he saw something that was becoming all too familiar in his line of work. "Did you note the whitish lines in the fingernails?" he asked.

"I did not." Sir David walked to the other side of the body and removed spectacles from his jacket pocket. He picked up the hand and examined it. "I daresay I wasn't even looking for signs of arsenic poisoning, considering the nature of his death."

"What of his mouth?" Greydon asked, placing his brother's arm down.

Sir David opened Phineas' mouth and leaned closer. "There are white spots on the inside of the cheek, as well."

Greydon took a step back from the table and said, "Someone was poisoning my brother in small doses."

"Most likely, Lady Eugenie was poisoning him and she grew tired of waiting for him to die," Sir David responded, unconcerned.

"Perhaps," Greydon muttered. He wasn't fully convinced. Why go through the trouble of slowly administering poison if Lady Eugenie didn't intend to see it through?

"Regardless, this changes nothing," Sir David said as he

removed his spectacles. "Lady Eugenie killed Lord Rushcliffe by plunging a dirk dagger into his heart."

"What if Lady Eugenie had an accomplice?"

Sir David slipped his spectacles back into his jacket pocket. "There was no indication that she had one, and I don't have time for a witch hunt."

"What if I interviewed Lady Eugenie?" Greydon asked.

Sir David shook his head. "Absolutely not!" he replied. "Consider what I shared as a professional courtesy but that is where your involvement ends. I do not want you to jeopardize this case for me. It is too important for my career."

Greydon wanted to continue arguing but he knew it would get him nowhere. But that didn't mean he wouldn't investigate it on his own.

"I understand, and I thank you for your time," he said with a tip of his head. "I shall be looking forward to the verdict from the inquest."

"As will I." Sir David walked towards the door and opened it. "Will there be anything else, my lord?"

With a final glance at his brother, Greydon knew he couldn't just leave well enough alone. He needed answers, and he had to discover for himself if Lady Eugenie had been poisoning Phineas. Or did she have an accomplice?

Knowing Sir David was still waiting for a response, he said, "Not at this time."

Enid had just stepped into her family's townhouse when her father's booming voice came from the opposite side of the entry hall.

"Where have you been, young lady?" he demanded as he approached her with a purposeful stride.

Enid didn't dare admit that she had just been at the public

house visiting Lady Eugenie so she decided to keep her response vague. "I was running an errand."

"An errand?" her father asked, skeptically. "You, a disgraced woman, going about Town as if you have a right to be there."

"You need not remind me of that every time we speak," Enid said as she removed her gloves. She was tired of having the same conversation with her father.

"Did I not ask you to remain at our townhouse?"

"If I recall correctly, you forbade me from leaving," she remarked dryly.

Her father glowered at her, not bothering to hide the disdain that was written on his face. "Yet you still defied me."

"I did, because I had to see to something."

He folded his arms over his chest. "What errand could be so important as to risk your reputation even further?"

"It hardly matters now," Enid said, placing her gloves down on the table. "I am home and no harm was done."

And right on cue, her father's nostrils flared. At least her father was predictable in his anger towards her. "I demand that you show me respect in my own home."

"Respect is earned, Father," Enid said, holding his gaze. She was growing tired of being treated less than in her own home. If her father wanted her to leave, then so be it. She had an inheritance, and she could fend for herself.

"If you are unhappy here, you are more than welcome to leave," her father responded, gesturing towards the door.

It had become a battle of wills, Enid realized, and she didn't want to give him the victory. It was on the tip of her tongue to announce that she was leaving but then she thought of Marigold. Her daughter was happy here. Could she really take her away from her grandmother?

As she mulled over her thoughts, her mother's voice came from the top of the stairs. "George," she said, a warning in her voice. "I do hope you are not trying to run Enid out of our home."

Her father had the decency to look ashamed. "I am not," he replied. "We were just having a conversation and I'm afraid it got rather heated."

"It would be best if you continued this conversation in the privacy of the drawing room," her mother suggested as she descended the stairs.

"There is no need," her father grumbled. "I need to depart for the House of Lords."

Coming to a stop in front of her husband, her mother asked, "Will you be home for supper?"

Her father's face softened as he leaned in to kiss his wife's cheek. "I shall make every effort to do so."

"I will ask Mrs. Booth to prepare the pudding that you so enjoy," his mother said.

"Thank you," her father responded as he stepped back. The disdain came back to his eyes as he met Enid's gaze. "You will remain here for the time being."

Rather than fighting with him, she nodded. "I have no place that I need to be anyways."

Her father headed towards the main door and Osborne stepped out of an adjacent room. He opened the door and stood to the side as her father walked through.

Once the door was closed, her mother gave her a chiding look. "I do wish you wouldn't provoke your father, dear. You know how he gets."

"I do, and I am tired of tiptoeing around him," Enid said. "He will only ever see me as the irresponsible girl that eloped. I am not that girl anymore."

"I know, but these things take time."

"I fear that Father is incapable of change, at least when it comes to me."

Her mother stepped forward and placed a comforting

hand on her sleeve. "Don't give up hope. He will come around; I am sure of it."

"You are far too optimistic, Mother."

She smiled. "Without hope, what do you have?"

A knock came at the door, breaking up their conversation.

Osborne went to open the door and asked, "May I help you?"

Enid turned her head and saw Mr. Moore in the doorway as he extended Osborne a calling card. "Mr. Moore," she greeted as she approached the door. "What a pleasant surprise."

"I was hoping for a moment of your time, my lady," Mr. Moore said.

"Of course," she responded. "Do come in."

Osborne opened the door wide and Mr. Moore stepped into the entry hall. He bowed when his eyes landed on her mother. "Lady Everton," he murmured.

Her mother tipped her head in acknowledgement. "Mr. Moore, it is a pleasure to see you again," she said. "How is your mother?"

"She is well, and I have no doubt she would have sent her regards had she known I was coming here today," Mr. Moore replied.

"Lady Harrogate is a kind woman," her mother said.

"Yes, she is," Mr. Moore agreed.

Enid assumed that Mr. Moore wished to discuss Lady Eugenie and she didn't want him to reveal to her mother that she had just returned from The Brown Bear. She really didn't want another lecture on propriety.

"Would you care to take a tour of our gardens?" Enid asked.

Mr. Moore nodded. "I would be delighted." He offered his arm. "May I escort you?"

Enid placed her hand on his arm, and they started walking towards the rear of the townhouse. Once they had stepped outside, she removed her hands and clasped them in front of her. "I do appreciate your discretion on my visiting Lady Eugenie."

With a glance at her, he said, "I see that I correctly assumed you did not tell your mother what you have been up to."

"Heavens, no," she replied. "My mother is a very patient woman but even she has her limits."

"If that is the case, why did you go?"

Enid gave him a sheepish smile. "Surely you must know of my less than stellar reputation."

"I do," came his prompt reply.

She tried not to be affected by his swift reply. Her tarnished reputation was a known fact amongst the members of the *ton*, but it still hurt to be gossiped about. She had made a mistake, but no one, including herself, would let her forget it.

"Well, Lady Eugenie was my only friend that stood by me after I eloped with John," Enid shared. "We would write letters to each other, and they always bolstered me up, even when life seemed bleak. She never once condemned me for my actions, and I wanted to return the favor. She needs to know she is not alone in this."

Mr. Moore came to a stop on the path and turned to face her. "She is lucky to have you as a friend," he said.

"I have learned that a true friend only comes along every so often and one must not take that fact for granted."

"No, one should not," Mr. Moore agreed. "Which is why I need your help. Lady Eugenie is not being forthright about what took her to the late Lord Rushcliffe's apartment that day."

"What would you have me do?" Enid asked. She would do just about anything to help her friend, especially if it meant Eugenie would be found innocent of this terrible crime.

Mr. Moore looked conflicted as he ran a hand through his black hair. "I want you to speak to Lady Eugenie again and try to convince her of the error of her ways. I do not want to see an innocent woman hanged."

"I can try," Enid said, "but there are some secrets I would take to the grave as well." Prior to her elopement, she wouldn't have felt the need to keep such secrets. But she was not the same woman she was before. She didn't owe anyone anything. She would only give what she wanted to give to others.

"I would be remiss if I didn't tell you that if word got out, this could damage your reputation even further," Mr. Moore remarked.

"I doubt that," Enid responded. "I don't think my reputation could go much lower."

"I wouldn't ask this of you if I didn't think it was absolutely necessary," Mr. Moore said.

As she went to reply, she saw Lord Rushcliffe approaching them with a frown marring his features. He was a burly man, but he had never used his size against her. She felt safe with him, even if she didn't know everything about him, and that was enough for her.

"Lord Rushcliffe," she greeted as she executed a curtsy. "What a pleasant surprise."

He came to a stop next to her, his frown still intact. "Lady Enid, may I have a word?" he asked. His words were tight.

"You may." She gestured towards Mr. Moore. "Are you acquainted with Mr. Samuel Moore?"

Lord Rushcliffe shifted his gaze towards the barrister. "I am," he replied. "He lets criminals go free."

"Only the innocent ones," Mr. Moore corrected with a smile on his lips.

"I doubt that," Lord Rushcliffe muttered.

Mr. Moore turned towards her. "I shall send word when I have secured a meeting." He bowed. "Good day to you both."

Once Mr. Moore started to walk away, Lord Rushcliffe asked, "What were you discussing with Mr. Moore?"

"Aren't you the nosy one, my lord?" Enid teased.

Lord Rushcliffe didn't appear amused by her attempt to lighten the mood. "I do hope you were not making plans to see Lady Eugenie again."

She eyed him curiously. "How did you know that?"

"You insult me," he replied. "After all, I am a skilled investigator."

"I never doubted that."

Lord Rushcliffe gestured towards a bench that sat just off the path. "Would you care to sit down?"

"It depends."

"On what?"

She arched an eyebrow. "Do you intend to lecture me?"

"I do." He paused and gave her a stern look. "Have you no shame?"

Not taking any offense, she said, "I'm afraid I lost that a long time ago." It was a simple fact so why deny it?

Lord Rushcliffe's jaw clenched. "You traveled across Town to The Brown Bear and met with a woman that is about to go on trial for the murder of my brother."

"Lady Eugenie is innocent."

"So say you," Lord Rushcliffe said. "But the coroner is preparing for the inquest as we speak and he is confident the verdict will be in his favor."

"He is rushing to judgment without all the facts."

"Why should he not?" Lord Rushcliffe asked. "His case is strong, and Lady Eugenie has given him no reason to question that."

Enid bit the inside of her cheek as she tried to think of something that might sway Lord Rushcliffe's mind. But she was at a loss for words. Until Lady Eugenie revealed the full truth about what happened that day, no one could help her.

With a pointed look, Lord Rushcliffe asked, "So we are in agreement, then? You will stay away from The Brown Bear."

"I cannot agree to that. I will do whatever I can to help Lady Eugenie."

"To what end?" Lord Rushcliffe demanded.

Enid decided it would be best to appeal to his sense of decency. "Surely, you must have some doubt that Lady Eugenie could have done such a thing."

Lord Rushcliffe stepped closer to her. "I stray on the side of the law," he said, his gaze firmly set on her.

"But sometimes the law is wrong."

"Not in this case."

"How can you be so sure?" Enid pressed. "If Lady Eugenie is condemned, the Crown is killing an innocent woman."

Lord Rushcliffe watched her quietly for a long moment, and she wondered what he was thinking. "You are impossible," he finally declared.

"I have been called much worse, my lord," she said. "I know you are grieving your brother, but I assure you that Lady Eugenie had nothing to do with his murder."

"Where is your proof?"

"I have none."

Lord Rushcliffe looked heavenward. "I don't have time for this," he said. "Just stay away from The Brown Bear. A public house is no place for a lady."

"No," Enid responded.

"No?"

Enid squared her shoulders and hoped that her voice was somewhat confident. She wouldn't stand here and let Lord Rushcliffe tell her what to do. She had a voice and she intended to use it. "You have no right to dictate my actions, my lord."

"I am trying to help you."

"It feels like you are trying to control me," Enid said.

Lord Rushcliffe looked back at her with a scowl, which in

no way intimidated her, or her position. "Why are you being so stubborn on the matter?"

"Because, my lord, someone needs to advocate for Lady Eugenie," Enid replied.

"Why does it have to be you?"

Enid offered him a bright smile that she hoped rather perversely would grate on his nerves. "If not me, then who?"

Without waiting for his response, she started walking down the path towards her townhouse. There was no point in continuing to argue with him. They would never see eye to eye.

Chapter Five

Greydon knew the best course of action would be to let Lady Enid walk away and not engage her any further. But he was unable to do so. He didn't know why it was so important to him, but he needed her to see reason.

"Do you want to know what your problem is?" he shouted after her.

Lady Enid stopped and slowly turned around. Her expression was tight, giving nothing away. "I suppose you will tell me," she said dryly.

It was evident that Lady Enid was angry, but he decided to press forward. Whether that was a smart choice or not, he knew not. "You think you know what is best and you will fall on the sword before you admit you are wrong."

"Pardon me, but I find that a little hypocritical of you to say, my lord," she said as she closed the distance between them. "You won't even consider the possibility that Lady Eugenie is innocent."

"And *you* won't consider the possibility that she is guilty," he countered.

Lady Enid came to a stop in front of him. "Quite frankly, I do not think you are thinking rationally on this case."

"Me? You think I'm the one that is acting irrationally?" Greydon asked. How dare she say such a thing! Enid was only going off her feelings and not facts.

"I know you want the person who murdered your brother brought to justice—"

He spoke over her. "I do, and she is residing in jail." He leaned closer to her, making their faces inches apart. "Where she belongs."

Lady Enid's eyes narrowed slightly. "I daresay it is *you* that is impossible."

"I have been called worse," he said, using her own words against her.

Greydon was close enough to Lady Enid that he could see that her eyes were flashing with anger. He hadn't set out to upset her, but he couldn't just let bygones be bygones.

Lady Enid didn't shy away from him, but she stood her ground. "I will prove to you that Lady Eugenie is innocent."

"And how will you do that?" he mocked.

"I don't know yet, but do not underestimate me."

"I have never, and I will never, underestimate you, my lady, but you are on a fool's errand."

"Then so be it."

Greydon's eyes roamed over Lady Enid's face. He noted the long lashes that framed her blue eyes, her flushed cheeks and the gently defined jawline that was quite firmly set. Why did she have to be so contrary about this? Or so blasted beautiful?

Brentwood's booming voice came from next to them. "It is a fine day we are having, is it not?" he asked, his words curt.

It was only then that Greydon realized how close he had been to Lady Enid. He stepped back and turned towards Brentwood. "Yes, it is a fine day." How had he been so distracted that he had failed to hear his friend approach?

Brentwood watched them both with a stern look on his face. "Dare I ask what has you both so upset?"

Lady Enid's brow creased in a frown. "It is a trite matter."

"I doubt that," Brentwood responded. "Your tense argument suggests otherwise."

"It is nothing that concerns you, Brother," Lady Enid said, the slightest hint of a bite to her tone.

Brentwood regarded his sister for a moment before he shifted his gaze to Greydon. "Perhaps you can shed some light on this, Rushcliffe."

Greydon glanced at Lady Enid and could see the thinning of her lips. He had tapped into her anger, which was fine by him. But if she was going to make his life miserable, he might as well return the favor.

"We were discussing Lady Eugenie," Greydon said.

Brentwood's jaw clenched as he addressed his sister. "Yes, I heard that you visited The Brown Bear to visit Lady Eugenie."

"Mr. Moore told you that?" Lady Enid asked.

"No, Sir David Abbott did when I saw him at the club earlier," Brentwood replied. "You didn't think you could keep that a secret, did you?"

Lady Enid shrugged one shoulder. "I would have preferred that Sir David Abbott use a little more discretion."

Brentwood crossed his arms over his chest. "If it helps, he spoke to me in confidence. He did not want to ruffle any feathers, so to speak, but he said he wouldn't be so forgiving next time."

"I understand."

"You should be grateful that he sought me out and not Father," Brentwood said. "I think we both can agree that would not have ended well."

Some of the fight drained out of Lady Enid, but she still held her head high. "I agree."

Brentwood dropped his arms to his sides as he heaved a sigh. "Why did you go, Enid?" he asked. "A makeshift jail at a public house is no place for a lady."

"I needed to see Lady Eugenie," Enid replied.

"But, why?" Brentwood asked. "Has your reputation not suffered enough? Now you want to be associated with a murderer."

Enid visibly stiffened. "Lady Eugenie is not a murderer."

"Leave it," Brentwood encouraged. "Let Mr. Moore do his job. He is a very competent barrister, possibly one of the best in London."

She opened her mouth but then closed it. When she did speak, it was calm, collected, even, making her words that much more purposeful. "Mr. Moore asked me to go with him again to speak to Lady Eugenie."

"Absolutely not!" Brentwood exclaimed with a swipe of his hand. "You will never set foot in The Brown Bear again."

"You do not get to dictate my actions," Enid said.

Brentwood placed a hand on her shoulder. "I am trying to protect you, Enid," he responded. "Your tattered reputation cannot take another beating."

"There are some things more important than what my reputation is."

"Not for a woman," Brentwood stated. "You must think about your daughter."

Greydon didn't think it was possible, but Brentwood's words had caused Enid to go quiet. She lowered her gaze and said, "Do not bring Marigold into this."

"I'm afraid I must," Brentwood said. "Are you not fighting for her future, as well?"

Enid's eyes snapped up. "You know I am."

"Then you must stop all this nonsense about trying to help Lady Eugenie," Brentwood urged, compassion in his voice.

"Am I to just abandon Lady Eugenie in her time of need?" Enid asked.

Brentwood cast a look to Greydon, indicating that he could use some help.

Greydon had two options. He could go on as he had been and continue to be at odds with Lady Enid or he could help ease her conscience by offering to help Lady Eugenie- the woman that he believed killed his brother. A murderer.

But as he studied Lady Enid, he could see the raw, unflinching anguish on her face. She was not good at hiding her emotions, causing him to feel even more conflicted. Could he walk away and not help Lady Enid? He cared for her, and swallowing his pride seemed like a small thing compared to seeing her bright smile again.

Before he knew what he was about, he said, "If you would like, I can go speak to Lady Eugenie and see if there is any validity to her claims."

A line between Enid's brow appeared. "But you already think she is guilty," she said. "What good would that do?"

"I am willing to go into the meeting with an open mind." He smirked. "Need I remind you that I am a skilled investigator?"

"Why would you do such a thing?" Enid asked, her eyes searching his.

Greydon held her gaze as he said, "For you, I would do anything." It was the truth. It was complicated, but it was the truth. Lady Enid was so beautifully charming and full of life that it took his breath from his lungs.

An adorable blush came to Enid's cheeks. "That is kind of you to say," she said, lowering her gaze.

Brentwood cleared his throat. "Yes, that was rather kind, and completely out of character for you," he remarked.

As his words left his mouth, Lady Brentwood approached them and came to a stop near her husband. "I have come to extend Lord Rushcliffe an invitation to dine with us this evening," she said. "My mother-in-law was rather insistent on you coming, my lord."

Greydon tipped his head. "I would be honored."

Lady Brentwood smiled. "Wonderful."

He turned his attention back towards Lady Enid. "I will

seek out Mr. Moore before we dine this evening and I hope I will have something to report."

"Thank you," Lady Enid said with a brief smile.

Brentwood interjected, "Allow me to walk you to the door."

"That isn't necessary…" he attempted.

"I insist," Brentwood said, gesturing towards the townhouse. "After you."

Greydon bowed. "Ladies," he said before he started walking towards the townhouse.

Brentwood matched his stride and lowered his voice. "Do you have designs on my sister?" he asked.

"No, I do not," Greydon said.

"I don't believe you."

"It is true," he asserted. "Marriage is the farthest thing from my mind at the moment."

"Then why are you so eager to help my sister?" Brentwood pressed.

A footman opened the door to the townhouse and Greydon stepped inside. He couldn't explain his reasonings to Brentwood or else the man would see right through him. Brentwood would know that he had developed deep feelings for Enid, and that was something he just couldn't abide.

"I merely want justice for my brother," Greydon said as they walked through the corridor.

"But you don't believe Lady Eugenie is innocent."

Greydon glanced over at his friend. "No, but Lady Enid does and I shouldn't discount her feelings so easily."

"Interesting," Brentwood muttered. "I do believe I said something similar to you."

"Perhaps, but I tend to discount most of what you say."

Brentwood chuckled.

They arrived at the main door and the butler opened it. As he stepped outside, Brentwood's voice stopped him.

"Don't wait too long."

"For what?" Greydon asked.

Brentwood looked amused by his response. "If you don't know, I am not going to tell you. You will just have to work it out on your own."

Greydon looked heavenward. "As usual, our conversations are a mixture of vexing and not at all informative."

"I shall see you tonight," Brentwood said.

As Greydon walked towards his coach, he shook his head. His friend was infuriating with his so-called advice. What was he not supposed to wait for?

An image of Lady Enid came to his mind and that brought a smile to his lips. She was the best thing that he had never planned. But that didn't mean he would act on his feelings. He was much too sensible of a man to fall for a woman that he could fall in love with.

Love was a weakness and had no place in a marriage. That useless emotion could bring a man to his knees and he didn't need- or want- that in his life. It didn't matter that Lady Enid's smile, her beautiful smile, dared him to fall in love with her.

Greydon stared at the books that were in front of him as he tried to become familiar with their accounts. He had been reviewing them for what seemed like hours and he was growing tired. His father wanted him to start managing their estates while he immersed himself in politics. But he had no interest in running an estate. He wanted to solve crimes, not sit behind a desk.

He was not his brother, but his father didn't seem to notice- or care. Greydon rubbed his eyes as he leaned back in his chair. This is not the life that he envisioned he would have. He didn't want this life; he wanted to keep things the way they were. He wanted the freedom to come and go as he pleased, answering to no one but himself.

He felt trapped in his new life and he saw no way out of it.

His father stepped into his study with a drink in his hand. "Are you taking a break?" he asked.

Greydon used his hand to massage the ache in the back of his neck that came from being hunched over the desk. "I don't know how you can sit here, day in and day out, working on the accounts."

"It is what a man of my position does. It is a great responsibility." His father shifted in his stance. "You would know that if you were around more."

"Do you ever tire of doing what is expected of you?"

Shaking his head, his father frowned a bit. "You may not have been born into this life, but you inherited it when Phineas died. Most people would envy you."

"I know, and I do not mean to sound ungrateful, but I don't want this," he said, waving his hand over the books.

"Then what would happen to the hundreds of people that we employ?" his father demanded. "They would all be turned out and forced to seek other employment."

Greydon pushed back his chair and rose. "Perhaps we could hire a man of business to handle our accounts."

His father's frown deepened. "We do have a man of business- a Mr. Bingham. He is quite competent, but you still need to be acquainted with our accounts."

"I don't want to do this, Father," Greydon said.

"But you must!"

Greydon walked over to the window and sighed. His father was stubborn, but he wasn't wrong- at least in this instance. Someone needed to ensure all the people that they employed were taken care of and their estates continued to thrive. They needed a leader, someone to put their trust in. Could he be that man?

It was entirely too complicated, all of it, and for the

millionth time, he mentally cursed his dead brother for not being here. Which wasn't fair of him. Phineas was murdered. It wasn't as if he freely walked away from this life. But that didn't stop him from grumbling.

His father walked over to the desk and began to organize the books. "You can complain all you want but, in the end, you will do your duty. Lives are dependent on you, Son."

Greydon knew his father spoke true and it greatly irked him. This was now his responsibility. No amount of complaining could change that.

Davy stepped into the study and met his gaze. "Mr. Moore has arrived. Would you care for me to show him in?"

"Show him to the drawing room," Greydon replied. "I will be there momentarily."

"As you wish, my lord," Davy said with a tip of his head.

His father spoke up. "Why are you meeting with Mr. Moore?" he asked, gruffly. "Is he not Lady Eugenie's barrister?"

"He is," Greydon confirmed.

"Then what could you possibly say to him?"

Greydon didn't want to explain his promise to Lady Enid- a promise that even surprised him- so he replied, "It is complicated."

"It shouldn't be," his father said. "Do not do anything to jeopardize a speedy trial. I want to see Lady Eugenie hang, and quickly. It is no less than she deserves after she killed Phineas."

"I understand."

Greydon exited the study and headed down the corridor towards the drawing room. He had no doubt that this would be a very difficult conversation, but it needed to be done. He would say what needed to be said and hope Mr. Moore was smart enough to accept his assistance.

He stepped into the drawing room and saw Mr. Moore

was standing by the window. Judging by the frown on his face, he was not pleased to be there.

"Mr. Moore," Greydon greeted. "Thank you for coming to speak to me."

"What is it that you want, my lord?" the barrister asked, forgoing the usual pleasantries. "I am a very busy man and I do not appreciate being summoned by you."

Greydon raised a brow at the barrister, who was easily as broad through the shoulders as him. He had tanned skin, as though he spent entirely too much time outside. "That was not my intention."

"Then what was?"

Gesturing towards the settees, Greydon asked, "Would you care to sit?"

"I would prefer to stand."

Greydon decided it would be best to just be frank with the barrister. "I would like to offer my assistance on your case."

Mr. Moore stared back at him with thinly veiled contempt on his face. "You?" he asked. "Do you not believe Lady Eugenie is guilty?"

"I do, but I can put that aside to investigate my brother's murder."

"Surely, you cannot be serious."

"But I am."

Mr. Moore let out a disbelieving huff. "You are the brother of the murder victim. It would be entirely inappropriate for you to investigate the case. You would be biased from the start."

"I know I cannot officially investigate this case, but I can still help Lady Eugenie."

"How?" Mr. Moore demanded. "By putting the noose around her neck yourself?"

Greydon knew this was not going well, but he had to keep trying- for Lady Enid's sake. He decided he needed to try a different approach. "Did you know that someone was poisoning Phineas with arsenic?"

"That wasn't in the coroner's report," Mr. Moore said. "How did you come by that information?"

"I examined my brother's body and confirmed it for myself."

Mr. Moore grew silent, his brow furrowed in concentration. "This is the first welcomed news that I have heard since I was hired to represent Lady Eugenie."

"This doesn't mean that Lady Eugenie is absolved of guilt."

"No, but it is a start." Mr. Moore studied him before asking, "Why are you sharing this information with me?"

"I told you; I want to help with this case."

Mr. Moore shook his head. "I do not know what you are attempting to achieve with this charade, but I am a busy man. I do not have time for games."

"I am playing no game."

"Then why would you wish to let your brother's murderer go free?" Mr. Moore asked.

Greydon knew the best course of action was to tell the truth and hope that was enough. If not, then he could tell Lady Enid that he had done all that he could do. "Lady Enid believes that Lady Eugenie is innocent, and I made a promise to her that I would investigate her involvement."

"Why would you do something so foolish..." Mr. Moore's words trailed off. "You care for her, don't you?"

"As a friend, yes."

"I do not mean as a friend," Mr. Moore pressed. "You have feelings for Lady Enid because that is the only reason a man would act so irrationally."

Greydon tried to ignore the barrister's intense gaze as he tried to think of something that he could say that would appease Mr. Moore. He didn't dare admit that he held Lady Enid in high regard, at least, not yet.

Mr. Moore's lips quirked. "This is all starting to make sense."

"What is?"

"You are trying to impress Lady Enid by investigating this case," Mr. Moore pointed out. "But, as I said before, I do not have time for games." He bowed. "Good day, my lord."

Greydon could have let Mr. Moore go. He probably should have, especially since he wasn't entirely wrong, but he found himself saying, "Then I shall investigate this case on my own."

Mr. Moore turned back around to face him. "Why do you insist on making a nuisance of yourself?"

"I made a promise to Lady Enid and that means something to me."

"If word got out about your involvement—"

Greydon spoke over him. "It won't."

With a shake of his head, Mr. Moore grimaced. "You don't know that for certain and I can't risk Lady Eugenie's life over it."

"Lady Eugenie is going to hang unless you let me help you," Greydon said. "Sir David is already claiming victory and the verdict hasn't even been handed down from the inquest."

Mr. Moore's face fell slightly before he corrected himself. "It has, and the case is moving to trial."

"I know you have no reason to trust me but let me help you."

"Lord Rushcliffe, your reputation precedes you, but I cannot in good conscience bring you in on this case," Mr. Moore said. "I'm sorry."

"Then you have signed Lady Eugenie's death warrant."

Mr. Moore grew visibly tense. "I resent that fact. The truth will come out and Lady Eugenie will be set free."

"Sir David does not care a whit about Lady Eugenie or the facts about the case," Greydon asserted. "He is only interested in furthering his career with this case. He dismissed the arsenic poisoning as unimportant, and I doubt it will even make it into the report."

Mr. Moore ran a hand through his black hair. "If I did agree to this madness, you would answer to me, and me alone."

"I am only seeking the truth, just as you are."

The barrister shifted his gaze towards the darkened window. "All right," he said in a resigned voice. "We can start by going to your brother's apartment tomorrow. Perhaps another set of eyes would help."

"Thank you."

"Don't thank me yet," Mr. Moore said, bringing his gaze back to meet his. "I can't guarantee that this..." he gestured towards them both, "partnership will even work."

"Haven't you worked with Bow Street Runners before?" Greydon asked.

"I have, but this situation is entirely different and, dare I say, awkward." Mr. Moore walked over to the door and stopped. "Be at your brother's apartment at dawn."

Greydon tipped his head. "I will be there."

"Very good," Mr. Moore muttered before he departed from the drawing room.

After he heard the main door shut, he went in search of Davy. He saw the faithful butler in the entry hall.

"Ready the coach," Greydon ordered. "I am going out."

Davy had just left to do his bidding when his father stepped into the entry hall. "Where are you going?"

"Lady Everton invited me to dine with them this evening," Greydon revealed.

Disapproval dripped from his father's tone as he said, "I would prefer if you remained at home and continued going over the accounts."

"I need a break, Father."

"And you will get one, when you have earned it."

Greydon knew that nothing was ever good enough for his father, and he had stopped trying to win his father's approval years ago. "Goodnight," he said as he approached the door.

"You can't run away from your responsibilities," his father argued.

"I'm not," Greydon said. "I am going to Lady Everton's townhouse to dine with her family."

His father scoffed. "I have heard that their daughter, Lady Enid, has returned home. I do hope you won't give her any heed."

"If you must know, I consider Lady Enid a friend."

"A friend?" his father asked. "Surely you can't be serious. She is a ruined woman; a thorn in her parents' sides."

Greydon opened the door and leaned up against it. "You don't know what Lady Enid had to endure because of that poor decision."

"And you do?"

"I know better than most," Greydon replied, "and I will not hold her past against her."

"You are a bigger fool than I thought," his father said. "We have an image that we must maintain."

"I daresay that Phineas greatly diminished that image with his wayward behavior," Greydon asserted.

"You now have the ability to change that, but only if you stay far away from Lady Enid and others like her."

Greydon pushed off the door. "Here is the thing, Father," he smirked, "I don't care about my reputation."

His father harrumphed. "You will bring shame to this family, just as Phineas did."

"I am nothing like my brother," Greydon said before he walked out of the townhouse, slamming the main door behind him.

Chapter Six

Enid sat in the drawing room as she attempted to read a book, but it was proving to be an impossible feat. Her mind kept straying to Lord Rushcliffe and how he had agreed to help her, despite his earlier protests.

He was a walking anomaly. So why did her heart beat a little faster when he was around? It would do no good for her to develop feelings for Lord Rushcliffe because she would never act on them. She couldn't. She had learned the hard way that giving her heart away would only end in heartache and sorrow. That is why she had vowed never to trust her inconvenient heart again. It had deceived her once before.

Enid closed the book and set it down on the table. There was no point in trying to pretend to be reading, especially since she kept reading the same page, over and over again. No matter how hard she tried to banish Lord Rushcliffe from her thoughts, he was ever prevalent there, tormenting her, relentlessly.

She was grateful for his assistance in helping Lady Eugenie, and she believed him when he said he would investigate with an open mind. Why did she trust him so easily? She always had; from the moment she had first met him.

Rising, Enid ran a hand down her pale pink gown with a square neckline. She needed new gowns in darker colors, ones that reflected her widowed status, but those could wait. Her first priority was helping Lady Eugenie so she could return home to her sister, especially since she knew how her friend felt about her uncle. He may be Eugenie's guardian, but she had practically raised her sister since their parents had died.

Enid walked over to the window and stared out to the street. A coach came to a stop in front of their townhouse and a footman stepped off his perch to open the door. Once the door was opened, Lord Rushcliffe stepped out onto the pavement and approached the main door.

He cut a dashing figure in his fine clothing and she realized he looked really smart, indeed. He definitely looked the part of a lord, and she knew he would have no issue with finding a bride. Women would flock to him now that he was an heir to an earldom. She grew somber at that thought. She knew she had no right to him, but she also didn't want him to be with another.

Osborne stepped into the room and announced, "Lord Rushcliffe has arrived, my lady. Would you care for me to show him in?"

"Yes, please," she said.

The butler tipped his head in acknowledgement before he departed from the drawing room. It was only a moment later when Lord Rushcliffe stepped into the room. He stopped and bowed. "My lady," he greeted, cordially.

Enid dropped into a curtsy. "My lord," she murmured.

"I hope I am not too early."

"Not at all," she replied. "The dinner bell should be rung shortly."

Lord Rushcliffe looked at her the way all women want to be looked at, making her feel beautiful. "You look lovely this evening," he said.

"Thank you," Enid said, suddenly feeling very nervous. "Would you care to sit and have a cup of tea while we wait?"

"I would like that very much," Lord Rushcliffe responded.

A maid slipped into the room and went to sit in the corner, ensuring they were properly chaperoned. It was rather silly in her opinion but her mother insisted.

Lord Rushcliffe waited until she sat down before he claimed the seat across from her. "I spoke to Mr. Moore earlier and we are going to visit my brother's apartment tomorrow morning. With any luck, we will discover something that could aid in proving Lady Eugenie's innocence."

"That is wonderful news."

"I do not want you to get your hopes up, though," Lord Rushcliffe said. "We might find nothing of importance."

"I understand." Enid reached for the teapot and poured two cups of tea. Then she extended one towards Lord Rushcliffe.

As he accepted the cup, their fingers brushed up against one another and her breath hitched. Good heavens! This would never do. She needed to protect her heart, at all costs.

"Thank you," he said as he leaned back in his seat.

"You are most kindly welcome."

They both sipped their tea and Enid was worried that the silence had stretched on for too long, causing her to blurt out the first thing she could think of saying. "It was a fine day today, was it not?" Drats. Did she just say something so incredibly dull?

"It was a fine day," Lord Rushcliffe agreed.

"I do hope tomorrow will follow suit." When the words left her mouth, Enid immediately wished she could take them back. What must he think of her?

Lord Rushcliffe nodded. "I agree." He leaned forward and placed his teacup and saucer onto the table. "But I would prefer if we discussed something else."

"What would you care to discuss?"

"Anything but the weather," Lord Rushcliffe replied with a smile.

Enid felt herself relax. There was no reason to be nervous around him. He had seen her at her worst, and he still came around.

"How has your daughter adjusted to her new life?" Lord Rushcliffe asked.

"She is thriving," Enid admitted, proudly. "She is talking more and is trying to assert her independence."

"Already?" Lord Rushcliffe asked. "That does not bode well for you."

"She is stubborn, just like me," Enid replied.

Lord Rushcliffe's eyes crinkled around the corners. "That trait has served you well. I hope it will do the same for Miss Marigold."

"I hope so, too," Enid agreed. "John wasn't appreciative of my stubborn nature and he tried to beat it out of me."

All humor vanished from Lord Rushcliffe's expression. "That was wrong of him to do so," he said firmly. "No one should have treated you so distastefully."

"I know, but it was my own fault. Had I not run off with him, my life would be very different," Enid sighed.

"Do you regret it?"

She shook her head. "No, because that pain-filled path gave me Marigold. She gave me the strength to leave John before he ultimately killed me."

"Then I am most grateful for your daughter."

"She is the most important thing to me in this whole world," Enid shared. "I find myself more times than not in the nursery. I must drive the nursemaid mad with all my attention towards her."

A reflective look came into Lord Rushcliffe's eyes. "My mother was the same as you," he shared. "She showered attention upon her children, and she even insisted on dining with us each evening."

"My father would never allow that," Enid said. "He can barely tolerate me sharing a table with him."

"Has he not embraced your return?"

Enid shook her head. "He has not."

"I'm sorry."

"There is no reason to feel sorry for me," she said with a wave of her hand. "I do not have the grand illusions that my father will ever forgive me for what I have done."

Lord Rushcliffe's eyes held compassion. "I would not give your father any heed," he said. "There are many people that are happy that you are home."

"For which I am most grateful. I find that I am most pleased at how much love my mother showers upon Marigold."

"I do believe my mother would have been the same way around her grandchildren, had she still been alive," Lord Rushcliffe said, a hint of sadness resonating in his voice.

Enid took a sip of her tea before saying, "My condolences on your mother's passing."

"It has been a few years now, and with each passing day, it gets easier to remember her without getting sad." He offered her a weak smile. "A part of me never wants to marry because I have seen how broken my father has become after losing my mother."

"You must not give up on love so easily."

"I said nothing about love," Lord Rushcliffe said. "Although, I have seen too many unhappy marriages that started as a love match."

Leaning forward, Enid placed her teacup and saucer down onto the tray. "Just because it doesn't work out for another doesn't mean it won't work out for you."

"It is a risk that I do not wish to take."

Enid nodded, knowing how Lord Rushcliffe felt. She had thought she had found her love match with John, but he had just been using her. "I doubt that I will ever trust another with my heart, as well," she said. "But that is only because it is irrevocably broken."

"Hearts can be mended," Lord Rushcliffe attempted.

"Not mine," Enid said. "How can I ever fully trust another after what John did to me? He took my innocence in his stride and used it against me."

Lord Rushcliffe moved to sit on the edge of his seat. "What your late husband did was wrong, but you should not give up so easily."

"Give up? Is that what you think I am doing?" Enid asked with a shake of her head. "No, I am protecting myself, and my daughter. Besides, even if I was foolish enough to dream of marrying, no one would want me."

"I do believe you are selling yourself short."

Enid offered him a grateful smile. "You are kind, my lord, but we both know that no sane man would want a ruined woman as his wife. And I have made peace with that."

Lord Rushcliffe looked as if he had more to say on the subject but Malcolm stepped into the drawing room with Rosamond on his arm.

Malcolm glanced between them. "Are we interrupting something?" he asked.

"Not at all," Enid said as she sat up straight in her seat. "Lord Rushcliffe and I were just discussing marriage." As soon as the words left her mouth, she felt her cheeks grow increasingly warm at her misstep.

Her brother's brow shot up. "You were?"

Enid jumped up from her seat as she rushed to explain. "No, I misspoke," she said. "We were discussing marriage, but not between us."

"But you were discussing marriage with someone else?" Malcolm asked.

"No, both of us have no intention of ever marrying," Enid replied, turning to address Lord Rushcliffe. "Isn't that right, my lord?"

Lord Rushcliffe had risen when she stood up and he was watching her with an amused look on his face, as if he were holding back laughter. "Yes, quite right, my lady."

"As you can see," Enid started, "our discussion about marriage was innocent and purely theoretical."

Malcolm bobbed his head. "All right," he said, eyeing her with a bemused look on his face. "I believe you."

"That is good," Enid remarked, wishing she could stop speaking. Why was she rattling on?

Fortunately for her, her mother stepped into the room and asked, "Shall we adjourn to the dining room?"

Enid let out a sigh of relief. With any luck, no one would revisit their previous conversation.

Lord Rushcliffe stepped closer to her and lowered his voice. "You handled that nicely," he said, mirth in his voice.

"A gentleman wouldn't comment on a lady's discomfort," Enid stated as she tried to keep some of her dignity intact.

"I think we can both agree that I do not always act like a gentleman." He winked at her, and that one move made her knees go weak. She swallowed hard and knew with complete certainty that she was in real trouble with him. Every glance, every smile, confirmed what she already knew—Lord Rushcliffe was a man that she could fall hopelessly in love with.

Greydon pushed in Lady Enid's chair before he went to claim the seat next to her. Lord and Lady Brentwood sat across from them and Lady Everton sat at the end of the long rectangular table. The footman had just placed their bowls of soup in front of them when Lord Everton stepped into the room.

"My apologies for being late, but I assure you that it

couldn't be helped," Lord Everton said as he moved to sit at the head of the table.

"No harm done," Lady Everton graciously responded. "Do you remember Lord Rushcliffe, the son of Lord Pendle?"

"I am acquainted with Lord Pendle. He is a staunch Tory," Lord Everton said as he went to address Greydon. "Are you a Tory?"

"I am," Greydon replied.

"Pity," Lord Everton muttered. "I am surprised that your father allowed you to come to dinner, considering my daughter's reputation."

Greydon saw Lady Enid purse her lips at her father's harsh comment, but she didn't say anything. "He voiced no concerns," he lied. His father had voiced many concerns, but he cared little about those. He would associate with who he wanted, when he wanted, and his father couldn't do anything about that.

Lady Everton interjected, "Perhaps we can speak of something much more pleasurable."

"What are your thoughts on how Parliament is handling the war?" Lord Everton asked him.

"I do not have an opinion," Greydon replied.

Lord Everton frowned. "You must have an opinion now that you are your father's heir. Soon, you will be immersed in politics and your vote matters greatly."

"My father still has many years ahead of him."

"I thought something similar when I was your age, but my father died of a heart attack quite unexpectedly." Lord Everton gave him a pointed look. "You would be wise to remember that. No one knows what the future holds. Death is no respecter of persons."

Lady Everton's voice was tight as she said, "Dear, I do believe we have spoken enough of politics this evening, and death."

Lord Everton nodded. "Very well." He picked up his

spoon and dipped it into the bowl. "Pray tell, Rushcliffe, how did you occupy your time before you became your father's heir?"

Greydon knew he couldn't reveal that he worked as a Bow Street Runner so he settled on, "I engaged in the usual pursuits of a second son, I suppose."

"Interesting," Lord Everton said before taking a sip of his soup. It was evident that he was not impressed by his admission. It was expected of younger sons to obtain employment to support themselves and their families. Not doing so would cause them to be a drain on their family's finances.

Malcolm spoke up. "Rushcliffe and I occasionally go boxing at Gentleman Jack's club," he shared.

"Is that what we do?" Greydon joked. "I thought it was just an opportunity for me to hit you and little else."

Rubbing his jaw, Malcolm responded, "It does feel an awful lot like that."

"You poor thing," Rosamond cooed as she placed a hand on her husband's shoulder.

Lord Everton glanced at Malcolm before saying, "That is foolhardy since Lord Rushcliffe appears to be twice your size."

Malcolm puffed out his chest. "We are of similar size," he said. "I'm surprised more people don't get us confused."

"I daresay that you need spectacles," Rosamond teased as she removed her hand.

"You wound me, my dear," Malcolm said, feigning outrage.

Rosamond laughed. "You will live."

Malcolm exchanged a look with his wife and returned her smile. "I am glad that you are here to keep me humble."

"Always, my love," Rosamond said, her words leaving little doubt of how much she adored her husband.

Greydon noticed that Lady Enid was eating her soup and she had a sad look in her eyes. He leaned closer and whispered, "Is everything all right?"

"It is," she replied quickly, making him think that everything was most assuredly not all right.

But before he could press her, Lord Everton asked, "Have you scheduled your brother's funeral yet?"

"Not to my knowledge," Greydon replied. "But the body has not been released by the coroner so it might be a few more days."

"Yes, Sir David is known to be rather thorough with his investigations," Lord Everton said. "I am just sure you want to close this chapter and begin a new one as quickly as possible."

"I am in no rush to bury my brother," Greydon admitted.

"Were you close with your brother?" Lady Everton asked.

Greydon shook his head. "Not particularly," he revealed. "We were very different people and that manifested itself as we grew older."

Lady Everton gave him a sad smile. "I am sorry to hear that."

"Brothers may share the same blood but they are not obligated to enjoy one's company," Greydon said. "Phineas' path was not one that I wished to join him on."

"Your brother was a cad," Lord Everton stated.

Lady Everton gave her husband a disapproving look. "That is rather harsh of you to say since Lord Rushcliffe is still grieving his brother."

Greydon put his hand up. "I take no offense. It is merely the truth."

"As a general rule, we do not like to speak ill of the dead," Lady Everton said.

Lord Everton flicked his wrist at the footmen to indicate that they were ready for the second course. The footmen stepped forward to retrieve their bowls and placed a tray in the center of the table.

Malcolm stood up to carve the meat and served the ladies first.

Lord Everton turned his attention back towards Greydon and asked, "Do you hunt?"

"I do," Greydon replied.

"We shall have to invite you to our country estate during hunting season," Lord Everton said. "Our lands are stocked with enough game that I can assure you that you won't leave disappointed."

"I would like that very much," Greydon responded.

Lord Everton continued. "Like all landowners, we have issues with poachers, but we deal with them swiftly. I insist that they are transported."

Lady Enid spoke up. "That seems rather harsh, Father."

"They are stealing from me. What would you have me do?" Lord Everton demanded. "Invite them over for a tea party?"

"No, but some of them might just be trying to feed their families," Enid replied.

"Then they should find a job and stay off my lands," her father snapped.

"It isn't always easy to find a job, especially right now," Enid said in a calm voice. "With the war going on—"

Lord Everton cut her off. "Ladies do not speak of the war in a man's presence. It is unsavory to do so."

"Regardless, the war has taken a toll on the people that are barely scraping by and there isn't enough food to go around," Lady Enid said.

"How does that concern me?" Lord Everton demanded.

Lady Enid lifted her chin stubbornly and her words became determined. "You could be a little sympathetic to the people that are caught poaching on your lands."

Lord Everton just stared at his daughter. "You know nothing of what you are speaking about. Poachers will ravage our lands and kill all the game, leaving us with barren wood-lands. Is that what you want?"

"No, but—" Lady Enid started.

"Yet you think I should show the poachers compassion?" Lord Everton asked, speaking over her. "Poachers could ruin us. Is that what you want?"

"Of course not, but—"

Lord Everton scoffed. "This is precisely why women should never be landowners. They do not think logically."

Lady Everton's firm voice came from the head of the table. "You have made your point, George," she said. Her tone brooked no argument.

Greydon had spent a considerable amount of time with other men and he had developed a keen ability to read them, and their intentions. He studied Lord Everton quietly for a moment, and he determined that he was a terribly unhappy man. He pushed people away for the sake of keeping up appearances, which wasn't uncommon in their circles, and tried to assert his dominance.

He shifted his gaze to Lady Enid and saw that she was using her fork to push the meat around her plate. She may pretend that her father being mean to her didn't bother her, but he suspected it did, more so than she would ever let on.

Meeting Lord Everton's gaze, Greydon said, "I do believe Lady Enid has a valid point."

Lord Everton's brows raised high. "Which is?"

"The poor are suffering, more so because of the war, and we need to show more compassion to their plight," Greydon said.

"The poor are suffering because they do not help them-selves," Lord Everton declared. "There is plenty of work to go around."

"But there isn't," Lady Enid asserted. "For many of them, working at a workhouse is their only option."

"What is wrong with a workhouse?" Lord Everton asked.

"It is a terrible place and people die all the time from the harsh work conditions and lack of food," Lady Enid said.

Lord Everton looked unimpressed. "Then they could move to the countryside and work in the fields."

"How would they travel to find work?" Lady Enid asked. "They can't afford to pay for a mail coach."

"They should work harder then," Lord Everton snapped.

"Father, with all due respect, you know not what you are speaking of," Lady Enid said.

Lord Everton dropped his fork onto his plate and glared at his daughter. "How dare you," he growled. "You are just an insolent child."

Greydon had just about enough of Lord Everton and his pretentious attitude. He needed to say something and stand up for Lady Enid. She wasn't wrong, after all. He had no doubt that she would have died at the workhouse had she stayed longer. Most people did.

He wiped the sides of his mouth with his white linen napkin and said, "Lady Enid is right. I have spent a fair share of my time in the rookeries, and it is not for the faint of heart. The things I have seen are not fit to share over a dinner table."

"Why do you frequent the rookeries?" Lord Everton asked.

"I wanted to see if the newssheets gave an accurate portrayal of what life was like in the rookeries," Greydon said.

"What did you discover?" Rosamond asked from across the table.

"It is far worse than what is being written about," Greydon replied. "The blackened homes are unfit for living, many with decaying foundations and broken windows. The rooms are so small and filthy that the air itself seems tainted. There are poles that are thrust out from the window that hold threadbare linens to dry."

"If that is the case, why do they live in such squalor?" Lord Everton asked.

"They have little choice in the matter," Greydon replied. "It is their way of life and they have no way out of it."

"That is not my concern," Lord Everton said.

Lady Enid leaned forward in her seat. "It should be all of our concerns, especially yours. You can enact real change in the House of Lords."

"You are mistaken," Lord Everton responded. "Lord Ashington has made it a crusade of his to provide access to clean water for the poor, but he does not have the support of the other lords. It is just a waste of time to advocate for the poor."

"I disagree," Lady Enid said.

"I will not trade the clout I have in Parliament to help the poor," Lord Everton declared with a swipe of his hand.

In a commanding voice, Greydon said, "But I will." He had been searching for a purpose. Perhaps he had found one. He could be an advocate for the poor and try to turn the hearts of the other lords to the plights of people that were suffering in the rookeries.

He had been there and seen what it was truly like. He had seen the desperation in the men and women's eyes and the frail bodies of the children that were begging on the street. He knew all too well of the deplorable conditions that the people worked in.

"I know you mean well, but wait until you become a peer," Lord Everton counseled. "You will see how difficult it is to get a bill passed."

Greydon sat back in the chair. "I do not back down from a fight."

Lady Enid smiled, and it was one that reached her eyes, causing the room to feel brighter as a result of it. "I find that admirable, my lord."

"Do not praise me since I have yet to start," Greydon responded.

"But I know what kind of man you are and I do believe you will bring around real change," Lady Enid said.

Finding himself curious, Greydon asked, "What kind of man do you think I am?"

"A good man, with a good heart," Lady Enid replied, decisively.

Greydon blinked. "Do you truly believe that?"

"With my whole heart," Lady Enid said.

As he took a moment or two to collect himself, Greydon realized that no one had ever called him a "good man" before. He strived to be honorable, but sometimes he found himself too close to the grey line as a Bow Street Runner.

But Lady Enid believed in him, and that meant everything to him.

Chapter Seven

Greydon stifled a yawn as he rode in the coach to Phineas' apartment. He had spent entirely too long with Lady Enid and her family the previous evening. They had played games well into the night and even Lord Everton played a game of whist.

But he did not regret it. He enjoyed every minute he could have with Lady Enid. She was like a breath of fresh air in his life. And when she smiled, it did something to his heart.

He was spending entirely too much time thinking about Lady Enid. A part of him wished he could banish her from his thoughts, and another part never wanted her to leave. It was a constant battle that he fought within himself.

The coach came to a stop in front of a brown-stoned building and a footman came around to open the door. Dawn had just broken and there was a white haze that hung low to the ground. It was eerily quiet, as it should be in this part of Town. The only people that were on the street were servants as they went about their business. Anyone of importance was still sleeping in their beds.

Greydon exited the coach and saw Mr. Moore was leaning

against the building. He did not look pleased to see him by the slight scowl on his face.

"It is about time you showed up," Mr. Moore grumbled. "I have been waiting far too long for you."

Greydon didn't dignify Mr. Moore's words with a response. He glanced up at the building and asked, "Shall we go in?"

"That would be for the best. We don't want to garner too much attention," Mr. Moore said, pushing off the building.

He held the door open for Mr. Moore and waited to follow him in. Once he closed the door, he approached the apartment that was labeled "102-A". A sign nailed to the door read- *No entry. By order of Sir David Abbott.*

Not deterred by the order, Greydon reached for the handle and turned it. Locked. But he shouldn't have expected any different.

Turning towards Mr. Moore, he asked, "You, by chance, don't have a key?"

Mr. Moore frowned. "It is your brother's apartment. Why would I have a key?"

"Very well," Greydon said as he removed two long pins from his jacket pocket. "Stand guard while I open it."

Greydon crouched down and slipped the two long metal pins into the locking mechanism. He turned them in a purposeful manner until he heard the distinctive click.

"I opened it," Greydon announced as he rose. He returned the pins to his jacket pocket and opened the door. "After you."

Greydon turned his head to make sure no one was about to witness them entering the apartment but the corridor was clear. He stepped inside and closed the door.

As his eyes roamed the small apartment, he saw that the coroner had done a decent job of leaving the crime scene intact. But why would he expect anything different? Sir David believed Lady Eugenie to be guilty so there was no need to search for any other incriminating evidence. To do so could jeopardize his case.

Mr. Moore disappeared into a room off the hall and shouted, "In here, Rushcliffe."

Greydon skirted the two settees that sat in the center of the hall and headed towards what he assumed was the bedchamber. He came to a stop in the doorway as he saw the large bloodstain that was on the feather mattress. That was his brother's blood.

But now was not the time to be sentimental. He had a job to do. He walked closer to the bed and looked for anything that was amiss. An empty teacup was overturned on the nightstand, and he picked it up. He sniffed it but he smelled only the remnants of tea. Not that he expected otherwise. Arsenic was odorless and tasteless. That is why it was so deadly.

He crouched down and looked under the bed. But there was nothing there. Surely there had to be something here that could help Lady Eugenie.

Mr. Moore picked up some crumpled papers from the desk. "Your brother was writing a love letter to 'his dearest Lottie'. Was that his wife?"

"No, her given name is Harriet," he replied. "I have no idea who Lottie is."

"There are some traces of blood on the paper," Mr. Moore said before he turned his attention towards the drawers.

Greydon walked over to the window and saw that it opened to the alley behind the apartment. He opened it and leaned out. It was possible, based on the location of the window, that people heard Lady Eugenie scream, just as the coroner said.

But why scream? If she had just killed Phineas, why wouldn't she flee from the scene? Why stay and incriminate herself?

Mr. Moore closed the last drawer and said, "There is nothing in here that is useful."

Greydon turned to face the barrister. "Did Lady Eugenie say why she screamed?"

"She was trying to get help for Lord Rushcliffe."

"And you believe that?"

"You don't?" Mr. Moore countered. "Why else would she scream?"

Greydon bobbed his head. "I am beginning to wonder the same thing. She could have just walked out the door and disappeared into the crowd. So why stay?"

"Sir David claims that she panicked and was trying to deflect blame off of her," Mr. Moore replied.

A water basin sat on the table in the corner, and he walked over to it. He could see a reddish tint to the water. "Did Lady Eugenie say that she attempted to wipe the blood off her hands?"

"No, why?"

"There is blood in this water," Greydon pointed out. "Based upon the amount, I would say that someone washed the blood off their hands."

"Someone else was here," Mr. Moore said.

"That is what I have concluded, as well," Greydon responded. "But was it the murderer or Lady Eugenie's accomplice?"

"Lady Eugenie is innocent."

"I credit your feelings, but I need to look at the facts, without bias," Greydon said. "I am, however, beginning to doubt the scenario that Sir David has created. It just doesn't make sense, based on what I have seen."

Mr. Moore shook his head. "Well, thank heavens for that," he mocked.

"Do you know how long Lady Eugenie had been my brother's mistress?"

"She wasn't his mistress," Mr. Moore said. "That is what Sir David wants people to think, but it is not true."

Greydon was still skeptical. Why would a lady lower herself to visit a known rakehell if she wasn't his mistress? "Then why was she here?"

"She won't say," Mr. Moore replied. "She says that she is willing to take the reason to her grave."

"She might have to," Greydon said.

"That is what I have been telling her as well."

Greydon's eyes roamed over the bedchamber until they landed on the fireplace. He saw the remains of a fire, but the hearth had not been cleaned in days. He suspected it hadn't been cleaned since the murder. He crouched down in front of it and saw the burned curled corners of papers in the soot. "Someone burned papers in here," he informed the barrister.

"Do you suspect your brother or someone else?" Mr. Moore asked.

"I don't know," Greydon replied. "But someone went to great lengths to ensure those papers were destroyed."

"With all of this evidence brought to light, it might create reasonable doubt in the minds of the jury," Mr. Moore remarked.

"I doubt it. Lady Eugenie was found standing over Phineas' body with blood on her hands," Greydon said, rising. "It is going to take more than reasonable doubt to help her at this point."

"What do you propose?"

"You need to speak to your client and try to convince her to tell you the real reason she came to my brother's apartment."

"I wish it were that easy," Mr. Moore sighed. "Lady Eugenie has been quite tight-lipped on that issue."

"Perhaps a few more days in jail might change her mind."

"I don't think it will, sadly."

Greydon crossed his arms over his chest as he retreated to his own thoughts. What, or who, was Lady Eugenie trying to protect? What was so important that she was willing to take it to the grave?

Men and women were naturally selfish. It had been his experience that people only cared about themselves. Some may claim they had principles, but that all changed when their backs were against the wall. So why wasn't Lady Eugenie being more forthcoming with information?

Mr. Moore spoke up, drawing back his attention. "What are you thinking?"

"Things are not adding up here," Greydon replied. "I am not quite ready to say that Lady Eugenie is innocent but there are too many anomalies that give me pause."

"That is good enough for now."

"I need to discover who Lottie is and I suspect that Lord William might know," Greydon said. "He was my brother's oldest friend and they shared similar interests."

Mr. Moore pressed his lips together. "Yes, but Lord William is a bigger cad than your brother was. No offense."

"None taken," Greydon said. "I was not blind to my brother's reputation, but he is not on trial here."

Mr. Moore nodded his understanding. "Would you care for me to join you when you speak to Lord William?"

"I would prefer to go alone," Greydon replied. "If you are there, he might start asking questions that we don't want to answer."

"Quite right," Mr. Moore agreed.

Greydon's eyes grew fixated on the blood-coated bed. He wished, and not for the first time, that things had been different between him and his brother. He might have been able to save him, had he but the chance.

Mr. Moore came to stand next to him. "For what it is worth, I am sorry about your brother."

"Thank you," Greydon murmured. "But this still doesn't mean that I like you."

"The feeling is mutual."

"I'm glad that we can agree on something," Greydon said as he pried his eyes away from the bed. "We should depart so we do not garner any attention when we leave."

Mr. Moore put his hand out, indicating he should go first. "After you, my lord," he said.

As they departed the apartment, they made their way towards the street. He noticed that Mr. Moore didn't have a coach out front. "Do you need a ride?" he asked.

"I will walk," Mr. Moore replied. "Walking helps clear my head."

"Suit yourself," Greydon said as he went to step inside of his coach.

Mr. Moore called out to him, causing him to pause on the step. "I would be remiss if I did not thank you for your help today," he said. "I am embarrassed to admit that I need all the help I can get on this case."

"I am happy to oblige."

Mr. Moore smirked. "Have you come to terms about your feelings for Lady Enid?"

Greydon's jaw clenched. "That is none of your concern."

"I will take that as a yes, then."

"You would be wrong."

"I don't think I am."

Greydon decided to end this ridiculous conversation and stepped into the coach, slamming the door behind him. Mr. Moore was the last person he wanted to discuss his feelings with. He could barely tolerate the man.

But his concern was- if Mr. Moore knew he had feelings for Lady Enid, who else knew?

———————⌇———————

Enid stepped out of the nursery, closing the door behind

her. She had just put Marigold down for a nap and she was beginning to think that she could use one as well. She had the most fitful night of sleep because she was afraid. Now that she knew her fickle heart could be so easily turned, she knew she needed to protect herself.

It didn't matter that Lord Rushcliffe was the most handsome man of her acquaintance or how time seemed to slow down every time she saw him. She couldn't act on her feelings, nor would she. Furthermore, Lord Rushcliffe had given her no indication that he favored her, and that was good.

Despite all that had happened to her, she believed in love… but for other people. She didn't dare presume she was worthy of finding a love match. It wasn't in the cards for her, no matter that her heart had been turned to Lord Rushcliffe.

Her focus should remain on Marigold, and she would push down the yearnings of her heart. She had meant what she had told Lord Rushcliffe over dinner the night before. He was a good man, and he deserved a woman that didn't have a tainted reputation.

Her heart would remain locked away. That was the safest thing for her.

As Enid glanced down the corridor that led to her bedchamber, she knew that sleep would elude her. It would be best if she went in search of her mother. She assumed her mother was in the drawing room right now, waiting for her callers.

She walked down the stairs and crossed the entry hall. Once she stepped into the drawing room, she saw her mother was sitting next to Rosamond on the settee and they were working on their needlework.

Her mother glanced up when she walked in. "Is Marigold down for her nap?"

"She is." Enid sat across from them. "I had hoped for a nap but I decided against it."

"Why is that?" her mother asked as she pulled the needle out of the fabric.

Enid sighed. "My thoughts are forever jumbled and I would just lie awake with my thoughts."

"Anything you wish to share?" her mother inquired.

"Not at this time," Enid replied. She didn't dare reveal her feelings for Lord Rushcliffe. Then her mother would start scheming and no good would come from that. It would be best if she remained quiet on the subject.

Rosamond spoke up. "Would you care to go to the opera this evening with us?"

"I am not sure if that is wise," Enid said. "I fear that I would attract far too much attention, and not the good kind."

"Let the people stare," Rosamond asserted, lowering the needlework to her lap. "You live your life as you see fit and do not give the naysayers any heed."

Enid knew that Rosamond was trying to encourage her, but even she couldn't change her damaged reputation. No one could help her. "I do not want your reputation to suffer by being associated with me," she said.

"Let me worry about who I associate with," Rosamond encouraged.

"You are kind, and I know you mean well—"

Rosamond spoke over her. "Is there a yes somewhere in there?"

"It is a no," Enid replied.

"Well, I do not accept that." Rosamond reached for a cucumber sandwich on the tray. "It would be a mistake if you didn't come."

"I think it would be a mistake if I *did* come," Enid corrected.

Rosamond took a bite of her sandwich and was silent for a moment. Then she said, "Malcolm thinks it would be for the best if you came. As do I."

Her mother interjected, "I agree. You should go."

Enid opened her mouth to object, but Rosamond continued. "Life is meant to be enjoyed, not just endured. You need to get out of these walls and live your life to the fullest."

"I am happy here," Enid asserted. "It is safe, comfortable."

"If you continue to play it safe, I promise you that you will die with regrets," Rosamond pressed.

Enid lowered her gaze to her lap as she fidgeted with her hands. "I already have too many regrets."

"Then don't make new ones," Rosamond said. "Come to the opera with us tonight. You can hide in the back of the box if you would prefer."

Enid knew that she had a choice. She could continue on as she had or she could try to be brave, which was something that was eluding her at the moment. If she went tonight, she knew the gossips would not be kind to her. But, on the other hand, she would be gossiped about no matter what. So why shouldn't she enjoy herself?

Her mother spoke up. "I will watch over Marigold this evening. You do not need to worry about her."

Enid brought her gaze up and said, "I would like to go to the opera."

Rosamond clapped her hands together. "That is wonderful news. Malcolm will be so pleased by your decision."

"What will Father say?" Enid asked. "I have no doubt that he will be furious about my decision."

Her mother gave her an encouraging smile. "Let me deal with your father."

A thought suddenly occurred to Enid. "I have nothing to wear for this evening," she confessed. "All my gowns are entirely inappropriate for an evening at the opera."

"You need not worry about that. I have already had my lady's maid alter one of my gowns for you to wear," her mother said.

"How did you know I would agree to go this evening?" Enid asked.

Her mother's eyes twinkled with mirth. "I had a suspicion."

Enid hoped that this evening didn't turn into a disaster. She may have been born into this life, but she had given it up when she had eloped with John.

Osborne stepped into the room and announced, "Lady Lizette Westcott and Miss Bolingbroke have come to call."

Rosamond rose. "Please send them in," she said.

After the butler went to do her bidding, it was only a moment before Lady Lizette and Miss Bolingbroke stepped into the room.

Lady Lizette embraced Rosamond and said, "It has been far too long since we last spoke."

Rosamond laughed. "We spoke yesterday."

"Yes, but I do miss you living under the same roof as me," Lady Lizette said. "It was much more fun."

Enid turned her attention towards Miss Bolingbroke, who was standing back. "How are you faring?" she asked.

"I am well," Miss Bolingbroke replied. "And you?"

She smiled. "I am well, as well."

"I am glad that we are both well," Miss Bolingbroke said, returning her smile.

Gesturing towards an upholstered armchair, Enid asked, "Would you care to sit?"

"I would, but I am afraid I am unable to," Miss Bolingbroke sighed. "My mother is forever going on about my wrinkled gowns. It would be best if I stand here and do not move to ensure I do not create more wrinkles."

"Surely your gown won't get too wrinkled by sitting down," Enid encouraged.

"One would think, but my mother believes the reason why I haven't found a husband is because of my wrinkled gowns,"

Miss Bolingbroke said. "That, or my questionable personality."

"There is nothing wrong with your personality," Enid pressed.

Miss Bolingbroke blew out a puff of air. "Tell that to my mother."

Rising, Enid walked closer to her new friend. "If you choose to stand, then I will stand with you," she said.

"Thank you," Miss Bolingbroke murmured. "That is most kind of you."

Her mother addressed Miss Bolingbroke. "Would you at least care for a cup of tea?" she asked. "Or a cucumber sandwich?"

"Thank you, my lady, but I will pass. I do not wish to soil another gown with my clumsiness," Miss Bolingbroke replied.

After her mother poured a cup of tea for Lady Lizette, they started engaging in conversation and Enid turned her attention back towards Miss Bolingbroke. "I am sorry that your mother is so hard on you."

"It has always been that way," Miss Bolingbroke said. "She was the diamond of the first water when she debuted, and I am just... me. I am unmarried and my parents fear I will become a spinster."

"You are still young."

"My mother was married at my age, and she still shines whenever she walks into a room. Whereas I am just dull."

Enid placed a hand on her friend's sleeve. "You must not be so hard on yourself."

"I'm sorry. I do not mean to complain." Miss Bolingbroke lowered her voice. "Did you go speak to Lady Eugenie?"

With a glance over her shoulder to ensure no one was paying them any heed, she matched Miss Bolingbroke's tone, and replied, "I did, and I am even more convinced of her innocence."

"How did you get in to see her?"

"I asked nicely," Enid said vaguely. She didn't want to reveal that Mr. Moore had lied to get her into the room with Lady Eugenie.

Miss Bolingbroke frowned. "I heard that they are transferring her to Newgate now that the case is going to trial."

"How awful for her."

"I do not think you will be able to see her in Newgate, not without word getting out. Besides, it is much too dangerous to go there."

Enid nodded. "I agree, but I do worry about Lady Eugenie. She doesn't deserve this kind of treatment."

"No, she most assuredly does not," Miss Bolingbroke agreed. "But what can we do to help her?"

"I am working on that."

Osborne stepped into the room and met her gaze. "Lord Rushcliffe would like a moment of your time, my lady. Are you available?"

A thrill of excitement coursed through her at the mere mention of his name. What was wrong with her? Hadn't she decided she needed to safeguard her heart? Trying to appear indifferent, she replied, "I am. Will you send him in?"

Miss Bolingbroke gave her a curious look. "I hadn't realized you were acquainted with Lord Rushcliffe."

"He is a family friend," she said, not wanting to go into any more detail.

Lord Rushcliffe appeared in the doorway, looking deucedly handsome in a fine blue jacket and buff trousers. He bowed and exchanged pleasantries with the ladies before turning towards her and asked, "Can I speak to you privately?"

Enid glanced at her mother, who nodded her approval. "We can speak in the entry hall," she said as she went to brush past him.

Once she was far enough from the door to keep their

conversation private, she turned towards Lord Rushcliffe and gave him an expectant look.

Lord Rushcliffe had a solemn look on his face. "I just came from my brother's apartment and I have found many things that are disconcerting, to say the least."

"Could these things exonerate Lady Eugenie?"

"No, it is going to take a lot more to prove Lady Eugenie's innocence," Lord Rushcliffe replied. "But I am going to continue with the investigation until I get to the bottom of this."

"If you need any help—"

Lord Rushcliffe shook his head. "Absolutely not," he said. "You will stay here where it is safe and I don't have to worry about you."

"I can do more than what you are asking of me."

"I know."

"If that is the case, why won't you let me help you?"

Lord Rushcliffe leaned forward and tucked a piece of errant hair behind her ear, his finger lingering on her skin. "You seem to think that I don't think you are capable of helping me," he said. "But that is the furthest thing from the truth."

Her eyes roamed over his smooth jawline and she could see every freckle, every scar. "What is the truth, then?" she asked, breathlessly.

"I can't abide the thought of putting you in harm's way, for any reason. I need you to be safe," Lord Rushcliffe responded. "I can't be out there, not knowing if you are safe or not."

The main door opened and Lord Rushcliffe straightened.

Malcolm stepped into the entry hall and glanced between them. "Dare I ask what you two were discussing?"

"The weather," Enid rushed to reply.

Her brother gave her an exasperated look. "That seems highly unlikely."

Lord Rushcliffe bowed and addressed Enid. "I shall call upon you tomorrow, if you have no objections."

"I do not."

"Very good," Lord Rushcliffe said before he swiftly walked out the door.

Enid's eyes remained on Lord Rushcliffe's retreating figure until the door was closed. What had just happened between them?

Malcolm crossed his arms over his chest and gave her his most accusatory look. "What was all that about?"

"Nothing," Enid replied.

"It appears to me that you and Lord Rushcliffe are growing rather close."

"You would be wrong," Enid responded. "We are just friends."

Malcolm dropped his hands to his sides and approached her. As he placed a hand on her shoulder, he said, "Just be careful, little sister."

"You don't need to worry about me."

"But I do, and I always will," Malcolm said, dropping his hand.

While her brother walked into the drawing room, Enid took a moment to catch her breath. The skin behind her ear still tingled from Lord Rushcliffe's touch.

Chapter Eight

Greydon sat in the coach as he headed towards the unsavory part of Town. He needed to speak to Lord William and he was all too aware of the establishments that the man frequented, especially since his brother would usually accompany his friend.

His thoughts strayed towards Lady Enid and he chastised himself for being so familiar with her earlier. What was he thinking? That was the problem- he wasn't. He always seemed to lose rational thought when Lady Enid was around. She bewitched him, body and soul, and he fought hard to free himself from these relentless feelings.

Why was it nearly impossible to banish Lady Enid from his thoughts? He couldn't act on them. He cared little about her tainted reputation, but he knew he couldn't marry a woman that he could grow to love. *Love.* What a useless emotion. He had seen how it had destroyed his father, and he refused to follow suit.

The coach came to a stop in front of a gambling hall that was known as *The Lucky Ace*. The red-brick building was unassuming, but it was not a place for the faint of heart. The vilest of things happened inside these doors.

Greydon exited his coach and approached the main door. He tried to open the door but it was locked. So he knocked and waited. And waited. When no one answered, he knew he would need to find another way in.

He went around the side of the building and saw an alleyway. It was dark and smelled of excrement but he continued on. He noticed a side door and went to open it. This one wasn't locked, and he stepped inside.

There was a guard at the door who greeted him. "What is yer business here?" he growled, taking a step closer to him.

"Nothing that concerns you." Greydon drew himself up to his full height, hoping to intimidate the man. If the man wanted a fight, he had one.

The guard's critical eyes swept over him, but he eventually took a step back. "Go on, then, but I will be watching you, Bloke," he said.

Greydon headed down the corridor to where he could hear loud laughter. He stepped into the hall and saw scantily clothed women walking around with trays in their hands. Some of the women were in the laps of the men that were playing cards at the tables, whispering into their ears.

Tables filled the room and men of all walks of life sat around them. A low-hanging cloud of smoke hung in the hall from all the cigars that were being smoked. Someone was playing a rowdy tune on the pianoforte in the corner and a few men that were into their cups were singing along.

He hated gambling halls. Their sole purpose was to deprive men of their money. But it was the place that his brother loved the most. These were the people Phineas preferred to associate with.

His eyes roamed the room until they landed on Lord William. He was sitting at one of the tables in the back and, by the looks of it, he was ahead at the moment.

Greydon skirted the tables but was stopped by a blonde-haired woman with a tray in her hand. "Can I help you with something?" she asked in a sultry voice.

"No, thank you," Greydon said. "If you will just let me pass…"

The woman stepped closer to him until they were just inches apart. "I would be happy to show you upstairs," she said. "The beds are quite comfortable."

No wonder why his brother came to The Lucky Ace. It acted as a brothel, as well. Phineas couldn't seem to help himself.

Greydon took a step back. "I am not interested in what you are offering."

The woman's lips turned into a pout, which he suspected was well-rehearsed. No doubt it was quite convincing to the men that were interested in that type of thing. "That is a shame. I am told that I am quite vigorous."

He cleared his throat, finding himself deucedly uncomfortable at that thought. "Yes, well, that is quite informative, but I am meeting a friend. And I am late. Do you mind?"

Annoyance flashed across the woman's face. "Yes, I do mind," she said before she spun around and walked off. It was evident that she was not used to being rejected.

Greydon continued to the table and saw Lord William toss his cards down. He came to a stop next to him and gestured towards the empty chair. "May I have a seat?"

Lord William looked up at him through bloodshot eyes. "Greydon?" he asked. "What in the blazes are you doing here?"

"I need to speak to you," he replied as he sat down.

"I thought you were too good for a place like this," Lord William mocked as he reached for his drink. "That is what your brother told me."

Greydon leaned closer to him. "I was hoping you would answer a few questions for me."

Lord William tossed back his drink and slammed the glass

onto the table. "And what kind of questions would those be?" he asked. "Because I am rather busy."

"Yes, I can tell," Greydon responded dryly. "But they will be quick."

Turning to face him, Lord William asked, "Do you know what I miss most about your brother?"

"I do not."

Lord William burped, loudly. "I miss how he would come in here as if he owned the place. He would sit right where you are sitting and play for hours. I could always count on him, and he is gone now."

"I'm sorry, but surely you have other friends that can play with you."

"Nah, these men are imbeciles," Lord William said, gesturing to the other men at the table. "They only care about winning and they do not think long term."

The men at the table scowled at Lord William, but they continued to focus on their cards.

Lord William continued. "I am lonely, Greydon. So lonely. I do believe I need the companionship of one of the lovely ladies here tonight."

"I won't stop you, but don't you think you have had enough for one day?"

Lord William stared blankly at him. "Why would you think that?"

"You are drunk," he pointed out.

One of the men interjected, "He usually is."

Lord William's eyes narrowed at the man who'd just spoken. "And your life is so perfect, John," he taunted. "You come here to escape that whore of a wife."

John shoved back his chair and shouted, "You will not speak of my wife that way!"

"I will speak of her however I want, and there is nothing you can do about it," Lord William spat out.

Greydon knew he'd better intercede or else things would

end badly. He rose and reached for Lord William's arm. "You are out of line."

"No, *he* is out of line," Lord William said, yanking back his arm. "John knows the type of woman he married. She shares it with everyone but him."

John came around the table and Greydon stepped in front of him. "Leave him be," he ordered.

"Why would I do that?" John asked.

Greydon knew this wasn't his fight but he needed to ask Lord William a few questions before he engaged in fisticuffs. "He has had too much to drink and he doesn't know what he is saying."

Lord William spoke up. "I know what I am saying, and I meant every word," he taunted.

John tried to push him out of the way, but Greydon remained rooted in his spot. It was going to take a lot more than that to move him. "Just walk away while you still can," he advised.

Lord William rose and put his fists up in the air. "You are lucky that Greydon is here or else I would have beaten you to a bloody pulp."

Why couldn't Lord William just be quiet? He kept trying to escalate the situation and he was in no position to fight.

John stared daggers at Lord William. "Your friend won't always be around to protect you, my lord," he growled.

"I don't need him; I don't need anyone," Lord William declared as he started swaying on his feet. "I can fight my own battles."

The guard from the main door approached them and asked, "Is there a problem, gentlemen?"

Lord William pointed towards John. "He is no gentleman, but I am. I am more of a gentleman than anyone else in this room."

The guard frowned. "I think it is time for you to go," he said. "You are drunk and are stirring up problems."

"No, *you* are stirring up problems!" Lord William exclaimed. "I was just sitting here, minding my own business."

"I doubt that," the guard said. "Come along."

Lord William puffed out his chest. "You can't remove me from here. Do you know who I am?" he demanded.

"I do, and I don't care," the guard replied.

Greydon turned towards Lord William. "It is best if you walk out of here, rather than be dragged out."

"Fine," Lord William shouted with a wave of his hand. "I was going to leave anyways. I have had enough of this paltry place."

John walked back to his seat and muttered, "Good riddance."

"What did you say?" Lord William asked.

With a lifted brow, the man repeated his words slowly. "I said 'good riddance'."

Lord William scoffed. "You are inconsequential to me. You are a nobody and you will die a nobody."

Greydon grabbed Lord William's arm. "Let's go." He had just about enough of Lord William's pretentious attitude. He had no doubt that Lord William needed a comeuppance, but it wouldn't be today. Not with him.

Lord William tried to yank back his arm, but Greydon held firm as he led the man towards the door.

"You are hurting me," Lord William whined.

The guard held the door open as Greydon shoved Lord William out the side door. Lord William straightened himself in the alleyway. "That was uncalled for, Greydon," he shouted. "Who do you think you are?"

Greydon came to stand in front of Lord William and said, "I just need to ask you a few questions and then you can go home and drink it off."

"Why would you think I would answer your questions?" Lord William asked as he stuck his haughty chin in the air.

"If you don't, then I will let John have a go at you," Greydon said.

Some of the defiance left Lord William and his shoulders sank some. "You wouldn't dare," he said with uncertainty in his voice.

"I wouldn't test me; not today."

"What do you want to know?" Lord William asked, resigned.

"Did Phineas ever speak of a Lottie?"

Lord William gave him a baffled look. "Yes, I heard him utter that name, once or twice, but I never met her. Which is unusual since I knew most of the women that Phineas had dalliances with."

"Do you know where I can find her?" he pressed.

"Why?"

"Just consider me curious."

Lord William brought a hand up to his forehead. "I don't," he said. "Do you mind asking your questions in a quieter voice?"

Ignoring his request, Greydon pressed forward. "Did my brother ever mention Lady Eugenie?"

Lord William huffed loudly. "Lady Eugenie was a nuisance to Phineas. She would come around at odd hours to harass him. It did not surprise me that he died at her hand. She was never going to release him from her grasp."

"Are you sure?"

Lord William nodded decisively. "I am, and that is what I told Sir David Abbott when he came around."

Greydon resisted the urge to groan. "When did he question you?"

"The day the news broke about Phineas." Lord William grew somber. "God rest his soul. He died entirely too young."

A man emerged from the gambling hall and emptied the contents of his stomach next to the door. He wiped his mouth with the back of his hand and went back inside.

Lord William scrunched his nose. "I think it is time we depart from this wretched alleyway," he said before he walked away.

Greydon followed Lord William as his mind started whirling. Something wasn't adding up, but he wasn't quite sure what it was.

———————◦———————

Enid sat in the darkened coach as it traveled to the opera. What was she thinking when she had agreed to come? She had no doubt that this was a mistake. The *ton* would never accept her back into their ranks. She would forever be an outsider looking in.

Rosamond's voice broke through her musings. "It will be all right," she encouraged.

"I doubt that," Enid responded. "I don't know why you brought me. Your reputation will be tarnished, right alongside mine."

Malcolm reached for his wife's hand. "I dare anyone to say a disparaging word about my wife," he said in a firm tone.

"Yes, but the *ton* can turn on anyone," Enid pressed. "One minute you are in their good graces, and then you find yourself on the outs. They can be ruthless and unforgiving."

"The *ton* can be manipulated, just like anything or anyone else. You must trust us on this," Malcolm said.

Enid glanced down at her clasped hands in her lap. She did trust her brother, but even he couldn't control how the *ton* would react when they saw her at the opera. She had loved being the center of attention when she was a debutante but it was different now. She was a widow and a ruined woman- in the eyes of the *ton*.

But she was doing this for Marigold's sake. She wanted to give her daughter a future that she could only dream of.

The coach came to a stop in front of the Royal Opera House and a footman stepped off his perch to open the door. Once it was opened, Malcolm assisted them onto the pavement.

Enid felt a pit in her stomach as she watched the other patrons exit their coaches and travel up the steps to the Royal Opera House. No one seemed to give her much heed and that was greatly appreciated.

Malcolm offered his arm and led her up the stairs. He glanced over at her and whispered, "Breathe, Sister."

"This is a mistake. I shouldn't be here," Enid said.

"It is too late now," Malcolm responded as he led her through the doors.

Once they stepped inside, the entire room seemed to erupt in hushed conversations and the women whipped open their fans as they stared at her with disapproval on their features. The men in the room shifted so their backs were towards her, further shaming her.

Enid felt the panic well up in her chest and she knew she couldn't do this. It was too much. The *ton* would never accept her and it was futile to even try.

As she turned to leave, Lord Roswell Westlake stepped out from the crowd and approached her. She was grateful to see a familiar face, especially one that she had known for many years. He may have been Malcolm's friend, but he had always treated her with kindness.

Lord Roswell stopped in front of her and bowed. "It is lovely to see you this evening, Lady Enid."

"You are the only one that feels that way," Enid said as she dropped into a curtsy.

"Do not give them any heed," Lord Roswell encouraged. "They are jealous of your beauty."

Enid shook her head. "I assure you that is not the reason."

The short, white-haired Lady Emma Keyes approached Enid with her haughty nose in the air. "Your kind is not welcome here," she declared. "You should go before you further embarrass yourself."

As Enid tried to think of a retort, Lord Roswell spoke up. "Lady Enid will be joining me in my box this evening, assuming she is agreeable to that."

Lady Emma pursed her lips. "Why would you sully yourself with a trollop, my lord?" she asked. "If you need a companion, I would be more than happy to introduce you to a few young women."

"That is not necessary," Lord Roswell replied.

"My lord," Lady Emma started, "you must think of your mother. If word ever got out that you were associating with women of loose morals, such as Lady Enid, she would be devastated. It could cause her to fall into an early grave."

Lord Roswell visibly tensed. "You know not what you speak of and I would encourage you to bite your tongue."

"I know precisely what I speak of," Lady Emma declared.

Taking a step closer to the infuriating woman, Lord Roswell asked, "How is your son doing? Last I heard, he got his mistress pregnant and then abandoned her."

Lady Emma's eyes darted around the room. "That is neither here nor there."

"But it speaks to his character, and yours, if I am not mistaken," Lord Roswell said. "After all, you raised him. One must question what was taught in your home."

She gave him an indignant look. "I am not my son's keeper."

Lord Roswell shrugged one shoulder. "No, but, out of all these people, you should not be the one casting the first stone."

"I am merely speaking what everyone is thinking," Lady Emma declared.

"How noble of you," Lord Roswell mocked.

Lady Emma narrowed her eyes. "I am going to call upon

your mother and tell her all about your deplorable actions this evening."

"I hope you do," Lord Roswell said.

With a huff, Lady Emma declared, "Well, I never." She spun on her heel and walked back towards her female companions.

Malcolm tipped his head at his friend. "Well done, but I do hope Lady Emma doesn't cause too much trouble for you."

"I can assure you that my mother will give her little heed." Lord Roswell turned to address Enid. "How are you faring?"

Enid offered him a sad smile. "You can't fight off everyone that doesn't approve of me."

"No, but I can do so to the peskier ones," Lord Roswell responded. "Now, would you care to accompany me to my box or was I too presumptuous in my invitation?"

"That is kind of you to offer but—"

Malcolm interrupted her. "I think that is a wonderful idea."

"You do?" Enid asked, turning to face him. "What of our box?"

"Roswell's box is much grander than ours and it would go a long way for everyone to see you with him," Malcolm replied.

Enid recognized that her brother had a point, albeit reluctantly. She had been hoping to sit behind her brother and sister-in-law in the box and not draw too much attention to herself. But if she went with Lord Roswell, everyone would surely notice her.

Lord Roswell put his arm out. "If you are worried about your reputation, my sister is in the box with her companion," he said with mirth in his voice.

Knowing if she refused his proffered arm it would draw even more unwanted attention, she decided the best course of action would be to go with Lord Roswell, without voicing any further complaints.

She placed her hand on Lord Roswell's arm and allowed him to lead her towards a corridor, all while keeping her head held high. She refused to show the gnawing feeling of insecurity that was growing inside of her as she passed by women whispering behind their fans about her.

Once they had broken away from the crowd, Lord Roswell leaned closer and encouraged, "You are doing just fine, Enid."

She glanced over at him. "Is my discomfort so terribly obvious?"

"It is," Lord Roswell replied. "But you managed to take the first step, and you did so spectacularly."

She let out a slight huff. "I see that you are prone to exaggeration."

"Perhaps, but the *ton* will adore you soon enough," Lord Roswell said as he came to a stop by a door.

Enid followed suit and removed her hand. "The *ton* hates me."

"The *ton* hates everyone." Lord Roswell opened the door. "You should consider yourself fortunate."

"Do be serious."

"I am," Lord Roswell said as he held the door open wide. "Being accepted by the *ton* isn't as wonderful as people perceive it to be."

"I know, but I must think about my daughter's future."

Lord Roswell lifted his brow. "But what about your own future?"

"That is the least of my concerns," Enid replied. "I had my chance and I squandered it. I will not have my actions ruin my daughter's, as well."

"Your future and Marigold's will always be intertwined no matter how much you try to fight that."

Enid sighed. "I was afraid you might say that."

A familiar voice came from inside the box. "Are you two going to chat during the whole performance?"

Turning, she saw the dark-haired beauty, Lady Octavia,

standing there with her hand on her hip. She tried to keep her face expressionless, but her eyes gave her away. They were filled with humor, just as they always were. In the next moment, she was wrapped in Octavia's arms.

"I have missed you," Lady Octavia said as she stepped back. "I will never forgive you for eloping and abandoning me in the process."

"I didn't think you would receive me," Enid replied honestly.

Lady Octavia's lips twitched. "You know what they say about women and thinking…" She paused. "It is a terrible combination."

Lord Roswell groaned. "That was terrible."

"I thought it was quite clever," Lady Octavia said.

"Well, you would be wrong," Lord Roswell said. "We should get to our seats before the performers step on stage."

As Enid stepped inside, Lady Octavia looped her arm around hers. "You will sit by me."

"You are the worst to be sitting next to," Lord Roswell said from behind them. "Octavia likes to talk throughout the performance."

"Hush, Brother," Lady Octavia ordered. "Enid is old enough to make her own decisions and I won't have you making disparaging comments."

As they went to sit down, Enid claimed the center seat and noticed an older woman was leaning her head against the wall, her mouth hanging partly open.

Enid pointed at the woman. "Is she all right?"

Lady Octavia followed her gaze. "Yes, that is my companion, Mrs. Harper," she replied. "She may look like she is dead, but she is just resting. Trust me. I have made that mistake a time or two."

"Can anyone rest during the opera?" Enid asked.

"That is the best time to rest one's eyes," Lord Roswell said. "The lights are dim and everyone is paying attention to the performers on stage. No one cares a whit about what I am doing."

Lady Octavia shook her head at her brother. "People care, but it is *you* that does not care."

"Precisely," Lord Roswell said with a smile.

Shifting in her seat, Lady Octavia addressed Enid. "You eloped, your father disowned you, your husband died, and now you are back home where you belong. Did I miss anything?"

Enid laughed softly. "You left the part out about my daughter."

Lady Octavia's eyes grew wide. "You have a daughter?"

"I do," Enid said. "Marigold is a year old and I just adore her."

"Can I see her?" Lady Octavia asked.

"You may."

"What kind of tricks can she do?" Lady Octavia asked.

Lord Roswell chuckled and chimed in. "Marigold isn't a pet. She is a baby."

"They are similar, are they not?" Lady Octavia defended. "Both are dependent on someone else to survive."

"Heaven help us if you are ever responsible for raising a child," Lord Roswell joked.

With a shrug of one shoulder, Lady Octavia responded, "That is what nursemaids are for."

Lord Roswell leaned closer to Enid. "Run, Enid, run while you still can," he whispered. "It is too late for me, but save yourself."

Lady Octavia leaned in and matched his low tone. "I can hear you, Brother."

"I am well aware," Lord Roswell said as he straightened in his seat.

"Just ignore Roswell, everyone does," Lady Octavia advised with a smirk on her lips.

Enid watched a performer step onto the stage and the room went quiet. Well, all except for Lady Octavia.

"Did Roswell inform you that I acquired a peacock as a pet?" she asked.

"He did not," Enid replied.

Lady Octavia shuddered. "Do not be fooled by their beautiful feathers. Peacocks are mean, vile creatures."

Lord Roswell put his finger up to his lips. "Do be quiet," he said in a hushed voice.

"Why?" Lady Octavia asked. "Has something happened on stage yet?"

"No, but it will," Lord Roswell pressed.

Lady Octavia leaned back in her seat. "I do not know why you talked me into going to the opera. It is dreadfully boring."

"Not this again," Roswell muttered. "Is it possible for you not to complain until after the performance?"

"Forget I said anything, and I do apologize for existing," Lady Octavia said in such a dramatic fashion that only she could get away with.

As the curtains opened, Enid turned her attention towards the stage and she found herself grateful that Malcolm had talked her into coming this evening. How she had missed this. She hadn't been to the opera in years, not since she was a debutante. It felt good to do things that used to bring her so much joy.

Chapter Nine

With the morning sun streaming through the windows, Greydon sat at his father's desk in the study as he went through the accounts. He had gotten up at an early hour since sleep kept eluding him. He wanted to sleep, but his thoughts kept straying towards Lady Enid.

He had many more important things to do than to dwell on Lady Enid. So why couldn't he stop himself? He had been around beautiful women before, though, they usually lacked the traits he found most desirable. Traits like intelligence, compassion and confidence. But Lady Enid was in possession of these traits, and more.

Botheration.

He needed to focus on what was important- the case. He would need to do some more digging into Lady Eugenie's past and hoped it yielded some results. That was the only logical course of action at the moment. But, to do so, he would need to speak to Lady Enid, which was not entirely unappealing to him.

His tall sister, Helena, stepped cautiously into the room. Dark curls framed her face and swayed back and forth as she glanced around the room. "Is Father home?" she asked.

"He is still sleeping."

Helena let out a sigh of relief. "Good, because I need to speak to you," she said as she closed the door. "Has Father decided when the funeral will be taking place?"

"It is to be in three days' time." Greydon glanced curiously at her. "Did Father not send word?"

"No, of course not," Helena exclaimed, tossing up her hands. "Why would he keep his daughter informed of such a thing?"

Leaning back in his chair, he said, "I should have known."

Helena sat across from him in an armchair. "What has had you so preoccupied of late?" she asked. "I have come by on multiple occasions only to discover you are not home."

"I am rarely home," he pointed out.

"Yes, but it is different," Helena pressed. "Phineas just died and you have assumed his title."

Greydon frowned. "Do not remind me."

"I apologize if I am being insensitive, but Phineas' death did not come as a surprise to me, considering how he lived his life," Helena said. "I halfway expected him to drink himself to death or be found in a ditch somewhere."

"I had been hoping he lived a long, fruitful life," Greydon admitted. "I never wanted his responsibilities." He waved his hand over the desk.

"Well, you have them now and I can only imagine how unbearable Father is being about it. Our family's legacy is the most important thing to him."

Greydon could hear the hurt in his sister's voice and it made him sad. His father hadn't always ostracized Helena. It wasn't until their mother died that his father started keeping Helena at arm's length. She was the spitting image of their mother.

"Father will come around," he attempted. It was an empty promise. They both knew that their father was incapable of change. The grief had consumed him, taking every ounce of happiness that he had once enjoyed.

Helena could see right through him and made a face. "Father will never come around, and we both know that. He stopped being a father to me the moment Mother was buried."

"If it helps, I prefer when Father was cold and distant to me," Greydon said. "He has been far too attentive as of late. He is demanding that I become acquainted with all of our accounts."

"You poor thing," Helena mocked. "What a burden you must bear."

Greydon chuckled and it felt good to do so. "I have missed you, Sister."

"I am only but across Town. You are always welcome in my home."

"I thank you for that, and I will visit soon, I promise," Greydon said.

Helena cocked her head. "What burdens are you bearing right now?" she asked. "You look more troubled than normal."

Not taking offense, he replied, "No more than I usually am."

"That did not answer my question."

Greydon had always confided in his sister, but he didn't dare speak of Lady Enid to her. He was worried if he did so that Helena would see right through him. And that was a risk he did not want to take.

With an expectant look, Helena asked, "Is this about your work as a Bow Street Runner?"

"It is," he replied. That was partially true so he wasn't technically lying to his sister.

"Do you wish to expand at all?" Helena prodded.

Greydon hesitated. He wasn't quite sure how she would respond to the fact that he was looking into their brother's murder. Should he keep that from her and protect her from the truth?

Helena shifted in her seat and said, "I know that look."

"What look?" he asked innocently.

"You are trying to decide how much to reveal because of my delicate constitution," Helena said. "But I assure you I am much tougher than I look."

Greydon grinned. "I agree with that."

"Now, out with it."

His grin disappeared as he leaned forward in his seat and he rested his elbows on the desk. "I am looking into Phineas' death."

"Why would you do such a thing?" Helena asked. "The case is going to trial and everyone is saying that Lady Eugenie killed him."

"I have some doubts."

Helena lifted her brow. "You are trying to prove Lady Eugenie's innocence?" she asked in disbelief. "She was standing over our brother's body with blood on her hands."

"That is true, but there were indications that another was at Phineas' apartment."

"Are you implying that she had an accomplice?" Helena asked.

Greydon knew how ridiculous he must sound to his sister, but he couldn't in good conscience just ignore the things that he had seen. "Perhaps, but there are some things that don't add up. And I just want to be sure Lady Eugenie is guilty before she gets a noose around her neck."

"Why do you care so much?" Helena asked.

"I don't care, per se, but I need to discover the truth," Greydon replied.

Helena pressed her lips together. "You don't owe Lady Eugenie anything. Why can't you just let this go?"

"I'm afraid I am unable to do so."

Leaning back in her seat, Helena studied him for a long

moment, her expression giving nothing away. Finally, she spoke. "All right, what can I do to help?"

"This is something I need to do on my own."

"Why do you insist on shouldering so many burdens?" Helena questioned. "Ever since Matthew died——"

Greydon cut her off. "I don't want to talk about him."

"That is no surprise. You never do."

"That is because that part of my life is over."

Helena gave a look that implied she didn't believe him. "For the past five years, you have been running from what happened. It wasn't your fault."

Shoving back his chair, Greydon rose. "You know not what you speak of."

"But I do."

Greydon walked over to the window and stared out. This was the last conversation that he wanted to have. What happened to Matthew had been imprinted on his very soul. It was why he worked as hard as he did, never wavering for fear of failure; fear of having to acknowledge what had happened was, in fact, his fault.

He was the one that had recommended going to the tavern, knowing that it was in the rookeries. What had started as a night of drinking turned into something much more sinister.

"Greydon..." his sister attempted.

He put his hand up, stilling her words. "I know you are trying to help, but I am fine."

"You don't seem fine."

Turning to face her, he went to lean back against the windowsill. "What do you want from me?" he asked, his voice rising. He knew his sister only had his best interests at heart, but he wasn't in the mood to discuss this. Why couldn't she drop it?

"I want you to acknowledge that Matthew's death,

although tragic, was not your fault," Helena said. "You won't be able to start healing until you do so."

"Who says that I want to start healing?" Greydon demanded.

Helena looked as if there were more things she wanted to say on the subject, but instead she said, "I did not come here to fight with you."

"It seems like you did."

"No, I just wanted to know when Phineas' funeral was," Helena said. "Spending time with you was just an added benefit." Her words were followed by a small smirk.

Greydon knew he was being defensive but he did not like talking about that fateful night when he had lost his best friend. It should have been him. He wanted it to be him. Instead, he was forced to relive that night, over and over, in his head.

Pushing off from the windowsill, Greydon said, "I would prefer if we would discuss something else."

"We could always discuss Lady Enid," Helena remarked with her smirk still intact.

He felt his body grow tense. "Why would we do that?"

"She is a perplexing choice, considering her past," Helena said.

"What do you know of her past?" he half-asked, half-demanded.

Helena put her hands up in surrender. "You forget that I owe Lady Enid a great debt. I have no ill-will towards her."

"I'm sorry… again," Greydon said. "But I would prefer not to discuss Lady Enid either."

"What can we discuss then?" Helena teased. "The weather? The state of the gardens? Or we could go practice our needlework together?"

Greydon shuddered. "That sounds dreadful."

Helena grew solemn. "Just promise me that you know what you are doing," she said, holding his gaze.

"I can't promise that. Quite frankly, I don't know what I am doing."

"You are playing a risky game right now, especially spending time with Lady Enid," Helena advised. "I have no doubt that when Father hears you are spending time with Lady Enid that he will grow irate."

Greydon nodded his acknowledgement. "I can handle Father."

"I hope that is true."

Rising, Helena smoothed down her black gown and asked, "If I may be so bold, why Lady Enid?"

"Pardon?"

"I don't think I can make my question any simpler," Helena said. "Why are you showing attentions to Lady Enid?"

Greydon pursed his lips together. "If you must know, I am not pursuing Lady Enid," he replied. "She was the one who asked me to investigate Phineas' murder. She is adamant that Lady Eugenie is innocent."

"Yet you indulged her request."

"Not at first, but I have since come around," Greydon said.

Helena considered him for a moment, and he was afraid of what she might be seeing. In an inquisitive tone, she asked, "Am I to assume you hold no affection towards Lady Enid?"

"None," he lied.

"But you are doing her bidding?" Helena pressed.

Greydon shook his head. "I daresay you are reading too much into this."

"Am I?"

Before he could reply, Helena continued. "As riveting as this conversation is, I must depart before Father wakes up."

"You will be seeing him at the funeral," Greydon reminded her.

Helena grimaced. "Do not remind me. I have no doubt he will say as few words as possible to me."

"Most likely."

Walking over to him, Helena leaned in and kissed his cheek. "Just be careful, Brother. Even you aren't invincible."

"I never claimed to be."

"But your actions say otherwise." Helena spun on her heel and departed from the room.

Greydon walked back over to the desk and sat down. He glanced up at the long clock in the corner and wondered how much longer he should wait before calling upon Lady Enid. He wanted to keep her informed of the ongoing investigation. At least that is what he was telling himself. He wanted to see her again. And that was the problem. It was always the problem.

Enid held Marigold in her arms as they strolled through the gardens. It was a bright, sunny day and there was not a cloud in sight. The flowers were in full bloom this time of year and the fragrant smell of roses wafted through the wind.

She lifted her head to the sky and took a deep breath. She was happy being back home. This is where she belonged, even if her father went out of his way to make her feel unwelcome. Most importantly, this is where Marigold deserved to be. She was an innocent in all of this, and Enid would fight for her daughter. She had to. That was her job as Marigold's mother.

Enid watched her mother approach from the townhouse with a purposeful stride. It wasn't long before her mother stopped next to her and said, "Lord Rushcliffe has arrived and has been shown into the drawing room."

A familiar twinge of excitement flowed through her at those words. "Oh, I hadn't expected him so early," she said, hoping her words didn't reveal her excitement at seeing him again.

Her mother, always the dignified one, clasped her hands in front of her. "You two have been spending a lot of time together as of late." Her words weren't accusatory, but they merely stated a fact.

"Have we?" Enid asked innocently. "I'm afraid I haven't noticed."

Lifting her brow, her mother asked, "You haven't noticed he has come to call the last few days?"

Enid knew she had been caught in a lie so she attempted to save face by saying, "Yes, well I have noticed *that*."

Her mother was not so easily fooled by her attempt to pacify her. "What are you keeping from me, Child?" she asked forthrightly.

"Nothing," Enid rushed to reply.

"I just worry that you and Lord Rushcliffe are growing too close and that would only end in tears."

"Why is that?"

Her mother unclasped her hands, and her eyes grew compassionate. "I do not wish to speak of such things but your reputation has been tarnished and I daresay that most gentlemen of the *ton* won't be able to look past that, especially when seeking a wife."

"A wife?" Enid repeated.

"Yes, I do not wish to be a naysayer but—"

Enid spoke over her mother as she rushed to correct her. "Lord Rushcliffe doesn't want me for a wife," she declared. "I can assure you of that."

"Then why is he coming to call so frequently?"

Enid bit her lower lip as she tried to think of something that would appease her mother. She couldn't reveal that he worked as a Bow Street Runner or that she asked him to investigate his brother's murder. It wouldn't make sense why he would do so unless she knew all the facts. And that was not her secret to share.

"I'm afraid I cannot say," Enid said.

Her mother frowned and lowered her voice. "Lord Rush-cliffe doesn't want you for a mistress, does he?"

"Heavens, no!" Enid exclaimed. "Lord Rushcliffe is a kind, honorable man. He would never ask such a thing from me."

A look of relief came to her mother's face. "I am glad to hear you say that. I have been so worried."

"You need not worry about Lord Rushcliffe. We are just friends."

"You must be careful, then," her mother said. "You wouldn't wish to tarnish Lord Rushcliffe's reputation."

"I have no intention to."

Her mother nodded in approval. "Very well. You mustn't keep him waiting for long," she encouraged, holding her arms out. "I shall finish Marigold's walk."

"Thank you, Mother," Enid said as she relinquished her hold on her daughter.

As she approached the townhouse, a footman opened the door and she stepped inside. After she walked down the corridor, she passed the open door to the study and she heard her father say, "A word, Enid."

Enid closed her eyes. What now? What could her father possibly want to say to her? Well, she should be grateful he was speaking to her today.

Begrudgingly, she took a few steps back and entered the study. "Yes, Father," Enid said as cordially as she could. She had no doubt that he was going to yell at her for something that she had done or even thought about doing.

Her father placed the quill he was holding down on the desk and stared up at her. "I have spoken to Lord Pendle and you are to stay away from his son."

"I beg your pardon?"

"You are to stay away from Lord Rushcliffe," her father replied sternly. "Do I make myself clear?"

Enid was not done with her questions and asked one of

her own. "Why does it matter to you or Lord Pendle who Lord Rushcliffe associates with?"

Her father looked at her like she was an imbecile. "Are you so cruel and selfish that you would have others impugn Lord Rushcliffe's honor by associating with him?"

"I would not, but—"

"Then run along and do try to avoid instigating another scandal," her father ordered in a dry tone.

Enid stared at her father for a moment, unsure of what she should say. Her father was so cruel to her and would never let her forget her past mistakes.

Her father glared at her. "Why are you still here?" he asked. "Can't you see that I have work to do?"

Taking a step closer to the desk, she ignored the annoyance that flashed on his features and she asked, "Why do you hate me?"

"Hate you?" her father asked with a shake of his head. "I don't hate you."

"You don't?" She almost sighed in relief at that news. Perhaps they could one day mend their relationship.

Her father continued. "But every time I look at you, I get disappointed all over again. You let this family down; you let *me* down. And that is something that one can never get over."

"I am sorry, Father," she said. "How can I ever make this right?"

"I'm afraid you can't."

"Are we just to go on living with one another as we have been?"

Her father picked up the quill and dipped it into the ink pot. "That is right," he replied. "Your mother and brother may want you here, but I do not. Remember that."

Enid was dismissed as he turned his attention to the documents on his desk and began to write. Her father had clearly put her into her place... again. But that didn't mean she wouldn't fight for change. She couldn't go on, day in and day out, tiptoeing around her father, afraid to incite his anger.

But what could she do? Her father had no intention of ever reconciling with her. Knowing there was no point in engaging her father any further, she hurried out of the study and down the corridor.

Once she arrived at the drawing room, she stepped inside and saw a maid was sitting in the corner and Lord Rushcliffe was standing by the hearth.

Enid took a moment to admire Lord Rushcliffe's handsome face and fine clothing before saying, "I apologize for keeping you waiting, my lord."

Lord Rushcliffe turned to face her and when their eyes met, her heart started to beat faster. "Lady Enid," he said with a bow.

Enid approached him but was mindful to keep proper distance. "Have you any news?"

"I do," he replied, glancing at the maid in the corner. "Can she be trusted?"

"She can," Enid replied.

Lord Rushcliffe took a step closer to her and in a hushed voice asked, "Did Lady Eugenie ever mention a Lottie?"

"No, but she does have a sister named Charlotte. Perhaps she goes by Lottie?"

"How old is Lottie?"

"I believe she would be about seventeen years old now." She paused. "Why?"

He grew solemn. "I found letters that were addressed to Lottie in my brother's apartment," he revealed.

"You don't think that Lottie was having an affair with your brother, do you?"

"It isn't inconceivable."

"But she is only seventeen."

Lord Rushcliffe pursed his lips. "I do not believe age mattered to my brother," he shared. "He was a cad and preyed on all women, at least the ones that were handsome enough to tempt him."

"That is awful."

"I won't disagree with you there." Lord Rushcliffe shifted in his stance. "Do you know if Lady Eugenie held affection for my brother?"

"I do not know, but she insisted that she wasn't his mistress."

"And you believe her?"

"I do."

Lord Rushcliffe ran a hand through his dark hair. "I was told that Lady Eugenie was rather possessive of my brother."

"That does not sound like Lady Eugenie," Enid said. "She is generally practical and logical in her approach to things."

"We might be going down a dangerous path on this one," Lord Rushcliffe warned. "I need to prepare you that you might not like what I find."

"I understand."

Lord Rushcliffe held her gaze for a moment before asking, "What is troubling you?"

She blinked. "What do you mean?"

"I can see it in your eyes," Lord Rushcliffe said. "You are terrible at hiding your emotions."

Enid should have known that she couldn't hide what she was feeling around a seasoned investigator. With a glance at the doorway, she replied, "My father spoke to yours and they have decided that it would be best if we did not associate with one another."

"I see," he responded, taking a small step towards her. "Is that what you want?"

"No, it is not, but I think it would be for the best," Enid replied. "I do not want you to damage your reputation by associating with me."

"Do I not get a say in this?" Lord Rushcliffe asked.

Enid bobbed her head. "Yes, but I do not want you to be friends with me out of pity."

"Is that what you think I am doing?"

"I cannot presume to know what your intentions are," Enid admitted.

Lord Rushcliffe's eyes crinkled around the edges. "I am friends with you because I want to be, not because of some misguided notion that I pity you. And I do not abandon my friends, for any reason, no matter the repercussions."

"But your reputation—"

"I care more about you than my reputation," Lord Rushcliffe said, speaking over her.

Enid stared up at him, unsure of his meaning. Did he care for her as a friend or, dare she believe that his feelings extended beyond that? Did she want that?

Lord Rushcliffe's eyes grew intense, more so than she had ever seen before. "I will decide who I associate with, not my father, and most assuredly, not the *ton*." His words were firm but held a gentleness to them. "Do you understand?"

All Enid could do was nod her head in understanding.

"You will not rid yourself of me so easily," Lord Rushcliffe said.

"I do not want to rid myself of you," Enid admitted, pleased that she found her voice.

Lord Rushcliffe smiled, and her heart took flight. "I am pleased to hear that, and I hope I am not being too presumptuous, but may I call you by your given name?"

"You may," Enid replied.

"Then you must call me by mine," he said.

Enid felt herself smiling in response. "I would like that... Greydon," she said, tripping up on his given name.

"That was a good first attempt, and I do believe it will get easier every time you say it, which I hope is often."

"As do I," Enid said.

Greydon held her gaze and something passed between

them but she wasn't quite sure what it was. She felt like they were in their own world, even for just a moment. It was pleasant and she wanted to linger there with him.

But Greydon must not have felt the same because he cleared his throat and took a step back. "If you will excuse me, I have things I must see to."

"Of course," she said with a slight curtsy.

Greydon bowed. "Good day, Enid. I shall call upon you shortly."

Before she could say another word, Greydon departed from the drawing room without a backward glance. It was only a moment later that she heard the main door open and close.

What an odd reaction, she thought. Why had he left so abruptly? Had she done something wrong? She truly hoped not.

Chapter Ten

Greydon had made a huge mistake. He had miscalculated his feelings for Enid… again. It was growing nearly impossible to be around her without the immense desire to pull her into his arms and kiss her senseless. Would she even welcome his advances?

No. He couldn't pursue her. He couldn't. To do so would be utter madness. He had meant what he had said about not caring a whit about her reputation. He was loyal to the people that mattered to him, no matter what. He would rather have a kinship with a few good, kind people than the admiration of the masses. He was not one that sought the approval of others.

But for how long could he continue on as he had, denying his feelings for Enid?

His coach came to a stop outside of his ancestral townhouse and he saw that Mr. Moore was standing near the black iron fence that surrounded his property.

Greydon exited his coach and approached Mr. Moore with a curious look. "May I ask why you are loitering outside of my townhouse?"

"I need to speak to you," Mr. Moore said.

"Can this not be done in the comfort of my drawing room?" Greydon asked.

Ignoring his question, Mr. Moore took a step closer and asked one of his own. "Do you have any leads on the investigation?"

"At this time, I am trying to get a sense of who Lady Eugenie was," Greydon admitted. "Was she a jealous lover or an innocent bystander in all of this?"

"What do you think she is?"

Greydon sighed. "I don't rightly know, and that is what is bothering me."

"I can assure you that she had nothing to do with your brother's murder," Mr. Moore asserted.

"I know, but I live in a world that requires actual proof. I do not rely on someone else's word," Greydon said.

Mr. Moore frowned. "I have been granted permission for you to join me this afternoon when I meet with Lady Eugenie in Newgate."

"I shall look forward to it."

"I was hoping you had discovered something that I could use because the case is stacked against Lady Eugenie."

"If she is innocent, the truth will come out."

Mr. Moore did not look convinced. "Yes, because we have never put to death an innocent person before," he remarked dryly. "I shall send word about our meeting at Newgate."

Greydon tipped his black top hat in response and headed towards the main door. It opened and Davy stood to the side to grant him entry.

After he removed his top hat, Greydon extended it towards the butler and asked, "Is my father home?"

"He is, my lord," Davy replied. "He is in the study with Lady Rushcliffe. She only just arrived."

"Will you see to refreshments being brought in?"

"Very good," Davy said before he went to do his bidding.

Greydon wasn't quite sure what he was about to walk into. Harriet was always poised and composed, but she had only lost her husband a few days ago. Would she be crying? He hoped not. He was never quite sure what to say or what to do when a woman cried in front of him.

As he approached the study door, he heard his father's gruff voice echoing in the hall. He wasn't sure what his father was upset about but no doubt it was a situation of his own making.

He stepped into the room and saw Harriet, who had tears streaming down her face, as she sat across from his father on a settee, dressed in a black gown. She was a beautiful woman with her black hair, thin face, and pointed nose.

A flicker of relief crossed his father's face when he saw Greydon. "Good, you are home," he said. "Will you kindly tell Harriet that she will not be receiving one penny of her dowry back?"

Money. That is what this was about. That is what it was always about to his father. If anything cost a farthing over what his father thought was fair, then he would feel as if he had been cheated.

Greydon smiled at Harriet, despite feeling deucedly uncomfortable by her show of emotion. "Good morning, Harriet," he greeted. "How are you faring?"

She swiped at the tears on her face. "I am well." Her words sounding anything but believable. "I just came to speak to your father and…" She stopped and started sobbing.

Addressing his father, he asked, "What does the marriage contract say about the dowry?"

"It is to be returned only if he dies within the first year of marriage," his father replied matter-of-factly. "Harriet and Phineas were married for almost two years."

Harriet hiccupped. "But how shall I live without Phineas for support?"

"You are entitled to a jointure, which is quite fair, considering the circumstances," his father responded. "We will continue to support you until you are wed."

"Where will I live?" Harriet asked.

"You will remain at the townhouse that you shared with Phineas. I will continue to pay for it until the end of the Season. After that, you can reside at the dower house at our country estate," his father replied.

Harriet stared blankly at him. "You wish to exile me to the dower house?"

Greydon reached into his jacket pocket and removed a white handkerchief. He extended it towards Harriet. "We do not wish to exile you," he said. "What of your parents? Can you not go live with them?"

"They are living in Russia since my father is an ambassador, and I do not wish to live there," Harriet revealed as she wiped her cheeks. "But I do not want to live at the dower house either. All of my friends are here in Town."

"You are a widow now and we are expecting you to mourn my son properly," his father said firmly.

"I know my duty," Harriet remarked as she clenched the handkerchief in her hand.

"It would be best if you retired to the dower house right after the funeral," his father said. "I shall see to the arrangements."

As his father rose, Harriet shook her head. "I would like to stay in Town until the end of the Season."

"For what purpose?" his father demanded. "You are in full mourning for a year and half-mourning for six months."

"This is true, but I am not ready to leave London," Harriet said.

His father looked displeased by her response. "You are not thinking clearly at the moment and I have work that I need to see to."

Harriet's voice was hesitant as she said, "I was hoping to discuss the possibility of me attending Phineas' funeral."

"Absolutely not!" his father exclaimed with a swipe of his hand. "Women's constitutions are much too delicate to maintain a stoic calm in the face of death. I will not have my son's funeral gossiped about."

"It isn't unfathomable for me to attend," Harriet said.

"I understand your need to say goodbye, but a funeral service is not the appropriate place for you to do so," his father asserted.

Harriet's eyes lowered to her lap, and her shoulders slumped. She looked sad, defeated, and Greydon knew that he couldn't just stand by and not intercede on her behalf.

"I do not think Harriet's request to attend the funeral is unreasonable," Greydon said.

His father scowled. "I disagree," he growled. "We would be a laughingstock if we allowed Harriet to attend."

"I daresay you are exaggerating," Greydon remarked. "It isn't entirely uncommon for a woman to attend."

"A woman, yes, but not a widow," his father pressed.

Rising, Harriet said, "I should be going."

"Would you like me to escort you back to your townhouse?" Greydon asked.

Harriet gave him a weak smile. "That won't be necessary," she replied. "There are some advantages to being a widow."

Greydon bowed. "I shall send word about the funeral."

"Thank you." Harriet turned towards his father and dropped into a curtsy. "My lord," she murmured.

After Harriet departed from the study, Greydon crossed his arms over his chest and asked, "Was your harsh treatment towards Harriet absolutely necessary?"

"I wasn't harsh," his father replied. "I was pragmatic. There is a difference."

"Would it be so terrible if she came to the funeral?"

His father walked around his desk and sat down. "Widows have no place at a funeral. Harriet would find it difficult to restrain her tears and it would be embarrassing- for both of us."

"So you are trying to protect Harriet?"

"I am."

Greydon dropped his arms to his sides. "I think that is a mistake."

His father opened a ledger that was in front of him. "Duly noted, but I have work I need to see to," he said. "Did you have a chance to review those documents I left for you?"

"I did."

"And?" his father asked expectantly.

Greydon sat down on a chair that faced the desk. "I signed them and had them delivered to our solicitor."

His father nodded in approval. "I am pleased by the progress that you have been making."

Leaning forward, Greydon knew he was about to stoke his father's ire but he didn't care. He had a few things that needed to be said. "I understand you spoke to Lord Everton about me."

"I did," his father said, keeping his head down. "We decided it would be best if you ceased all communication with his daughter, Lady Enid."

"And if I disagree with that?"

His father brought his gaze up and gave him a baffled look. "Lady Enid is a ruined woman. I do not know why you have been wasting your time with her, but it ends now. You have a duty to this family."

Greydon held his father's gaze as he said, "I have no intention of ending my friendship with Lady Enid."

His father harrumphed. "Your friendship?" he asked. "Men and women cannot be friends. One always wants something from the other."

"That isn't true."

"Lady Enid is just using you to help rehabilitate her image and it won't work. She will only damage your reputation."

Greydon rose from his chair. "You do not get to tell me who I can and cannot associate with," he said. "I have my own mind."

His father's eyes narrowed. "You are my heir and I expect you to behave honorably."

"You assume I am not?"

"I know having Lady Enid as your mistress sounds appealing, but—"

Greydon cut him off. "I have no intention of taking Lady Enid on as a mistress, or any woman, for that matter."

"Surely you do not wish to court Lady Enid?" his father asked, aghast. "It would be entirely improper for you to do so and it would bring ruination down on this family."

"I am not looking to court Lady Enid either."

His father looked visibly relieved by his admission. "Then why are you spending time with her?"

Greydon tugged down on the ends of his blue jacket. "My reasons are my own, and I do not need you prying into my business."

"Be careful, Son," his father advised. "No one may have given you heed as a second son, but you are now heir to an earldom. Your every move is being watched and scrutinized."

"What a delightful thought," Greydon muttered.

His father reached for a quill and dipped it into the ink pot. "I do not know what kind of hold Lady Enid has on you, but it will go nowhere. She is unfit to even be associated with you."

Greydon took a moment to compose himself before saying, "You are wrong about Lady Enid. It is I who is not worthy of being associated with her."

"That is ludicrous, and not at all true," his father barked.

He knew that this conversation would go nowhere, and it would be best if he departed before his own temper flared. No matter what he said, he would never be able to convince his father how remarkable Enid truly was.

She was his dream. She made him want to be a better man, and all he wanted was to hold her in his arms. He thought about her all the time. Even now, when he was arguing with his father, he was thinking about Enid. There could never be another.

And that is when he knew he had done something intolerably stupid. With every moment he spent in her company, he'd grown to this moment, and suddenly he knew. He had fallen in love with Enid.

Greydon checked his pocket watch as he stood on the corner of Newgate Street and Old Bailey Street. He had arrived at the appointed time to meet with Mr. Moore, but the infuriating barrister was late.

He glanced over his shoulder at Newgate Prison and he resisted the urge to grimace at the stone edifice. This was a place that he wouldn't wish upon his worst enemy. It was terribly overcrowded, dank, and many prisoners were chained to walls to languish and starve.

A hackney came to a stop in front of him and Mr. Moore stepped out onto the pavement. "My apologies for being late, but I assure you that it couldn't be helped."

Greydon doubted that, but he decided to keep that to himself. He was in no mood for excuses and Mr. Moore seemed to be in possession of quite a few.

Mr. Moore paid the driver and the hackney started rolling away. "Shall we go in?" the barrister asked.

"That is why we are here, is it not?" Greydon muttered.

"That it is," Mr. Moore agreed. "Have you been into Newgate lately?"

Greydon frowned. "I try to avoid Newgate, if at all possible," he replied.

"Smart, but I do hope you are prepared for the depravity that we are about to witness. It is not for the faint of heart."

"You do not need to concern yourself about me."

Mr. Moore shrugged. "Suit yourself, but I did warn you."

"I am more than aware of the conditions of Newgate," Greydon said.

"But have you been to where the women are housed?"

"I have not, but I imagine it is similar to the men's side."

Mr. Moore grew somber. "At times, as many as one hundred and twenty women are placed in a ward and they all sleep on the cold floor with only a thin layer of straw for bedding. Everything is filthy to the excess and the smell is horrendous."

"Again, I am aware."

"Good, because it is no place for a lady, or any woman, for that matter," Mr. Moore said. "I have been told that the governor and doctors are even reluctant to go amongst them."

Greydon gave him a pointed look. "Yes, but you seem to forget that these are criminals. They were sent to Newgate for a reason."

"They are still people," Mr. Moore retorted in a firm voice.

"I do not dispute that."

Mr. Moore offered him an apologetic smile. "Forgive me, I'm afraid I am rather passionate about this topic. I do believe our prison system needs to be reformed and the prisoners need to be treated more humanely."

Greydon nodded. "I agree, but your arguments will fall on deaf ears, considering people are starving on the streets. Why should the prisoners be treated better than most people that reside in the rookeries?"

"It doesn't make it right," Mr. Moore said. "Female prisoners are pining away for want of food, air and exercise."

"Then I suggest that they don't break the law."

Mr. Moore shook his head. "I take my apology back. I do not know why I expected more from you."

"I am a man of the law, at least I was, and I have seen some vile things," Greydon said. "But I am not without compassion. Perhaps we can enact change when we take our seats in Parliament."

"I would like that."

Greydon gave him an expectant look. "Can we go inside now, or would you like to debate religious reform as well?"

Mr. Moore's lips twitched. "We can go inside, but I do hope you brought your handkerchief that has been dipped in rose water with you."

"That won't be necessary."

"Very well," Mr. Moore said before he started towards the main door.

Greydon matched the barrister's stride and it wasn't long before they stepped into The Keeper's House. Two guards greeted them from behind a built-in desk.

"What is it that ye want?" the guard asked as he glared at them.

So much for hospitality, he thought. It was obvious that the guards did not want them here anymore than he wanted to be here.

A door opened from behind the desk and a familiar red-haired guard stepped into the hall. He met Greydon's gaze and asked, "Mr. Campden, what brings you by today?"

One of the other guards spoke up. "Do you know this bloke, Walker?"

"I do, Bourne," Walker replied. "He is a Bow Street Runner, and a good one at that."

"Then what is he doing with a lying barrister?" Bourne pressed.

Mr. Moore cleared his throat. "You know that I can hear you, right?"

Bourne shrugged. "I didn't mean to hurt your feelings. I was just merely stating a fact."

"Can we just see Lady Eugenie?" Mr. Moore asked.

Walker lifted his brow. "That woman may look like a lady, but she is as cold as a stone on the inside," he said. "You are wasting your time representing her."

"It is my time to waste," Mr. Moore said.

"Suit yourself," Walker stated as he went to open the door. "Follow me."

As Greydon followed the guard into the dark, narrow corridor, he tried to ignore the pungent smell of unwashed bodies. That was one smell that he would never get used to.

Walker stopped by a door. "Wait in here," he ordered. "I will bring Lady Eugenie to you."

Mr. Moore opened the door and stood to the side as Greydon walked into the small, square room. The only light came from a window on the far side and it had bars in front of it. A table sat in the middle and there were two chairs pushed in.

Greydon leaned his shoulder against the wall as he waited for the prisoner to be brought in. Mr. Moore pulled out a chair and sat down.

A short time later, the door opened and Lady Eugenie stepped into the room. She was dressed in a tan gown that hung loosely on her body. Her long, blonde hair looked unkempt and her face had splotches of dirt.

Walker grabbed Lady Eugenie's arm and walked her over to the table. He pulled out a chair and forcefully pushed her down onto it. "Stay there," he growled.

Mr. Moore met the guard's gaze and said, "I wish to speak to my client alone."

With a frown, the guard released Lady Eugenie's arm and took a step back. "I will be right outside," he grumbled.

Once the guard had stepped out, Mr. Moore gave Lady Eugenie a weak smile. "How are you faring?"

"As good as can be expected, I suppose," Lady Eugenie replied unconvincingly.

"I brought someone that I believe can help you," Mr. Moore said.

Lady Eugenie turned her attention towards Greydon. "Why did you bring Phineas' brother?" she asked.

Mr. Moore glanced between them. "I hadn't realized that you two were acquainted."

"As children, our families would attend house parties together and we would play games with one another," Lady Eugenie explained.

Greydon pushed off from the wall and straightened to his full height. "That was long ago, and I don't have time to rehash the past."

"Neither do I," Lady Eugenie said. "Which is why I am wondering why a son of an earl can help me."

"My reasons are my own," Greydon replied. He didn't want to admit that he worked as a Bow Street Runner, at least not yet.

Lady Eugenie arched an eyebrow. "And why would you help me?" she asked. "Everyone believes I killed your brother."

"Did you?" Greydon asked.

She shook her head. "I did not," she said. "Not that anyone believes me. The guards have marked me for dead since I got here."

Greydon approached the table and said, "I am still not convinced that you are innocent, but I gave my word to someone that I would see this investigation through."

Mr. Moore interjected, "Perhaps Lady Eugenie should start at the beginning and tell us what happened."

Lady Eugenie nodded. "I noticed that the door to Phineas' apartment was open—"

"Why were you there?" Greydon asked.

"I won't say," Lady Eugenie said.

"Whyever not?' Greydon pressed.

Lady Eugenie fidgeted with her hands in her lap. "As I was saying, I went inside Phineas' apartment and I saw a dagger sticking out of his chest. I tried to help him, but he was already dead. I started screaming for help, but it did no good."

Greydon cocked his head. "Did you try to wash the blood off your hands when you were in my brother's apartment?"

She gave him a blank look. "When would I have had the time? The people swarmed inside the apartment and accused me of killing him."

"Did you burn anything?" Greydon asked.

"Again, with what time?" Lady Eugenie responded. "Everything happened so fast and my only concern was trying to help Phineas."

Greydon watched Lady Eugenie closely for any signs of lying, but he saw nothing that would indicate she was not telling the truth. She held his gaze, and her words appeared forthright. Heaven help him, but he believed her account. But he had one more question to ask. "How does your sister, Lottie, play into all of this?"

Lady Eugenie's face paled. "Lottie has nothing to do with this," she said in a shaky voice.

Based upon her reaction, Greydon knew that Lottie had everything to do with this case. "Why was my brother writing her letters?"

"He wasn't," Lady Eugenie attempted.

Greydon crossed his arms over his chest. "I think it is admirable that you are protecting your sister, but not if she is a murderer."

Lady Eugenie shook her head. "Lottie is no murderer."

"Then what is she?" Greydon asked. "Was she Phineas' mistress?"

Mr. Moore interrupted, "If you don't tell us the truth, then you could be put to death for this crime and what would happen to Lottie?"

Indecision crossed Lady Eugenie's face as she stayed silent. Finally, after a long moment, she revealed, "I went to Phineas' apartment because I was looking for Lottie."

"And you thought she was at his apartment?" Greydon asked.

Lady Eugenie met his gaze and her words sparked with anger. "Your brother was a monster. Lottie was only sixteen years old when he first seduced her. He fed her lies about love and whatnot, and my sister believed them."

"Did you find Lottie when you arrived?" Mr. Moore asked.

"I did not," Lady Eugenie said. "Everything else was how I said it was."

Greydon uncrossed his arms and asked, "Is it possible that Lottie stabbed Phineas in a fit of rage?"

"No!" Lady Eugenie exclaimed. "My sister would do no such thing. She loved him!"

The door to the room opened and Walker stepped back in. "Time is up," he said. "The prisoner needs to be returned back to her cell."

Mr. Moore rose from his seat. "That is unacceptable. I need more time with Lady Eugenie."

Walker approached Lady Eugenie and grabbed her arm. "You can speak to her tomorrow, assuming she behaves," he said as he yanked her out of her seat.

After Lady Eugenie departed from the room, Greydon turned his attention towards Mr. Moore. "I believe Lady Eugenie to be innocent."

"That is a relief," Mr. Moore muttered.

"But I will be paying Lottie a visit," Greydon said.

Mr. Moore rose from his seat. "I will accompany you."

Greydon put his hand up. "I think it would be best if I

asked Lady Enid to join me. Lottie might feel more comfortable in her presence when I ask her a few questions."

"I agree," Mr. Moore said. "Now can we leave this blasted place?"

"After you," Greydon replied, gesturing towards the door.

Chapter Eleven

With a book in her hand, Enid sat in the nursery while her daughter slept. It was a quiet, peaceful sound to hear Marigold's deep breathing. Her daughter was safe and that was all that mattered to her.

The door opened and her father stepped into the room. His eyes widened when they landed on her. "Enid," he greeted in a hushed voice.

"Father," she said, unsure of why he was here. He had made his thoughts known about how he felt about Marigold. The little girl was no more welcome in the home than she was.

Her father's eyes darted towards Marigold and they softened, which was something she never thought she would witness. He cleared his throat. "I just wanted to ensure you were in the house and not causing more problems for others."

Enid remained quiet, knowing nothing that she said would appease her father.

"Good day," her father said in his usual gruff voice before he departed from the room.

What an odd thing, she realized. She didn't usually sit in the nursery during Marigold's nap, making her wonder if her father visiting was a normal occurrence. She hoped so. How could he not love his granddaughter?

Enid placed the book down and quietly departed the room. As she passed by the nursemaid, she asked, "Does my father come to visit Marigold?"

Marie lowered her gaze. "I cannot say, my lady. He swore me to secrecy."

"I understand," Enid said, having no desire to make Marie uncomfortable.

She exited the nursery and headed down the corridor towards the stairs. She had just started to descend them when a knock came at the door.

The butler crossed the entry hall and opened the door, revealing Greydon. He stepped inside and his eyes met hers, causing a fluttering in her stomach. Or was that just her imagination? He had shown no sign that he held her in high regard. Which was fine by her. She couldn't- no, she wouldn't-give her heart away again.

So why did Greydon have such an effect on her?

Greydon bowed. "Lady Enid," he said cordially.

She dropped into a curtsy. "Lord Rushcliffe."

"May I speak to you privately for a moment?" he asked.

Enid nodded. "We can speak in the gardens," she replied.

Greydon approached her and held out his arm. "It would be my honor to escort you, my lady," he said.

After she placed her hand on his sleeve, he escorted her towards the rear of the townhouse. A footman opened the door and followed them out onto the veranda.

They stepped down onto the path that led through the center of the gardens. Enid removed her hand, clasping it in front of her, and glanced over at Greydon. "Did you speak to your father?"

"I did, and I informed him that I would not end my friendship with you," Greydon replied.

"Did he take issue with that?"

Greydon chuckled dryly. "He takes issue with everything that I do. This is not the first time that my father and I disagreed on something."

"I am sorry that I am the source of the contention."

"My father and I stopped seeing eye to eye a long time ago, I'm afraid," Greydon admitted. "He took issue with me becoming a Bow Street Runner. He even threatened to disown me."

"Did he?"

"No, because that would cause a scandal and my father would never do anything that would cause our family's legacy to be tarnished."

Enid could hear the hardness in Greydon's voice and it concerned her. "I think your father has hurt you more than you have let on."

"No more than what your father did to you."

"Perhaps, but I did bring shame to my family."

"You made a mistake," Greydon said.

Enid huffed. "I wish it was as simple as that," she said. "I hadn't even considered what would happen to my family as a result of my elopement. I was entirely self-absorbed."

"But you aren't anymore."

"I can't be because I have Marigold to tend to," Enid said. "I won't let her down."

Greydon smiled over at her. "I believe that to be true."

Enid found herself returning his smile. "The moment I held Marigold in my arms, I changed. I knew it was my job to keep her safe."

"And you have."

"Yes, but one day she will start asking questions about her father; questions that I can't answer," Enid said.

Greydon stopped and he turned to face her. "You did nothing wrong."

"I killed John," Enid said.

"No, four of us took that shot and no one knows which

bullet killed him," Greydon argued. "Besides, you were cleared of any wrongdoing by the coroner."

Enid gave him a grateful look. "Thank you," she started, "but I still played a role in his death."

"Do you regret it?"

"Heavens, no!" Enid exclaimed. "That is what has me worried."

Greydon placed a hand on her sleeve. "You were in an impossible situation and you did the best that you could. No one faults you for that."

Enid lowered her gaze. "Is it so wrong of me to be relieved that John is gone?"

"Not at all."

"He ruined my life, and he did all of it for money," Enid said. "He didn't love me and he made me feel as if I wasn't worthy to be loved."

Greydon took his finger and placed it under her chin, tilting it up until she met his gaze. "You are worthy of being loved, Enid," he said. "Do not let John's words continue to have a hold on you. For they are just that- words. Allowing his words, or the voice from within, to paralyze you will resolve nothing."

"How can I not?" Enid asked, her eyes searching his.

"You are an extraordinary woman, and I have never met anyone quite like you," Greydon said as he lowered his finger.

Enid smiled up at him. "Was that a compliment?"

"It most assuredly was." He took a step closer and now she had to tilt her head to look up at him. "But I made a terrible mistake."

Her smile dimmed. "I doubt that."

"No, it is true," Greydon said. He leaned closer until their faces were just inches apart. "I find myself in the uncomfortable position of developing feelings for you. I'm starting to think about you all the time."

"You do?" she asked breathlessly. Her words seemed to escape her as she stared deep into his eyes.

"Yes, and I do not know what we should do about it." His eyes dropped to her lips for a moment before bringing his gaze back up. "Tell me that you do not feel the same and I will walk away."

"I am unable to do so, but it would be much simpler if you walked away," she said.

"It would, but is that what you want?"

Enid felt tears burning in the back of her eyes as she admitted, "I am scared to show you the sore, crumpled pieces of my heart."

"Do not be scared, my dear, but allow me to care for you," he whispered gently.

Greydon had admitted that he cared for her. Her heart should take flight, but instead she couldn't stop the fear that was encompassing her. She had trusted another with her heart and he had abused it. She couldn't risk having that happen again. For if she did, and she was wrong, her heart would be irrevocably broken.

Enid placed a hand on his chest, stilling him. "I'm sorry but I cannot do this."

"Do what, exactly?"

"Kiss you," she replied.

"I said nothing of kissing."

A slight blush came to her cheeks. "But you spoke of affection."

"Those are two different things," Greydon said with a smirk on his lips. "But I would be happy to kiss you."

Enid took a step back and dropped her hand. "I am quite fond of you as well, but nothing can come of it."

"Pray tell, why not?" Greydon asked.

Her eyes grew downcast. "I am still picking up the pieces of my shattered heart from when John abused it."

"Allow me to help you with that."

With a shake of her head, Enid said, "You deserve someone who isn't ruined; someone who can love you with a whole heart."

"But I choose you."

Enid gave him a sad smile. "You are everything that I have ever wanted, and if my situation were different, I would be more than happy to accept your tokens of affection."

Greydon furrowed his brow. "Did I do something wrong?"

"You did nothing wrong," Enid replied. "John gave me hope with so many promises, and I was so naïve to believe all those things. He broke my heart in such a way that I do not think it will ever recover."

"I am not John," Greydon asserted.

"No, you are not, but I can't risk it; not again," Enid said.

Greydon ran a hand through his dark hair. "You will find that I am not one to give up so easily."

"I wish you would because my position will not change, not now, not ever," Enid asserted. "You are heir to an earldom and need to marry a woman that is above repute."

"Regardless of what you think I want, it is *you* that I need."

The tears started rolling down her cheeks but she made no attempt at wiping them away. "I'm sorry, Greydon. I cannot give you what you want."

Greydon reached into his pocket and removed a handkerchief. He extended it towards her and said, "I do not mean to upset you, my dear. I will drop it… for now. But I am determined to make you my wife."

Enid used the handkerchief to wipe away the tears. "You will be disappointed, then."

A smile came to Greydon's lips, as if he were privy to a secret. "I won't give up so easily, but I will not pressure you to do anything that you don't want."

"Thank you," Enid murmured.

Greydon took a step back and revealed, "I did manage to meet with Lady Eugenie at Newgate."

"You did?" she asked, grateful for the change in subject. "When was this?"

"I went with Mr. Moore and I do believe she had nothing to do with the murder of my brother," Greydon said. "But I cannot rule her sister out as a suspect. I must speak to her and I was hoping you would go with me."

"You suspect Lottie is a murderer?" Enid asked. "That is impossible. She is only seventeen."

"Age does not preclude her," Greydon said. "She may have been the last person that saw him alive, or she killed him."

"I will go with you, but only because I want to prove that Lottie is not capable of murder," Enid said.

Greydon stepped forward and placed a hand on her arm. "I shall call upon you tomorrow, assuming you are in agreement."

Enid wanted to close her eyes and relish his touch, but she didn't dare show Greydon how much he affected her. She loved him, she knew that now, but she refused to succumb to her desires. Greydon deserved better than her, and she wouldn't allow him to settle for a woman such as her.

———————～———————

Greydon sat in a comfortable armchair at White's but he was anything but. He'd had a fitful night of sleep and couldn't seem to wrap his head around what he had done yesterday.

What in the blazes had he done? He had confessed to Enid that he had feelings for her and offered for her. Yet the worst part of it all was that he didn't regret it. Not one bit. He loved her, and he wanted her as his wife. But he knew that was going to be an uphill battle since her scars ran deep.

How could he convince Enid to marry him? He needed a plan, but he couldn't seem to formulate one. He had always relied on logic, but love was not logical. There was no reasoning to it. It seemed to have a mind of its own and it always trumped his way of thinking.

Leaning forward, he placed his full glass onto the table. Drinking away his woes would solve nothing. He needed a clear head when he went to see Enid.

Lord Roswell approached him with an obnoxious smile on his face. "Rushcliffe," he greeted. "I did not expect to see you here."

"I needed a drink," he said.

His friend glanced down at his glass. "Yet you have hardly touched your drink."

"I have been thinking."

Lord Roswell smirked. "It is always hardest the first time."

Greydon looked heavenward. "What is it that you want, Roswell?"

"I have come to keep you company," Lord Roswell replied as he sat across from him.

"Surely there is someone else that could benefit from your company," Greydon asked.

With an amused look, Lord Roswell said, "You looked troubled."

"It is nothing that I can't handle," he asserted. He was hoping that Lord Roswell would get the hint that he did not want to engage in conversation. He was content being alone.

But he was not so lucky.

Lord Roswell leaned back in his chair. "Is it your brother's case that is bothering you or something else?"

"I would rather not say," Greydon muttered.

"Then it must be about Enid."

Greydon stared at him in astonishment. How in the blazes did he know that? Had he been so obvious in his affection for Enid that other people had noticed?

Lord Roswell chuckled. "It wasn't hard to deduce that you two care for one another."

"Regardless, I do not wish to discuss it with you."

A server came to a stop in front of the table and asked, "Would you care for something to drink?"

Lord Roswell nodded. "Brandy."

The server turned his head towards Greydon. "Anything for you, sir?"

"No," he replied. "I still have a drink."

"Very good, sir," the server said before he walked away.

Lord Roswell gave him an expectant look. "Pray tell, what went awry with Enid?"

Had his friend always been this astute, he wondered. "Nothing," he replied.

"You are a terrible liar."

"I am an excellent liar," Greydon insisted. "I make my living lying to the people closest to me."

"Then you need to work on that."

Greydon glanced around the room. "There must be someone else in this room that you can bother."

"I know many people in this room, but none are in need of me as much as you are."

"Why do you think I need you?"

Lord Roswell grinned. "I am rather good at providing advice. Some might even call me an expert on love."

"Now you are just spouting nonsense."

"Perhaps, but I am an excellent listener," Lord Roswell said.

Greydon reached for his drink. "What will it take for you to go away and leave me in peace?" he asked as he brought the glass up to his lips.

"There is only one reason why you are so ornery, and it is a woman," Lord Roswell said matter-of-factly.

"You aren't wrong," Greydon admitted.

Lord Roswell's smile grew. "The love master is all knowing."

"Will you stop calling yourself that?" Greydon asked, lowering the glass to his lap. "No one will ever call you that."

"I don't think that is true. It is rather catchy, if you ask me," Lord Roswell joked.

"But no one is asking you," Greydon stated.

His friend's smile disappeared but the mirth was still in his eyes. "Will you tell me what happened between you two?"

Greydon let out a sigh. He might as well tell Lord Roswell the truth. With any luck, it would cause him to leave faster. "I offered for Enid, but she turned me down."

"Interesting," Lord Roswell said. "Why do you suppose she did that?"

"She still harbors scars from her first marriage and she doesn't believe she is worthy of me," Greydon admitted.

"What do you intend to do about that?"

"I intend to fight for her," Greydon replied. "She is my match, my other half, and I won't allow her to walk away."

"But what if it is for the best?"

Greydon reared back. "How can you even say that?"

Lord Roswell shrugged. "Lady Enid is ruined, and your reputation will suffer as a result of it."

"I care little of my reputation."

"But perhaps you should," Lord Roswell said. "If you are a laughingstock amongst high Society, how do you expect to get any serious work done in the House of Lords?"

"I have no intention of playing the political game."

"You say that now, but things could change when you inherit your father's earldom," Lord Roswell said.

Greydon shook his head. "I would rather have Enid for a wife than approval from the *ton*."

Leaning forward, Lord Roswell said, "I just want you to acknowledge that you will be fighting an uphill battle if you wed Lady Enid. Your friends might abandon you, you could stop receiving invitations to social gatherings, and the *ton* will turn against you."

"What would you have me do?" Greydon asked. "Turn my back on the woman that I love?"

"You love her?"

Greydon bobbed his head. "I do."

"Then you must fight for her," Lord Roswell said.

"That is what I am trying to do, but it is proving to be a difficult task."

"Try harder."

Greydon huffed. "You are useless," he said. "Why do I even bother to listen to you?"

"Because you recognize my genius."

"That is most assuredly not it."

"The love master knows all," Lord Roswell said.

With a glance heavenward, Greydon responded, "You are an idiot."

Lord Roswell accepted a drink from the server before he took a sip. "Perhaps Brentwood will have some insights on this."

"I hope not."

Lord Brentwood's voice came from behind him. "What insight are you looking for?'

Greydon pressed his lips together. Could this morning get any worse? Why couldn't his friends see that he just wanted to be left alone with his own thoughts?

Lord Roswell rested his glass on the armchair. "Rushcliffe is asking for some advice on love and he has come to the love master."

"That is the furthest thing from the truth," Greydon said.

Brentwood came around the chair and sat next to Rush-cliffe. "I assume this is about my sister, and I must say, it is about time."

Greydon resisted the urge to groan. Did everyone know how much Enid meant to him?

Brentwood continued. "Have you offered for her yet?"

Lord Roswell spoke up. "He did, but she turned him down."

"That doesn't surprise me," Malcolm said. "Enid is fighting demons from her past, and she is struggling to find a new path."

"Greydon just needs to be patient, but constant in his affection," Lord Roswell said. "Enid must know that his intentions are honorable."

Brentwood nodded. "I concur."

A smug look came to Lord Roswell's face. "It is a shame that more people do not seek out my advice, especially on matters of the heart. I am hardly ever wrong."

"You are a jackanapes," Greydon muttered.

Lord Roswell brought a hand up to his chest. "You wound me, sir."

"I doubt that," he said, rising. "If you gentlemen will excuse me, I have had just about enough of you two."

"But I only just got here," Brentwood pointed out.

"And that is all I can handle of you," Greydon responded. "I am taking Enid on a carriage ride this morning."

Brentwood nodded in acknowledgment. "I do hope you can win Enid's approval."

"I hope so as well."

As he turned to walk away, Lord Roswell said, "If you need any more advice, the love master is always available."

Greydon rolled his eyes. His friend was an idiot, but he wasn't wrong. He did need to fight for Enid and prove to her that his intentions were genuine.

After he exited White's, he stepped into his carriage and drove towards Enid's townhouse. A footman came out of the townhouse to secure his horses and he headed towards the main door.

The door opened and the butler stood to the side. "Do come in," he encouraged. "Lady Enid has been expecting you."

Greydon stepped into the entry hall and waited for the butler to close the door.

"Follow me, my lord," the butler said as he started walking towards the drawing room.

Once the butler announced him, Greydon stepped into the room and saw Enid was sitting next to her mother. She was dressed in an alluring green gown with a square neckline. Her hair was piled atop her head and pearls were weaved throughout. To say she looked beautiful would be an understatement.

He bowed and greeted them politely.

Enid smiled, but it appeared guarded. "Good morning, Lord Rushcliffe," she said as she averted her gaze.

Lady Everton interjected, "Would you care for some tea?"

"Thank you for the kind offer, but I was hoping to take Lady Enid on a carriage ride this morning," he said.

"She is looking forward to it," Lady Everton responded with a slight nudge of her elbow. "Aren't you, dear?"

"I am," Enid replied unconvincingly.

Greydon stepped forward and held his arm out. "Shall we, my lady?"

Rising, Enid approached him and placed her hand on his sleeve. "Thank you," she murmured.

As he led her from the room, he said, "You look quite lovely today."

"That is kind of you to say, my lord," she responded, keeping her gaze straight ahead.

Greydon knew that Enid might not love him yet. But there were some things in life that were worth fighting for to the end. And Enid was one of those things.

Chapter Twelve

Enid's back was rigid as she sat in the coach next to Greydon. She didn't quite know what to say or do now that she knew the extent of his feelings for her. She wished she was strong enough to profess her love and to run into his arms, but she wasn't. She was scared. And that fear was consuming her, body and soul.

Greydon's voice broke through her musings. "I am sorry if my bold speech from earlier upset you."

"You didn't upset me," she attempted, hoping she sounded somewhat convincing.

He gave her a pointed look. "I think we both know that isn't true."

She offered him a sheepish smile. "Perhaps you upset me just a little." She should have known that he would see right through her.

"I do intend to press my suit."

"I wish you wouldn't," Enid said. "My position hasn't changed."

Greydon adjusted the reins in his hand. "We shall see."

"We shall *not* see," she argued. "I do not think I will ever marry again."

With a glance at her, Greydon asked, "When are you going to stop blaming yourself for what happened with John?"

"I don't think I ever will," she admitted softly. How could she? It was all her fault that she had fallen for his charms. She should have been better and seen through his lies.

"That is a sad way to live."

Enid shook her head. "I am still dealing with the consequences of eloping with John. My father hates me and the *ton* gossips relentlessly about me."

"You need to focus on what you can change."

She tossed her hands up in the air. "What can I change?" she asked. "Need I remind you that the only reason why my father agreed to have me come home was because my brother blackmailed him? He doesn't want me there."

"Do you want to be there?"

"I do, because it gives Marigold a home."

"Then who cares how you got there?" he asked. "Your father might never change, but that is on him, not you."

A brief smile came to her lips. "My father came to see Marigold and I suspect that he has done it before."

"That is wonderful."

"It is," she agreed. "I am hoping my father's heart is softening towards his granddaughter."

"I hope to meet Marigold one day."

"You will, at least when the time is right." Enid turned her head and watched the people walk along the pavement, skirting the vendors who were hawking their goods.

Greydon spoke up, drawing back her attention. "Are you close with your mother?"

"My mother is a saint, and I adore my brother, Malcolm," she replied. "They have been rooting for me this entire time."

"It is good when you have people that you can rely on."

"I agree, wholeheartedly," Enid said. "I should have come to my brother straightaway when John started beating me but I was too embarrassed to admit that I was wrong."

"I can understand that."

"You?" Enid asked. "You do not seem like the prideful type."

Greydon chuckled. "My father was furious when I started working as a Bow Street Runner. He threatened to disown me over it, but I didn't care. I refused to let my father tell me what to do. I was going to prove him wrong, even if it killed me."

"My father disowned me because he wanted to distance himself from the scandal."

"No one knows that I worked as a Bow Street Runner," Greydon said. "And who would have even suspected such a thing?"

Enid bobbed her head. She had to agree with him there. "It does seem rather far-fetched that a son of an earl worked as a Bow Street Runner."

"As a younger son, I had more leeway than Phineas did. His life was mapped out from the moment he was born. I didn't want that life," he admitted. "I wanted adventure."

"Did you find it?"

Greydon offered her a boyish grin. "I did, and then some," he said. "I was forced to put my life on the line more than once."

"That sounds rather terrifying."

"Says the person that dared to defy her husband and tell him no," Greydon said with a knowing look.

Enid shrugged. "I had little choice in the matter. I didn't want him to control me anymore."

"And you succeeded."

"That I did, but it came at a great cost."

Greydon shifted on the bench to face her. "You are stronger than you think you are."

"I am not strong."

"I disagree," Greydon said. "You drew a line in the sand and stood your ground. That is brave to me."

"I did so only because of my daughter."

"It doesn't matter why you did it but that you did do it."

Enid lowered her gaze to her lap. "You flatter me, but I am not as strong as you think I am. I am weak and have made far too many mistakes for you to ever praise me."

Greydon pulled back on the reins in front of a white-washed townhouse. "I know exactly who you are, Enid," he said. "I have never met a braver woman than you."

"I contend that is not true."

As he secured the reins, he remarked, "You risked your life for Marigold. Nothing is as strong as the love a mother has for her child."

"And I would do it again."

His lips twitched. "That is why I know how truly remarkable you are."

A blush came to her cheeks. Why did his words have such a profound effect on her? "You shouldn't say such things to me."

"I have to because it distracts me from what I truly want to do with you."

"Which is?"

His eyes dropped to her lips.

Enid felt her heart start pounding in her chest and she feared that he might be able to hear it. Good heavens, she hoped not.

Greydon exited the carriage and came around to her side. As he assisted her onto the pavement, she could feel the warmth of his body next to hers.

Once she was on the pavement, she removed her hands and clasped them in front of her, pretending that his touch had not affected her. But it did. It always did.

They walked up to the main door and Greydon knocked. It was promptly opened and a light-haired butler answered.

"How may I help you?" the butler asked with a hawk-like gaze.

Greydon reached into his jacket pocket and removed a calling card. "Is Lady Charlotte available for callers?"

"Who is asking?"

Greydon extended the card as he replied, "Lady Enid and Lord Rushcliffe."

The butler accepted the card. "I'm afraid not. Perhaps you could come back at another time," he said as he went to close the door.

Greydon put his hand out and held the door open. "I'm afraid we must insist," he stated in a firm tone. "We have come on behalf of Lady Eugenie."

The butler frowned as he opened the door. "Wait inside and I will go speak to Lady Charlotte at once. I can't promise anything, mind you."

"I understand," Greydon said as he followed Enid into the entry hall.

As the butler disappeared into a room off the hall, Greydon turned towards her and said, "Let's hope that this visit is not in vain."

"It won't be."

"How can you be so sure?" Greydon asked.

Enid held his gaze and said, "I have great confidence in your investigative skills, my lord."

Before Greydon could reply, the butler stepped back into the entry hall and announced, "Lady Charlotte will see you now."

Greydon put his hand out, indicating she should go first. Enid headed towards the door where the butler was standing and stepped inside. She saw the thin-faced Lady Charlotte was sitting on a settee and her blonde hair was tied into a loose chignon at the base of her neck.

Lady Charlotte jumped up from her seat. "You have received word from my sister?" she rushed out.

"We did," Greydon replied. "Lady Eugenie is doing the best that she can in Newgate."

"How is it that you were able to see her and not her own sister?" Lady Charlotte asked with a slight pout of her lips.

Greydon came to stop next to Enid. "I accompanied Mr. Moore to see your sister," he explained.

"Are you a barrister, as well?" Lady Charlotte asked.

"No, but I just want to ensure that the truth comes out," Greydon said.

"But you are the brother of the person that my sister is claimed to have murdered," Lady Charlotte pressed.

"I am, but I just want justice for my brother, nothing more, nothing less," Greydon responded.

Lady Charlotte shifted her gaze to Enid. "Do you vouch for him?" she asked.

Enid bobbed her head. "I do. Lord Rushcliffe is the most honorable man that I know, and you can trust him."

"Very well," Lady Charlotte muttered as she dropped back down onto the settee. "Thank you for coming."

"Before we go, I was hoping to ask you a few questions," Greydon said.

Lady Charlotte looked at him skeptically. "What kind of questions?"

"Your sister was arrested when she went to my brother's apartment to look for you and she found him dead," Greydon said. "Were you with him earlier?"

Lady Charlotte's eyes grew defiant. "How dare you accuse me of such a thing!" she exclaimed. "I am not a harlot."

Enid came to sit down next to Lady Charlotte on the settee. "We are not accusing you of anything. We are just trying to ascertain the truth." She paused. "Please. It is very important that you tell us everything about that morning."

The young lady bit her lower lip. "I was with Lord Rushcliffe but I left before my sister arrived."

Greydon stepped closer. "In what condition was Lord Rushcliffe when you left?"

"He was asleep," Lady Charlotte replied with a wave of her hand. "I left as soon as the dawn broke."

"We found a letter that was addressed to you that we suspect my brother was writing to you," Greydon said.

Lady Charlotte smiled. "Phineas always wrote me notes. That was just one of the many reasons that I loved him."

"You loved him?" Enid asked.

She placed a hand on her belly. "I do," she replied. "I just don't believe my sister would have killed him."

Enid glanced down at the hand covering Lady Charlotte's stomach before asking, "How far along are you?"

Lady Charlotte removed her hand quickly. "I don't know what you are referring to," she said firmly.

"I think you do," Enid pressed. "Is that why Eugenie went to go see Phineas? Was she going to confront him about your condition?"

Rising abruptly, Lady Charlotte declared, "It is time for you to go."

"Charlotte—"

Lady Charlotte spoke over her. "I have nothing more that I want to say to either of you," she said, crossing her arms over her chest.

Greydon rose. "We are just trying to help Eugenie."

"How is that exactly?" Lady Charlotte asked. "You are just on a witch hunt."

"I assure you that is not the case," Greydon responded.

Lady Charlotte started tapping her left foot. "Leave my home and never come back. If you do, I will call for the constable."

Greydon looked as if he had more that he wanted to say but he closed his mouth and nodded. "As you wish."

Neither of them spoke as they exited the townhouse and stepped into the carriage. Once Greydon urged the team forward, he said, "That was odd."

"I agree," Enid responded. "I do believe that Lady Charlotte knows more than she is letting on."

"That is what I surmised, too."

"Why wouldn't she want to help her sister?"

Greydon's jaw clenched. "It makes me wonder in what condition Phineas truly was in when she left."

Enid's eyes grew wide. "You don't think Lady Charlotte had anything to do with his murder, do you?"

"Either the murder itself or she was poisoning him with arsenic."

"But she is so young."

Greydon huffed. "That means little when you are dealing with matters of the heart. Charlotte had means and the opportunity to kill Phineas."

Enid glanced over her shoulder at Lady Charlotte's townhouse and wondered if that young lady could be guilty of such a horrific crime. She might have been angry enough to have killed him, especially if he wouldn't acknowledge their baby.

Greydon broke through her musings. "I do think Eugenie came to the same conclusion as we did and is trying to protect her sister."

"With her own life?" Enid asked.

"Wouldn't you do the same for someone you loved?"

Enid grew quiet, knowing that Greydon spoke true. She would do anything to help Marigold, even give her own life to save her.

Greydon exited the carriage and extended the reins to the footman. Then he proceeded inside his townhouse. He had just come from escorting Enid home and he had only walked her to the main door. He didn't want to become a nuisance but he had no intention of dropping his suit, no matter how much Enid objected. He knew that she cared for him. She had said as much, but he could see the fear in her eyes.

He had to prove to her that he would never betray her. But how was he to do that, he wondered. He had confessed his deep feelings for her, stopping short of revealing he was in love with her. He didn't want to scare her off by being too brazen.

The butler stepped out from a room off the hall and said, "Your father is requesting your presence in his study, my lord."

Greydon's foot stilled on the first step. He didn't want to talk to his father, but it was best that he got this over with. No doubt his father would criticize him for something he had done, or perhaps he was just in his usual cantankerous mood.

He shifted his course and started walking towards the rear of the townhouse. He had just stepped inside of the study when his father glanced up, his expression growing hard.

"There you are," his father grumbled. "Where have you been?"

"I have been busy," he replied.

"Busy with what?" his father demanded.

Greydon walked further into the room. "I would rather not say."

His father's eyes narrowed. "Have you been spending time with Lady Enid?"

"I have," he said, seeing no reason to deny it.

"You are being foolhardy. Take Lady Enid as your mistress and find a respectable young woman to marry."

Greydon shook his head. "I intend to marry Lady Enid."

His father's mouth dropped. "You can't be in earnest," he said. "Lady Enid is ruined and her reputation will tarnish ours."

"I think Phineas did a good enough job with that," Greydon remarked.

"Phineas acted no different than what his rank allowed him to do."

"You are justifying his behavior?"

His father frowned. "Of course not, but even he married a young woman with an unblemished character."

"Phineas was a cad, and I have no desire to follow in his footsteps."

"You would rather have this family disgraced?"

Greydon sat down on the chair that faced the desk. "That is not my intention, but I love Lady Enid."

Scoffing, his father said, "Love is an impractical emotion. It drives sane men mad."

"Did you not have love with Mother?"

His father's face softened slightly at the mention of his mother. "I did and look where it got me. I can't go to sleep without thinking of your mother. Besides, we started off as an arranged marriage. Our love was cultivated over time and experiences."

"I used to think as you do about love, but I decided I would rather have Lady Enid in my life than be afraid of being vulnerable," Greydon admitted. "Furthermore, Lady Enid made a mistake when she eloped but that mistake shouldn't define her."

"It most surely should. She is a weak female and abandoned her family."

"And she has learned from that."

His father leaned back in his seat and studied him for a moment. "Regardless, I will not allow you to marry her."

"You have no say in whom I marry."

His father puffed out his chest, no doubt in an attempt to intimidate him. "I am your father and you will do as I say!" he exclaimed, his words taking on a harsh edge.

Greydon lifted his brow at his father's attempt to manipulate him. It would take much more than that to change his mind. "That may have worked when I was little, but I am not some weak-willed man. I will marry Lady Enid, assuming she will have me."

"Are you prepared for the repercussions of your actions?" his father demanded. "The invitations will dry up and you will be left as a lone, dreary man."

"I care little of social events."

"You must care because this will all be yours one day," his father said, waving his hand over his desk. "But without support from your peers, you will get little accomplished in the House of Lords."

Greydon tugged down on the ends of his waistcoat. "I will find a way to accomplish my goals."

"You are a fool, Son, and you aren't thinking with your head," his father stated. "Marriage is a transaction that is supposed to benefit both parties."

"I cannot disagree more with you. Marriage is more than a transaction. I want to spend my life with Lady Enid because she makes me a better man."

His father huffed. "No, she has managed to insert her claws into you and you are too weak to pull them out."

"Au contraire," Greydon said. "Lady Enid has already turned down my offer of marriage because she is worried about damaging my reputation."

"That is the first sensible thing that girl has done," his father muttered.

"I won't lose her. I will prove to her that I am the man for her."

His father shook his head. "You are such a disappointment."

Rising, Greydon said, "I am sorry you feel that way, but my mind is made up. You may as well resign yourself to that fact."

"You are making a mistake."

"I don't believe I am," he said. "But if I am, it is my mistake to make."

His father reached for a piece of paper and held it up.

"Have you at least had a chance to look over the accounts that I left for you to review?"

"I have not, but I shall do so today."

His father rose and walked over to the drink cart. "You are going to put me into an early grave," he said. "Speaking of which, Phineas' funeral is in two days' time. Are you going to grace us with your presence?"

"I am, but it was in bad form that you only sent word to Helena about the arrangements."

Picking up the decanter, his father asked, "What would you have me do? Should I roll out a red carpet for her?"

"You are neglecting Helena, your daughter."

"I know she is my daughter," his father snapped. "How could I forget, considering she is the spitting image of her mother?"

"That isn't her fault."

"No, but I don't have time to run across Town every time I need to speak to her," his father argued as he poured himself a drink. "It is much easier to have a servant send word."

Greydon gave his father a knowing look. "You are putting her off on purpose, but it won't work."

"You know not what you speak of."

"I know more than you realize."

His father placed the decanter down and picked up his glass. "Fine," he said. "If you are so insistent, we shall invite them to dine with us this evening."

"That would be a start."

"I do not know what good it will do," his father muttered as he brought the glass to his lips.

Greydon knew he shouldn't engage his father, but when had he done what he should have? "You have changed, Father."

His father gave him a bored look. "I am the same man I have always been."

"That isn't true," Greydon contended. "You used to smile, but I haven't seen one since Mother passed away."

"What is there to be happy about?" his father demanded.

"You still have me and Helena."

"Oh, happy day," his father declared. "Should I run up and down the streets and scream 'Hallelujah'?"

Greydon shook his head. "You are pigheaded."

"As are you."

"I am nothing like you."

His father chuckled. "You and I are more alike than you realize," he said. "I was the second son as well. I lived my life the way I wanted to, but it all changed when my older brother died. I was forced to grow up, just as you will."

"I am doing just fine as I am."

"I used to say that, but the relentless work of running various estates takes a toll on you," his father said. "Fortunately, I had Abigail as a companion, and she helped me. I am afraid that I am lost without her."

"You aren't lost. You are just grieving."

His father's back grew rigid. "Do not tell me what I am doing," he shouted. "You have no idea what I have given up for you."

Greydon put his hand up. "Forgive me, Father, but I did not mean to sound insensitive."

"You should be more grateful for what you have been given," his father said. "With Phineas' death, you are a wealthy man now."

"I would rather have my brother here."

"Why, so you could ignore him?" his father asked. "Do not think for one second that I wasn't aware that your relationship with Phineas was strained."

"We were still brothers."

His father took a sip of his drink. "Yet you are trying to let his murderer go free," his father said. "Sir David told me that you are investigating the case."

"I am."

"Why would you do something so foolish?" his father demanded.

Greydon rose from his chair. "I am not entirely convinced that Lady Eugenie murdered Phineas."

"Are you mad?" his father asked.

"No, I am quite sane."

His father harrumphed. "You are determined to bring ruination down upon this family. We will be made a laughing-stock if anyone discovers you worked as a Bow Street Runner."

"No one will find out."

"You are naïve and foolish," his father declared. "Why can you not just behave within the bounds of propriety?"

"Where is the fun in that?" Greydon smirked.

His father waved his hand in front of him. "Leave me," he ordered. "I have had just about enough of you."

Greydon performed an exaggerated bow. "As you wish, Father."

His father pursed his lips together. "There will be a day of reckoning for you and I hope I am there to see it."

"I shall see you for supper." Greydon turned on his heel and exited the study. He knew no good would come in continuing his conversation with his father.

Chapter Thirteen

Greydon had just started to descend the stairs when a knock came at the main door. The butler crossed the entry hall and opened the door wide, revealing Helena and her husband, the Earl of Darlington.

Helena stepped inside and smiled up at him. "Good evening, Brother," she greeted.

Greydon approached his sister and gave her a kiss on the cheek. "Sister." He turned his attention towards his brother-in-law. "Darlington."

Darlington was a lanky man who tended to say the most uncouth things. There was no guile to him, but he appeared more clueless than anything. Despite this quirk, he was a good man and treated Helena very well.

Darlington tipped his head. "Rushcliffe." He paused. "I must admit I find it rather odd to address you as such."

"It has been difficult to come to terms with," Greydon admitted.

Helena placed a hand on his sleeve. "I have no doubt you will do far more good with your title than Phineas ever would have."

"I hope that is the case."

Darlington interjected, "With your title comes a great responsibility."

"Do not remind me, or my father," Greydon said. "He has been relentless trying to get me familiar with the accounts."

Helena lowered her hand to her side. "That doesn't sound at all like our father," she remarked with a knowing look.

Darlington gave her a baffled look. "That sounds precisely like your father."

"I know, but I was being facetious," Helena said.

With a chuckle, Darlington remarked, "I should have known. You have quite the quick wit, my dear."

Helena smiled at her husband. "I am glad that you find me so amusing."

Darlington reached for her hand and brought it up to his lips. "You are the only person who never fails to make me smile."

Greydon felt a twinge of jealousy at how much his sister and Darlington loved one another. They both seemed to radiate happiness. He hoped one day that he could convince Enid to love him as much as he did her. He knew it would be difficult, but it would be worth it in the end.

Helena turned her attention towards Greydon. "How is your suit going with Lady Enid?"

"I offered for her, but she turned me down," Greydon replied.

Her brow lifted. "She turned *you* down?" she asked incredulously. "Did she give a reason as to why that was?"

"Enid is worried that associating with me would tarnish our reputation."

"She isn't wrong," Helena stated.

Darlington glanced between them. "Was Lady Enid the one who eloped and her husband recently died?"

Helena nodded. "That is the one."

"You must stay away from her," Darlington counseled as

he placed a hand on Greydon's shoulder. "Women like that do not deserve a second chance."

"Women like her?" Helena repeated. "What do you mean by that?"

Darlington blinked. "What if she killed her husband?" he asked. "Does anyone know how he died?"

"I doubt that Lady Enid killed her husband," Helena pressed. "She is far too kindhearted for that."

"I am just saying that there are plenty of respectable women that would love to marry you," Darlington said. "If you are looking to marry, my cousin would be a good choice."

An image of Darlington's cousin came to his mind. She looked just like Darlington in a dress and she wore these round spectacles that hid most of her face. She would probably be the last person he would ever consider for a bride. But he couldn't very well admit that to Darlington.

"Thank you for that kind offer, but I intend to marry Lady Enid," Greydon said.

"But she turned you down," Darlington pointed out. "I can promise you that my cousin would be overjoyed with an offer from you. And she is quite good at needlework. If you need anything mended, she can do it quickly."

"I shall keep that in mind."

Darlington removed his hand and took a step back. "Just do not get my cousin to start laughing when she is drinking tea. She will snort and the tea will come out her nose."

Helena shook her head. "Dear, you shouldn't say such things about Hannah."

"Why? Is it not true?" Darlington asked.

"Yes, but no man is interested in a girl that can shoot tea out from her nose," Helena pointed out.

"Ah," Darlington said, wagging his finger. "You make a good point, Wife."

Helena exchanged a look of love with her husband before

saying, "I must admit that I was surprised to get an invitation from Father to dine with him tonight."

"I told him that he needs to try harder with you," Greydon shared.

"What is the point?" Helena asked. "He will try for a bit, then it goes back to the way it always was."

"Give him a chance," Greydon encouraged.

"I do, and he always manages to let me down, time and time again. At what point do I stop trying?" Helena asked with sadness in her voice.

Darlington reached for his wife's hand and said, "You have a good heart, and I hate to see you so disappointed."

Before Helena could reply, their father's voice came from the opposite side of the entry hall. "Shall we get this dinner over with?" he asked gruffly.

"Lovely sentiment," Helena muttered.

His father closed the distance between them. "Helena," he greeted.

"Father," she replied with a tip of her head.

Shifting his gaze towards Darlington, his father said, "Darlington."

Darlington acknowledged him in kind.

His father's eyes flashed with annoyance as he turned to face Greydon. "I noticed you have not spent any more time with the ledgers today."

"I did not have time."

"You would have time if you weren't wasting it on worthless pursuits," his father declared.

Greydon didn't feel like arguing with his father, not now. Why did his father always insist on being difficult? "They are not worthless, Father."

His father scoffed. "Did you tell Helena that you are pursuing Lady Enid?" he asked cynically. "A woman that is not even worthy to have us utter her name."

"That is your opinion," Greydon said.

His father straightened to his full height. "That is a fact," he shouted. "You are either too blind or stupid to realize it."

Helena spoke up. "Father, perhaps we can discuss something more pleasant?" she attempted.

"I am tired of being the only one that cares about this family's reputation," his father said. "Do you know how hard I worked to ensure you both had a good life?"

"And we are thankful for that..." Helena started.

Their father spoke over her. "Let's eat before I must retire to bed." He spun on his heel and headed towards the dining room.

Helena rolled her eyes as she accepted her husband's arm. "I see that Father is in a fine mood this evening," she whispered.

"Isn't he a delight?" Greydon joked.

Darlington pressed his lips together. "I don't find him to be in a pleasant mood at all. He is rather ornery if you ask me."

Helena patted her husband's sleeve. "We were teasing, dear."

"Why can't you just speak plainly then?" Darlington asked as he led her into the dining room.

Greydon saw that his father had claimed his spot at the head of the table and he was placing his napkin onto his lap. He went to sit to the right of him and hoped that his father would be in a better mood. But he was not so lucky.

His father leaned to the side as a footman placed the first course in front of him. "Are you increasing yet?" he asked Helena.

"I am not," Helena replied, her eyes turning downcast.

"You have one job as a wife," his father remarked.

Darlington cleared his throat. "You do not need to concern yourself with that," he said, his voice taking on a warning.

Greydon hid his smile behind his napkin. Good for Darlington, he thought. The man did have a backbone and he was standing up for his wife. His respect for the man had just gone up immensely.

His father frowned. "At least Helena did her duty and married well." He shifted in his seat to face Greydon. "I hope to say the same about you one day."

"You have no say in who I choose to marry," Greydon said.

After his father picked up his spoon, he remarked, "At least your mother isn't here to see what a disappointment you turned out to be."

Greydon tensed. "You have no right to mention Mother."

"Whyever not?" his father asked, his voice rising. "She was my wife, after all."

"If anything, you are the disappointment, Father," Greydon said.

"How dare you—"

Greydon continued. "You have forgotten Mother. You are a shell of the man you once were."

His father shoved back his chair and jumped up. "I have not forgotten Abigail. She is all that I think about."

"While you are wallowing in your grief, you have turned your back on us," Greydon said. "You don't even know who we are anymore."

"I know who you are!" his father exclaimed. "You are a man that only lives for himself."

"No, that is you," Greydon contended.

His father tossed his napkin onto the table. "I do not have to take this from you. I loved your mother dearly."

"I don't dispute that, but it is time to move on. You must accept that Mother is gone."

"Don't you think I know that?" his father asked. "Every morning, I wake up to disappointment when I remember that she is no longer with us."

Rising, Greydon said, "We miss her, too."

His father's face softened and his eyes grew moist. "Not as much as I do," he said softly.

As he went to respond, his father walked out of the room without saying another word. The silence was deafening as Greydon stared at the empty doorway. Why couldn't his father realize that they were all hurting since their mother's death?

Darlington's voice broke through the silence. "Should we eat before our soup gets cold or are we expected to wait until your father returns?"

"I do not think my father plans on returning," Helena replied softly.

Greydon gave them an apologetic look. "I'm sorry. I should have never pressed Father."

Helena's eyes held compassion. "You did nothing wrong," she said. "Until Father realizes his own misery, he won't ever change."

"I am not sure if he is capable of change," Greydon admitted.

"Perhaps not, but that doesn't mean we stop trying to help him."

Greydon returned to his seat and reached for his spoon. "We may as well enjoy the dinner our cook prepared."

"That sounds lovely," Helena said. "For the record, this is precisely how I thought dinner would go." Her words held amusement.

———————

With the bright, afternoon sun cascading through the windows, Enid sat in the drawing room as she worked on a cap for her daughter. She was embroidering flowers onto the white cap but she was moving at a slow pace. Her mind kept turning to Lady Eugenie and her impossible situation. No doubt, she was trying to protect her sister and she respected that choice. But her heart ached for her friend.

Rosamond's voice came from next to her. "That is lovely," she said, pointing at the cap.

"Thank you," Enid responded. "It is turning out much better than I expected."

Her sister-in-law held up a handkerchief with her husband's initials on it. "I do think Malcolm will be pleased with his new handkerchief."

As Enid admired the needlework on the handkerchief, she remarked, "You are very talented at needlework."

"I had to be," Rosamond said, lowering the handkerchief. "I wasn't raised in a grand house where servants tended to my every whim. My mother taught me how to mend my own clothes from a young age."

"Where were you raised, exactly?" Enid asked.

"In the countryside," Rosamond responded vaguely.

Enid decided to let the matter drop, but she found she was curious about Rosamond's past, which was something she rarely spoke about. She knew there was more to her sister-in-law than what she was letting on, but it wasn't her place to pry. She had secrets, too.

Osborne stepped into the room and announced, "Lord Rushcliffe has come to call. Are you accepting callers this afternoon?"

Enid hesitated as she tried to keep the excitement out of her voice. It would do no good if she acted like an overeager, love-craved debutante. "I am. Will you please send him in?" she asked.

Osborne tipped his head in acknowledgement. "Yes, my lady."

Enid leaned forward and placed the cap onto the table before she rose to greet Greydon. She took a moment to smooth down her pale-yellow gown. She really did need to get a more refined wardrobe, but she had yet to make the time.

Greydon stepped into the room and he smiled at her. That's it. All he did was smile, and in that moment, if it were possible, it reminded her that she loved him. And she always would. But love was not enough to risk everything. She had made that mistake before.

She dropped into a curtsy as she attempted to calm her racing heart. "My lord," she greeted politely.

He bowed. "My lady," he said with mirth in his eyes.

They stared at one another for a moment, both daring the other person to look away. Her mind whirled with things that she wanted to say but she couldn't seem to formulate the words. Not when he was looking at her like that.

Rosamond spoke up. "Would you care to join us for a cup of tea?" she asked, addressing Greydon.

Enid blinked and she was embarrassed by the fact that she had forgotten Rosamond was in the room. She had been so distracted by Greydon. How was that possible?

Greydon shook his head. "Thank you kindly, but I was hoping to invite Lady Enid on a carriage ride."

She knew that Greydon was not one to parade himself around Hyde Park during the fashionable hour so there must be more to this carriage ride than he was letting on. "I would enjoy that."

Greydon's eyes strayed towards the cap on the table. "Are you making a cap for yourself?"

"No, it is for my daughter," she rushed, reaching for it. "It is much too small for my head."

He smiled again. It was that same smile that she knew would be engraved on her heart from this day forward. "I was just teasing you."

"Oh, I should have known," Enid said. And she should have. It was obvious that the cap was for a small child so why had she not seen through his attempt at humor? She knew why. Greydon affected her in a way that no one had ever before.

Greydon stepped forward and offered his arm. "Shall we, my lady?" he asked. "My curricle is outside."

Enid placed the cap down before she placed her hand on his sleeve. "I think that sounds like a wonderful idea."

"Careful, it almost sounds like you are going to enjoy yourself."

"That has yet to be decided," she joked.

Greydon led her from the room and out of the main door that was being held open by Osborne. They stepped outside and he went to assist her onto the bench. Then he came around the curricle and claimed the seat next to her.

As he reached for the reins, he said, "I hope you do not mind my subterfuge, but I secured us a meeting with Lady Eugenie."

"How did you accomplish such a feat?" she asked.

He shrugged. "I paid off the guards for their discretion."

"That was ingenious."

"Not really," Greydon replied. "I have learned that people will say or do anything for the right amount of money."

Enid detected a hardness in his voice as he said his words. It hadn't been there a moment ago. Finding herself curious, she asked, "Who taught you that?"

Greydon's jaw clenched. "My father," he replied. "He always threw money at a problem, but he wasn't wrong. I used to pay off informants all the time as a Bow Street Runner."

"But paying off informants is very different from what your father did," Enid argued.

"He did no different than what he thought was best, especially when he felt he had no other options."

"Everyone has a choice."

Greydon adjusted the reins in his hand. "I was a troubled youth," he admitted. "My father sent me to Eton and I was sent home more than I care to admit for fighting. But my father kept sending me back, each time with a generous donation to the school. He didn't want me home, any more than I wanted to be home."

"I'm sorry," Enid said, unsure of what she should say.

"Unfortunately, Phineas made it nearly impossible for me to remain at Eton, considering his reputation with the ladies," he revealed. "He would sneak out at night and go to the village nearby to meet a young woman. Sometimes he would get caught but, most of the time, no one cared. Or they looked the other way because of who he was."

Greydon continued. "I vowed then and there that I would never be like my brother."

"You are nothing like your brother," Enid assured him.

"I know, but doubt can creep in. Phineas wasn't always a cad." He paused. "At least, I hope I speak true."

Enid shifted on the bench to face him. "Actions define a man, and your daily actions prove that you are honorable."

"I wish it were simple to believe that."

"It is," Enid said. "I have no reason to lie to you."

Greydon glanced over at her, his eyes sparking with vulnerability. "Will you always tell me the truth, no matter the consequences?" he asked.

How could she deny him something so simple? She wanted honesty between them- always. He deserved that. Frankly, she deserved that, too. And the thought of no secrets between them was something that she desired. "I promise," she said, hoping her words conveyed her sincerity.

His expression grew solemn. "I do not have very many people that I trust."

"I understand that feeling all too well."

"I know you do, which is why I am so comfortable around you," Greydon said. "You are unlike any other woman that I have ever met."

Enid decided it was time to lighten the mood since it was growing much too serious for her taste. "You must not have met very many women, then," she teased.

Greydon chuckled. "How is it that you can always make me laugh?'

"I am quite amusing, you know. Lots of people have told me so."

"Lots of people?" Greydon questioned. "May I ask who those people are?"

Enid smirked. "Marigold, Malcolm, a lady at the shop..." Her voice trailed off. "Those are just a few that I just came up with."

"Well, if a lady at the shop told you as much, as did a little child, who am I to argue?" Greydon joked.

She laughed, and when she did so, she felt freer somehow. As if some of her burdens had been lifted off her shoulders; burdens that had been there for some time, bogging her down.

Greydon pointed towards Newgate. "We are almost there," he said. "I wish you did not stand out so much."

"Is the pale yellow too much?" she asked as she adjusted the sleeves.

He turned towards her and met her gaze. "It is your beauty that I am referring to. No one can compare to you. No one."

Enid felt a blush creep up her neck as she held his gaze. "You are being very complimentary this afternoon."

"I am just merely stating the truth, my dear."

"Truth is in the eye of the beholder," Enid argued.

Greydon's lips twitched. "Aye, but surely you have noticed all the people who have stared at you as we passed by them," he said. "I can assure you that they were not looking at me."

Now the blush had taken hold and her face grew warm under his watchful eye. "You shouldn't say such things to me."

"I thought we promised that we would never lie to one another."

Enid knew that they didn't need words, not anymore. They could just look at one another and smile, knowing there is nothing else to look at.

Greydon pulled on the reins and the curricle came to a stop, rocking on its wheels. "I feel as if I should warn you about Newgate."

"There is no need," Enid said. "I lived in a workhouse for two months. Surely it is not much worse than that."

"I cannot speak on that," Greydon said as he secured the reins. He hopped down and came around to her side to assist her out of the curricle.

Once her feet were on solid ground, she removed her hands off his broad shoulders and took a step back, creating more than enough distance between them to be considered proper. Although, nothing about this outing was proper. They were going into a prison together and she only hoped that Sir David did not discover that she had come. He had warned her off from visiting Lady Eugenie.

Greydon offered his arm. "May I escort you inside?" he asked.

Enid glanced down at his proffered arm. "Are you sure that is wise? It isn't as if we are taking a stroll through Hyde Park. We are going into Newgate."

"True, but it does give me a reason to touch you, and I always look forward to those moments," Greydon said.

"You are incorrigible," Enid chided lightly, even though she was secretly pleased by his words. Just by his touch, he made her forget the rest of the world.

He took a step closer to her. "To be honest, I would prefer it if you remained close to me. A prison is not a place to be complacent."

Enid tried to appear as if she were put out. "All right, then," she said, placing her hand on his. "But only since you insisted."

Greydon reached for her hand and moved it to the crook of his arm. "I will keep you safe. You do not need to worry."

Enid knew he spoke true, making her grateful for his presence.

Chapter Fourteen

Greydon knew that he was being bold in his advances towards Enid, but the time to act was now. He could see the cracks in the mask that she showed the world. She was softening towards him, but he still had so much work left to do. She had been jilted before by love and it would take more than flattery to win her heart.

Everything he had said to Enid had been true. He didn't have very many people that he could trust and he knew that Enid was special. When she spoke, he listened and took her words to heart. He wanted to know what she thought. No, he *needed* to know what she thought. Her happiness was his greatest priority.

As he led Enid into The Keeper's House, Bourne stood up from behind the desk. "Well, well, look who it is, Stevens," he said.

Stevens glanced up from the desk. "Ah, the high and mighty Bow Street Runner has decided to grace us with his presence," he mocked. "Welcome to our humble prison."

Greydon tried to keep his tone cordial as he said, "Gentlemen."

Bourne let out a dry bark. "There are no gentlemen here. We are just doing our best to survive here."

Reaching into his jacket pocket, Greydon removed a handful of gold coins and placed them on the desk. "We are here to see Lady Eugenie, per our arrangement."

Bourne and Stevens moved quickly to scoop up their share of the money.

As he slipped the coins into his pocket, Bourne said, "Thank you for your donation, sir. It is greatly appreciated."

Stevens spoke up. "You will be given ten minutes with Lady Eugenie."

"I need more time than that," Greydon argued.

"My advice is to speak quickly," Stevens said. "If your presence is discovered here, it would spell trouble for all of us."

"I understand," Greydon said.

Stevens' eyes shifted to Enid and he straightened in his seat. "Who did you bring with you?" he asked with a flirtatious smile.

Greydon felt Enid step closer to him but she was showing no outward signs of discomfort. "That is not important," he said.

"Is she mute?" Stevens asked.

Enid's voice was calm as she replied, "I am not."

Stevens tossed up his arms. "She speaks!" he exclaimed. "And what a lovely voice it is."

Bourne came around the desk and approached Enid. His eyes perused the length of her as he said, "You are like a mirage in the desert. I think you brightened the entire room when you stepped inside."

Enid offered him a gracious smile. "You are too kind, sir, but if it wouldn't be an imposition, I would like to see Lady Eugenie now."

Bourne nodded. "Very well, but only because you asked nicely." He gestured towards Greydon. "Your companion could use better manners."

"I have told him as much," Enid joked.

With a chuckle, Bourne spun on his heel. "Follow me and do not dillydally," he ordered. "We will get in and get out, without anyone the wiser."

Greydon escorted Enid through the back door as they followed behind Bourne. The guard came to a stop outside of a door and reached for the handle. "Wait here. I will go retrieve Lady Eugenie."

After they stepped inside the small, square room, Enid slipped her hand off his arm and she walked over to the barred window. She looked out and shared, "I can see the gallows from here."

Greydon went to stand next to her. "We will find a way to keep Lady Eugenie alive."

"How can you promise such a thing?" she asked. "We both know the odds are stacked against her."

He placed his hand on her arm and gently turned her to face him. "Are you losing hope?"

"Is there any hope in a place like this?" she asked softly.

"I understand your reservations but you mustn't let Lady Eugenie see you despair," he replied. "She needs a calm, reassuring voice that all will be well."

Enid squared her shoulders. "You are right," she said.

"Of course I am," he remarked with a smirk. "But I do wish you would recognize my genius on more occasions."

"I said nothing about you being a genius."

"You didn't have to, but we both know you were thinking it."

Enid smiled. "You are a cocky man."

"Yet you still choose to spend time with me," he teased. "What does that say about you?"

As she went to reply, the door opened and she closed her mouth. Bourne had a firm grip on Lady Eugenie's arm as he led her into the room.

Bourne dropped Lady Eugenie's arm and said, "You have ten minutes. Use them wisely."

Greydon took in Lady Eugenie's haggard appearance. Her eyes were red and swollen and her blonde hair looked no better than a rat's nest. A film of dirt coated her fair skin and there was a pungent odor that had followed her into the room.

Enid seemed to have no reservations and closed the distance between them. She embraced Eugenie warmly and whispered, "I am so sorry this is happening to you."

Lady Eugenie dropped her arms and stepped back. "You shouldn't have done that," she argued as she went to scratch her head. "I have lice and I do not want you to get it."

"I have had lice before," Enid said. "You need not worry about me."

Greydon walked over to the table that sat in the middle of the room and pulled out the two chairs. He gestured towards them as he said, "We have much to discuss. Why don't you both have a seat?"

After they had both sat down, Greydon crossed his arms over his chest, not knowing how this conversation would go. He needed to be direct but he didn't want Enid to accuse him of being too forceful with his line of questioning. But he did not like being lied to.

He decided that the best course of action was to state what they knew and hope Lady Eugenie would fill in the gaps.

"We visited your sister, Lady Charlotte, yesterday," he shared.

Lady Eugenie looked displeased by that news. "You shouldn't have done that. Lottie knows nothing that would help me."

"I think she knows more than she is letting on," Greydon pressed.

"Lottie is just a young girl and can't understand the complexity of the justice system," Lady Eugenie attempted.

"She is not so little," Greydon argued.

Lady Eugenie abruptly rose. "I would prefer not to talk about Lottie."

Enid looked up at her friend. "Did Phineas know about the baby?"

Her face paled beneath the layer of grime. "What baby?" Lady Eugenie asked unconvincingly as she lowered herself back onto her chair.

"Lottie was rubbing her stomach, just as I did when I was pregnant with Marigold," Enid told her. "We are assuming that Phineas is the father."

Lady Eugenie's eyes grew frantic. "You must not tell anyone or she could be ruined."

Greydon huffed. "I do think her sister being accused of murder might have tarnished her reputation."

"I told Lottie that I would protect her but I can't do that from here," Lady Eugenie said.

"No, but you can tell us the real reason why you went to visit my brother," Greydon encouraged.

"For what purpose?" she asked. "If I tell the truth, then I could implicate my sister in all of this. That is something I do not want to do."

Enid reached for Lady Eugenie's hand. "I know you think you are doing what's best for Lottie, but what happens if you are found guilty? You will be executed and what will happen to your sister?"

"I know what you are thinking and Lottie did not kill Phineas," Lady Eugenie asserted.

"She was the last person to see him alive," Greydon said. "What if she stabbed him and fled before you arrived?"

Lady Eugenie shook her head vehemently. "No, Lottie would not have done that. She was happy about the baby and couldn't wait to tell Phineas."

"What if Phineas did not share in her excitement?" Enid asked. "It might have led her to do something drastic."

"You are wrong," Lady Eugenie said as she pulled back on her hand.

"But what if we aren't?" Enid insisted.

Rising, Lady Eugenie walked over to the window and stared out. "I must protect Lottie, at all costs."

"At the risk of your own life?" Enid asked.

"So be it," Lady Eugenie replied.

Enid cast Greydon a helpless look and he decided he needed to try a different tactic on Lady Eugenie. He needed to earn her trust or else they would get nowhere. It would be best if he tried to sympathize with her.

Greydon uncrossed his arms. "I understand the desire you have to protect your sister. It is something that is engraved inside of you. It is your purpose."

"Yes, that is right," Lady Eugenie said as she turned to face him.

"But we need to know everything about that day, no detail is too small. The more information you give us, the more we can help you," Greydon advised. "We want to help you, and your sister. We are not trying to condemn anyone."

Lady Eugenie pressed her lips together and it looked as if she were going to refuse his request. After a long, drawn-out moment, she sighed. "I went to Phineas' apartment with the intention of asking him to break things off with my sister. Lottie fancied herself in love with him and I knew it would only end badly for her, and him. When I arrived, I found a knife sticking out of his chest. I swear I did not kill him."

Greydon had made it a habit to know when people were lying to him. It was a matter of life or death for him, and he had gotten very good at it. But it was the way that Lady Eugenie held his gaze, without hesitation, that he knew she was telling the truth.

"I believe you," he said.

Lady Eugenie looked pleased by his admission. "Lottie adored Phineas and hung on to his every word," she shared.

"I knew there was no point in reasoning with her. She had the ill-conceived notion that she would one day become Phineas' wife."

Greydon cocked his head. "But he was already married."

Lady Eugenie shrugged. "That is what I told my sister as well, but I couldn't seem to convince her of it. I don't know what kind of promises Phineas made to her, but she believed him, wholeheartedly."

Enid interjected, "It wouldn't be the first time someone lied to control another person." Her voice was sad.

Lady Eugenie's face softened. "I'm sorry. You know that all too well."

The door flew open and it banged up against the wall, startling the ladies. Bourne stepped into the room and announced, "Your time is up." The guard went to grab Lady Eugenie's arm and yanked her out of the seat. "We need to get her back before she is missed by the other guards."

Enid rose. "Wait. We need more time with her."

Bourne scoffed. "Just be grateful for the time you got to spend with her," he declared as he led Lady Eugenie out of the room.

Greydon approached Enid and said, "She will be all right."

Enid didn't look convinced. "We need to get her out of here."

"I agree, but it would be wise if we departed before anyone else notices our presence," Greydon said as he offered his arm.

As Enid took his arm, Greydon could see that her shoulders were slumped slightly. He had no doubt that she knew what an impossible situation they found themselves to be in. Even if they were able to prove that Lady Eugenie didn't kill Phineas- and that was a big "if"- he knew that she would never turn on her sister. It didn't matter what the facts were.

This was a matter of the heart. And that was much more complicated to decipher.

The rain fell against the windows as Greydon sat at the desk in the study. He had just returned from Phineas' funeral, and he was emotionally exhausted. It had been one thing to know his brother was gone, but it had been entirely another thing to say goodbye.

The chapel had been filled with London's best, who had come to offer their condolences at the loss of one of their own. But he would gladly wager his inheritance that there wasn't a genuine mourner amongst them. Phineas wouldn't have cared either. He would have just wanted a big show. It had always been about appearances to his brother.

Greydon's stomach rumbled as he tried to get some work done. He had decided to forego his midday meal because he'd found he wasn't in the mood to eat. He just needed to keep his mind occupied, which was proving to be nearly impossible.

His thoughts kept straying to Lady Eugenie. She had been wrongly accused but it was going to take more than his word to get her out of Newgate. The people were against her, too. The newssheets confirmed that by the articles that were written about her.

He suspected Lady Charlotte had murdered Phineas, but how could he prove it? He needed to ascertain the truth for himself, but would Lady Charlotte even be willing to see him again?

Davy stepped into the room. "A Mr. Moore is here to see you, my lord…"

His words had just left his mouth when Mr. Moore barged into the room. "You went to see Lady Eugenie without me!"

"Good afternoon, Mr. Moore," Greydon said. "Would you care to have a seat?"

Mr. Moore approached the desk. "You had no right to visit with Lady Eugenie without me being present."

Greydon frowned as he addressed his next comment to the butler. "That will be all, Davy."

After the butler departed, Greydon leaned back in his seat. "I needed to speak to Lady Eugenie and I did not think you would mind."

"Mind?" Mr. Moore asked. "Good gads, are you daft?"

Greydon didn't take offense to Mr. Moore's insulting remarks because he knew what he should say to dispel his anger. "I do believe that Lady Eugenie's sister killed Phineas."

Mr. Moore blinked. "Surely you can't be serious?" he asked. "She is only seventeen."

"It did not take much to plunge a knife into his heart, especially if he was weakened by the arsenic."

The barrister dropped down into the chair. "Can you prove this?"

"No," he replied.

"Do you have any proof that can verify this accusation?"

"I do not."

Mr. Moore tossed up his hands in frustration. "You want me to accuse Lady Charlotte of murder with no proof?" he asked. "Are you mad?"

Greydon gave him a pointed look. "I am going to get proof."

With a shake of his head, Mr. Moore asked, "Do you just make things up? I am just curious to know if I put my faith in the wrong Bow Street Runner."

"I know it sounds far-fetched but if you will just hear me out," Greydon said.

Mr. Moore huffed. "By all means, explain to me this preposterous theory."

"Lady Charlotte was pregnant with Phineas' baby and she was the last person to see him alive that morning."

"How do you know that?"

"By her own admission she admitted she was at Phineas' apartment that morning," Greydon said. "I do believe she killed him and slipped out before her sister arrived."

Mr. Moore's brow rose. "I'm not saying I agree with you, but do you truly think Lady Charlotte is callous enough to let her sister hang for a murder that she committed?"

"I do, and Lady Eugenie is going along with all of this to protect her sister."

The barrister grew silent. "I daresay you might be on to something, but how can you prove it?" he asked. "I am not sure if you remember, but courts generally rely on evidence."

Greydon closed a ledger and placed it on the stack of books. "I need to speak to Lady Charlotte again."

"Can I at least be present this time?" Mr. Moore mocked.

"I take no issue with that," Greydon said. "But we do have an issue. Even if we can prove Lady Charlotte did murder Phineas, will Lady Eugenie allow her sister to be tried for murder?"

Mr. Moore pursed his lips together. "All I do know is that she has helped raise her sister since their parents died a few years back and is fiercely protective of her. Their guardian, which is their uncle, is a drunk and he has washed his hands of them."

"There must be some way to convince Lady Eugenie to accept the facts."

"What facts?" Mr. Moore asked. "Did you mention some when I wasn't listening?"

Greydon inched forward to sit on the edge of his seat. "Now that I have a working theory, I will get some," he said. "I just need time."

"Time is not a luxury that we have. The judge is pushing

to move this case up because people are demanding justice. They want Lady Eugenie to pay for what she did."

"It sounds as if they are seeking vengeance more than anything."

"Vengeance? Justice? It is all in the eye of the beholder," Mr. Moore said with a slight shrug of his shoulders.

A knock came at the door before Davy stepped into the room. "Mr. Libbey has come to call, my lord," he informed him.

"Who the blazes is Mr. Libbey?" Greydon demanded.

Davy held up a calling card. "He was your brother's solicitor."

Greydon flicked his wrist as he said, "Send him in."

Mr. Moore rose and tugged down on his green waistcoat. "I will set up a meeting with Lady Charlotte."

"She may refuse to see us."

"I won't give her that option to do so," Mr. Moore said.

As the barrister walked out of the room, he was passed by Mr. Libbey, who was a short, round man with blond hair greased to the side. He had red splotches on his face and a hint of stubble on his chin. A satchel hung over his left shoulder, and he was carrying papers in his hand.

Mr. Libbey came to an abrupt stop in the doorway. "Thank you for agreeing to see me, my lord."

"What is it that you want, Mr. Libbey?" he asked, hoping he sounded somewhat cordial.

Mr. Libbey held up the papers in his hand. "I have a copy of your brother's will. I thought you might want to see it."

"Bring it to me, then," Greydon ordered.

The solicitor approached the desk and extended the papers towards him. "He hadn't updated his will in some time but it does reflect how much he wishes to be left to his wife."

"Where, pray tell, is that?"

Mr. Libbey leaned forward and ran his finger down the writing. "The late Lord Rushcliffe requested ten thousand pounds to be left to his wife and a jointure of a thousand pounds a year."

Greydon's eyes roamed the document, confirming what the solicitor had said. "I shall inform my father."

"I already gave him the will for his review but he thinks it is far too generous. He says the estate cannot support that loss."

Placing the papers down, Greydon said, "I shall speak to my father about this at once."

"Very good," Mr. Libbey responded. "I am pleased that the couple did work out their differences in the end."

"I beg your pardon?" he asked. "What differences?"

Mr. Libbey gave him a blank look. "Did your brother not tell you about the divorce proceedings he was starting to instigate?"

"I know nothing of a divorce."

"Your brother came to me and asked me to draw up papers for a divorce settlement," Mr. Libbey shared.

Greydon was stunned. His brother had intended to divorce his wife? But they had only been married for two years. He had a sneaking suspicion about the answer to his next question but he asked it nonetheless. "Did my father know?"

"Yes, of course, considering he was preparing to help his son by pushing it through Parliament."

"Parliament would not have granted a divorce without proper grounds."

Mr. Libbey bobbed his head. "He claims that he never consummated the marriage between him and his wife."

Greydon looked at the solicitor in astonishment. "But they went on a wedding tour for months. Surely Lady Rushcliffe will contend that was not the case."

"I cannot speak as to what she would say, my lord," Mr. Libbey said. "All I was asked to do was to prepare the documents."

"Have they been filed yet?"

"No, your brother still had to acquire his wife's signature," Mr. Libbey said. "When I hadn't heard from him, I assumed that he had changed his mind on the divorce."

Greydon now realized that his brother had been paving the way for Lady Charlotte to be his wife. He was planning on divorcing Harriet. What a horrible blackguard! Did he not care a whit about what that would do to Harriet, or her reputation? She would be a shunned woman in high Society. No man would want to associate with her.

But Phineas had not given the divorce contract to Harriet for her to sign. If Lady Charlotte thought Phineas had backed out of divorcing Harriet, would she be furious enough to kill him? It was plausible, giving her a motive for killing him.

He shoved back his chair and walked over to the door. "Davy," he shouted.

The butler appeared only a moment later. "Yes, my lord."

"Bring my carriage around front," he ordered. "I wish to visit Lady Rushcliffe."

"I shall see to the preparations," Davy responded before he walked off to do his bidding.

Chapter Fifteen

Enid sat in the drawing room as she worked on embroidering a dress for Marigold. It was a lazy afternoon but her mind was far away. No matter how hard she tried, she couldn't stop thinking about Greydon. She loved him, and she always would, but she couldn't act on her feelings. Hadn't she learned from her mistakes? Yet she couldn't do anything but wish that things were different.

Rosamond's voice broke through the silence. "Are you all right?" she asked with concern in her voice.

Enid brought her gaze up and replied, "I am. Why do you ask?"

"You seem deep in thought," Rosamond said. "Is there something bothering you?"

"Nothing in particular," Enid lied.

Rosamond gave her a look that implied she didn't believe her. "You will find that I am an excellent listener."

Enid knew she could trust her sister-in-law, but she was scared. What if Rosamond thought she was foolish for developing feelings for Greydon? It hadn't been so long since her husband had died.

"Is this about Lord Rushcliffe?" Rosamond asked.

Was she so transparent, she thought. "How did you know?"

Rosamond smiled. "I would be blind if I didn't notice the growing attraction between you two. I think it is sweet that Lord Rushcliffe looks at you like you are the only one he sees."

Leaning forward, Enid put her needlework onto the table as she found the strength to say her next words. "He offered for me, but I turned him down."

If Rosamond was surprised by what she had just revealed, she didn't show it. "May I ask why you turned him down?" she asked. "It is obvious that you have feelings for him."

"I do, but I do not deserve him," Enid replied.

"I see, and did you tell him as much?"

Enid nodded. "I did, but he is still pressing his suit," she said. "He needs a wife that doesn't have a tarnished past."

Rosamond watched her for a moment before asking, "Does Lord Rushcliffe know of your past?"

"I have told him everything."

"And yet he still loves you."

Enid pressed her lips together. "He has said nothing about love."

With a knowing look, Rosamond asked, "Do you love him?"

"I do, with everything that I am," she admitted, seeing no reason to deny it any longer.

"Then you must do something about it," Rosamond advised. "Love is the greatest gift of all and should not be dismissed so easily."

Enid shook her head. "I have been down this road before and I was jilted."

"I am not saying it isn't scary to give your heart to another since you are risking that they will misuse it. But what if he gives everything to treat your fragile heart with love? Is that not worth the risk?"

"I don't know if I am strong enough to try," Enid admitted.

"There is only one way to find out," Rosamond encouraged. "Take the first step and see where the journey leads you."

Osborne stepped into the room, interrupting their conversation, and announced, "Lady Esther Harington has come to call. Are you accepting callers?"

Rosamond bobbed her head. "Please send her in."

"Very good, my lady," Osborne said as he departed from the room.

It was only a moment before Lady Esther walked into the room and went to drop down onto an upholstered armchair. "My stepmother is impossible!" she exclaimed. "She is trying to arrange a marriage for me. Can you imagine?"

Lady Esther leaned forward and reached for the teapot on the table. "I need something that will soothe my nerves," she declared as she poured herself a cup of tea. "I know I am being terribly rude but I am at my wit's end."

"No harm done," Rosamond assured her. "We do not stand on formalities here."

After Lady Esther placed the teapot down, she reached for the cup of tea and took a long sip. "Thank you," she said. "This is precisely what I needed."

Rosamond picked up the plate that held biscuits and held it out to her. "Would you care for something to eat?"

"I would." Lady Esther reached for a biscuit and took a bite. "My stepmother has informed me that she wants me out of the house before the baby comes. What nerve!"

"What does your father say?" Rosamond asked.

Lady Esther shrugged. "He does whatever he is told. Susanna has bewitched him and has turned him against me." She paused. "I need chocolate. Do you have any?"

"I can see if the cook can warm some up for you," Rosamond said.

"That won't be necessary. Tea and biscuits should be sufficient." Lady Esther turned her attention towards Enid and blinked, as if she had just noticed her. "I do apologize for the intrusion. You must be Lady Enid."

"I am," Enid said.

Lady Esther gave her a weak smile. "I'm afraid I made a terrible first impression on you. I am not usually so brazen, but I am very frustrated at the moment."

"Rightfully so," Enid assured her. "I would be irate if my parents tried to arrange a marriage for me."

Rosamond interjected, "Did you come alone?"

"I walked here, but a maid trailed behind me," Lady Esther replied. "My stepmother made sure of that."

"You walked here?" Rosamond asked.

Lady Esther gave her an amused look. "It is only a few blocks."

"Yes, but I was told that a lady does not walk to make calls," Rosamond said.

"Well, if I am lucky, everyone noticed and no one will want to marry me," Lady Esther responded. "Although that would create a whole bunch of new problems."

Rosamond shifted in her seat as she explained, "Esther's stepmother is of a similar age to her and she was appalled when her father married the woman."

"I was more than appalled!" Lady Esther shouted. "I was blasted angry. I apologize for my strong language, but it is true."

"I think we can handle your strong language," Rosamond teased.

Lady Esther put her empty cup and saucer onto the tray. "What am I to do?" she asked, her shoulders slumping slightly.

"Your stepmother can't force you to marry," Enid replied. "It is against the law."

"We both know that being a woman puts us at a disadvantage," Lady Esther said. "We are entirely at the whim of others."

Rosamond pushed the plate of biscuits towards Lady Esther. "Do not give up hope. Perhaps your stepmother will come around."

Lady Esther huffed. "There is a better chance of having a rhinoceros as a pet."

Her father stepped into the room and said in his usual gruff voice, "A word, Enid."

What now, she thought as she rose. She had no doubt her father wanted to criticize her for something she had done.

They didn't speak as she followed him into his study. Once they arrived, her father closed the door and crossed his arms over his chest. "I thought I told you to stay away from Lord Rushcliffe."

"You did, but I'm afraid that is impossible."

Her father's nostrils flared slightly, a telltale sign that he was barely holding on to his anger. "You will cease all contact with Lord Rushcliffe, and that is an order."

"No."

"No?" her father demanded. "You have no right to refuse my request. Furthermore, it has come to my attention that you visited Newgate. Are you determined to ruin this family?"

"That is not my intention—"

He cut her off. "Your actions suggest otherwise," he shouted.

Enid was done. She was tired of fighting with her father. He would never see her for who she was now. He would always judge her because of her past. "Is it always going to be like this?" she asked in a resigned voice.

A baffled look came to his face. "Like what?"

"You are always going to find fault with me, no matter what I do," Enid said. "It is exhausting, Father."

Her father pursed his lips. "If you just behaved better, I wouldn't have to chide you as much as I do."

Enid knew what she needed to do. It was time, but was she strong enough to take the first step? A feeling of peace swept over her and she knew that she was. "I think it is for the best if I used my inheritance to maintain my own household."

"Surely you don't mean that," her father said.

"I do," Enid said. "I can't take this constant fighting. It is time that I forge my own path."

Her father uncrossed his arms and some of his anger dissipated. "And who will take care of Marigold?" he asked. "I doubt you will have the funds for a nursemaid."

"I can take care of my own child."

"You are just spouting nonsense," her father said with a swipe of his hand. "You couldn't manage being on your own."

Enid tilted her chin. "You seem to forget that I survived an abusive husband and life inside of a workhouse for two months. I am more than capable of taking care of myself."

"Enid…" her father started.

She put her hand up, stilling his words. "I am sorry, Father, but my mind is made up. I will speak to my solicitor about finding appropriate accommodations."

Her father's back grew rigid. "Fine!" he exclaimed. "Do as you like but do not come groveling back to me."

"I have no intention of doing so."

He reached for the door handle and opened the door. "Be off with you. I have work that I need to see to."

Keeping her head held high, Enid walked through the door and tried to appear unaffected as her father slammed the door behind her.

Her eyes roamed over the grand entry hall that she had called home for as long as she could remember. This may have been her home, but she would establish her own household. A place that she could finally breathe without the fear of upsetting her father.

Enid walked up the stairs and stopped outside Marigold's bedchamber. She slowly turned the handle and stepped into the room. It was quiet as she made her way to Marigold's side. She was sleeping so peacefully.

She had wanted her daughter to grow up with her grandparents, but her father was impossible. He would never just let her be. Why couldn't he let go of her past? As she thought about that, she realized that she hadn't let go of her past either. Perhaps it wasn't as easy as she thought.

Greydon exited the coach in front of his brother's brownstone townhouse and let out a sigh. He had no doubt this was going to be a most difficult conversation with Harriet since there was no way he could delicately ask about the divorce. His best course of action would be to say what needed to be said and hopefully she wouldn't turn into a simpering miss.

He approached the main door and knocked. It was only a moment before the door opened and a tall, fair-skinned man asked, "May I help you?"

"I am Lord Rushcliffe and I would like to see Lady Rushcliffe," he announced. There was no point in removing a calling card.

The butler tipped his head and opened the door wide. "Yes, my lord."

Greydon stepped into the entry hall and was surprised to hear Harriet's laughter drifting out from a side room. His curiosity was piqued even more when a male's voice followed the laughter.

Rather than wait to be announced by the butler, he wanted to see for himself what was so amusing. He followed the sound of the voices and approached the door. He glanced inside and saw Harriet sitting on the settee and she had a bright smile on her face. Her companion had his back to him, but there was something familiar about him.

As he headed into the room, Harriet looked over at him and her smile vanished. She jumped up from her seat with a guilty look on her face. "Greydon. What a pleasant surprise," she said in a light, cheery voice.

"Isn't it though?" he asked.

Her companion rose and turned to face him. It was none other than Lord William, his brother's best friend. "Rushcliffe," he greeted.

Greydon didn't bother to respond to Lord William's greeting but instead directed his question towards Harriet. "Dare I ask what was so amusing?"

Harriet's eyes darted towards Lord William before saying, "We were just discussing the weather."

"The weather?" Greydon repeated. Surely she did not think he was so intolerably stupid that he would fall for that explanation.

Lord William interjected, "Yes, we were discussing the weather."

Greydon resisted the urge to groan. They did think he was that stupid. "Pray tell, what is so funny about the weather?" he pressed.

"It is just so fickle," Harriet replied with a nervous laugh.

"Yes, but I fail to see how that is so amusing," Greydon said.

Lord William smiled, no doubt in an attempt to disarm him. "You must use your imagination if you want to imagine a sunny day in London."

Greydon lifted his brow. "Why are you here?" he demanded. He was tired of their lies and hoped they would speak the truth.

"I'm visiting an old friend," Lord William responded. "I am doing nothing wrong by calling upon Harriet."

Again, they thought he was an idiot. They didn't think he could see through the charade that they were playing. Their innocent act was just that- an act. It was evident that they were closer than Lord William dared to admit.

Lord William took a step back. "I should be going," he said.

"By all means, you should stay," Greydon responded dryly. "It is obvious to me that you do as you please- with whom you please- anyways. Isn't that right?"

"I would, but I'm afraid I am late for a meeting," Lord William said before he rushed out the door.

Coward.

Greydon crossed his arms over his chest and stared at Harriet. He had so many things he wanted to ask her and he wanted the awkward silence to make her feel uncomfortable. He had learned people tended to let things slip when they were caught off guard.

Harriet tried to appear indifferent, but he could tell that she was nervous by the fidgeting of her hands. "Is this truly necessary?" she asked.

"Is what necessary?" he repeated. He had no intention of making this easy on her.

With a wave of her hand, she said, "This whole judgmental persona you have about you right now."

"You hardly know what I am thinking."

"No, but I can see the disapproval written on your face," Harriet stated. "It is very unbecoming of you."

Greydon narrowed his eyes. He was done playing the fool. "Did my brother know about you and William?"

Her mouth dropped, as if she couldn't believe he had pieced together this puzzle, but she quickly recovered. "I do not know what you are referring to—"

"Don't lie to me," he ordered, his voice rising. "Did my brother know?"

Harriet lowered her gaze to her lap as she admitted, "He had some suspicions, but he did not know."

Uncrossing his arms, he held her gaze. "I think he did know, which is why he intended to divorce you."

Harriet put her hand in front of her. "No, you have it all wrong," she said. "Phineas presented me with a divorce contract, but I talked him out of it."

"That doesn't sound at all like my brother," Greydon remarked. Phineas was stubborn to a fault, much like their father.

"I knew all about his affairs and I pretended that it didn't bother me. I knew what I was getting into by agreeing to marry Phineas. But it was different when he met his latest lightskirt," Harriet said with disgust. "She sunk her claws into him and refused to let him go. She was the one that convinced him to get a divorce. He didn't truly want one since it would ruin both of us."

"Phineas' solicitor claimed the divorce was based on the assumption that you two had not consummated the marriage."

Harriet smirked. "We took care of that within a few hours after we signed our marriage contract. I can assure you that he had no complaints either."

Greydon frowned. "Did you know about his other apartment?"

Harriet nodded. "Whenever we came to London, Phineas would go his way and I would go mine, but we always came back together when we retired to our country home."

"You took no objections to his..." he cleared his throat... "indiscretions."

"I took issue, but little could be done about it," Harriet said, the hurt evident in her voice. "Phineas was not the type of man that could be faithful to one woman."

"I'm sorry." Greydon knew his words were wholly inadequate at a moment like this, but he felt sympathy for Harriet.

No woman should be treated as terribly as she had been by her husband.

Harriet gave him a weak smile. "At least I got a title out of it. That is all that my father cared about when he arranged the marriage."

"You should know that Phineas did leave a will."

Lowering herself onto the settee, Harriet said, "I know, but it means little until your father agrees to the terms."

"I will speak to him about it."

"Thank you, Greydon," she said. "It might be best if you leave out what you witnessed today. I do not think your father is the understanding type."

"No, he is not," Greydon readily agreed.

Harriet waved her hand over the tea service on the table. "Would you care for some tea?"

"I would not, but I would be remiss if I did not warn you against continuing your liaison with William. You are in mourning."

"I am well aware of my situation."

Greydon gave her an expectant look. "If my father did discover the truth about you and William, he would show no mercy."

Harriet looked displeased. "I understand, but I am a widow now. We are allowed some indiscretions, assuming we are discreet."

Knowing that nothing else needed to be said between them, Greydon said, "Good day, Harriet."

She replied in kind.

He turned to leave but stopped himself. He had one more thing he needed to ask her. "Have you ever been to Phineas' apartment?"

She pursed her lips. "Why would I ever have set foot into that place?" she asked, as if the mere thought insulted her.

"Fair enough," Greydon replied.

Harriet leaned back in her seat. "Is it true that you are pursuing Lady Enid?"

"I do not wish to discuss that with you."

She gave him a haughty look. "I would not cast the first stone at me since you are entangled with a ruined woman."

Greydon grew rigid. "I did not ask for your opinion on the matter."

"You did not, but I see the contempt in your eyes for me," Harriet said. "I am doing no different than what my husband did."

"We both know it is different for a woman."

"How is that fair?" she asked.

Greydon sighed. "I never said it was fair—"

She spoke over him. "No, it most assuredly is not."

With a shake of his head, he said, "Just be careful, Harriet. You are playing with fire, and I worry that you might get burned."

"Isn't that the fun of it all?"

He had just about enough of this conversation. They were getting nowhere, and he was beginning to see a side of Harriet that he did not like. He had always considered her to be prim and proper, a very capable wife of a viscount, but he had been wrong. She was no better than his brother. Harriet just did a better job of hiding it.

Greydon turned and walked out of the room. The butler hurried to open the main door and he stepped out onto the pavement. He took a deep breath. He found that he needed a walk to clear his head.

A footman stepped off his perch and went to open the coach door.

He put his hand up to stop the man. "I do believe I shall walk home."

The footman tipped his head in acknowledgement. "Very good, my lord," he said.

As he started walking down the pavement, he realized that

he didn't want to go home right away. He wanted to see Enid again. Besides, he needed to update her on his investigation. He knew that he could make up a million reasons as to why he needed to see Enid, but the truth was, he just wanted to be with her. His best moments were when he was with her. They made him smile no matter what was transpiring in his life.

Chapter Sixteen

Enid sat on her settee in her bedchamber as she read her book. She was grateful for the silence that was afforded to her because she knew she wouldn't be residing in the lap of luxury for long. She would move out of her parents' townhouse, and she would be responsible for running a household- a small household.

She had enough of an inheritance to live for the remainder of her days, assuming she lived frugally. Which was not something she was opposed to. She could buy a small cottage in the countryside and have her own garden. It sounded simple. It sounded perfect. But she felt guilty taking Marigold from her grandmother.

She couldn't remain under the same roof as her father. It wasn't working. She was tired of the fighting and it was time she proved to him that she was not the same selfish girl that eloped in the middle of the night.

A knock came at the door.

"Enter," Enid ordered as she placed the book onto a side table.

The door opened and her mother stepped into the room

with a sad look in her eyes. "I just heard the most distressing news from your father." She paused. "Is it true?"

Enid knew precisely what she was referring to. It was amazing to her that it took her this long to find out. "It is."

Her mother's hand flew up to her mouth. "You cannot leave," she said. "What of Marigold? She is thriving here."

"I know, but I can't remain here with Father."

"Your father can be difficult…" her mother started.

She huffed.

"… but he doesn't want you to go either."

Enid lifted her brow. "I somehow doubt that to be true. He has done everything in his power to force me to leave."

Her mother came to sit down next to her on the settee. "I shouldn't tell you this but he visits Marigold every day."

"I was wondering about that."

"I do believe that Marigold has won over his heart."

Enid rolled her eyes. "If he even has one."

Her mother reached for her hand. "Your father is a complicated man, but he does have a good heart. He has just forgotten how to use it," she said. "And he is making an effort, at least with me."

"I am glad that things between you have improved."

A smile came to her mother's lips. "They have and I am most grateful that I gave him a second chance. I thought my trust in him had been misplaced but I was wrong."

"Father will never see me as anything but the girl that eloped. He doesn't think I have changed."

Her mother released her hand and sat back. "You and your father have always been at odds with one another. I daresay it is because you are very similar."

"Similar?" Enid repeated. "I think not."

With a knowing look, her mother said, "You both are stubborn, almost to a fault, which served you well when you were on your own. But you are home now and don't need to be so obstinate. Furthermore, you both are scared to be vulnerable."

"There may be some truth to that," Enid admitted with a slight shrug of her shoulder. "I don't have the luxury of being vulnerable since I have Marigold."

"Being vulnerable is not a weakness. It is quite brave, in fact."

Enid shook her head. "Nothing good comes from being vulnerable. I must protect my heart at all costs."

"That is a sad way to live."

"It is a sensible way to live," Enid countered.

Her mother's eyes held compassion as she responded, "You have been hurt, there is no denying that, but there is so much joy in this world. All you have to do is look at Marigold to see it."

"Precisely, which is why Marigold is enough for me."

"Don't be so quick to dismiss Lord Rushcliffe's advances," her mother said.

Enid felt her back go rigid. Was she so obvious with her affection that everyone knew that she held him in high regard? "I said nothing about Lord Rushcliffe."

"You didn't have to," her mother said. "He is enamored with you, and I suspect you feel the same about him."

Before she could reply, a knock came at the door.

"Enter," she ordered.

The door opened, revealing a young maid, and she announced, "Lord Rushcliffe has come to call, my lady. Are you accepting callers?"

"I am," Enid said. "I will be down shortly."

After the young maid left, closing the door behind her, her mother's lips twitched. "Speaking of the devil..." her words trailing off.

Enid rose. "You are reading too much into his visits."

"Am I?' her mother asked innocently. "Or are you not reading enough into his visits? He does seem to come rather frequently."

She didn't want to go into detail that Greydon was visiting

her to update her on the investigation. Knowing her mother was still waiting for her response, she said, "I cannot speak for him as to why he comes. Perhaps he is just bored."

"He is most assuredly not bored," her mother contested, rising. "He comes for you, my dear. I just pray you see it before it is too late."

Enid was done with this conversation. She didn't want to explain how scared she was to open her heart again. She loved Greydon but the fear of the unknown terrified her. And even if she did follow her heart- which she wouldn't do- she was not worthy of him. She would only drag his name down through the mud and that wasn't fair to him. He deserved better.

"I shouldn't keep Lord Rushcliffe waiting any longer," Enid said as she walked over to the door.

"Just think on what I said," her mother attempted.

Enid opened the door. "I will," she lied before she stepped out of her bedchamber.

As she walked down the corridor, she knew that her mother meant well, but Enid was jaded. Life hadn't always been kind to her, and she had been burned before. That was not something that she could just get over and move on from.

She descended the stairs and saw Greydon standing in the entry hall, his top hat in his hands.

He greeted her with a smile. "Hello, Enid," he said.

She returned his smile. "Greydon."

"I was hoping to speak to you privately, assuming you have no objections."

"I have none." She gestured towards the rear of the town-house. "Would you care to take a stroll in the gardens?"

His smile grew, making him devilishly handsome. "I would greatly enjoy that." He placed his top hat on and offered his arm. "May I escort you?"

Enid placed her hand on his sleeve. "Thank you, kind sir." And right on cue, her heart started racing at his mere touch and she wondered if she would always have this reaction.

They walked to the rear of the townhouse and a footman held the door open, promptly following them out onto the veranda.

Once they started walking down one of the paths, Enid resisted the familiar urge to remove her hand and create more distance between them. But she found she didn't want to. She wanted to be close to him.

Greydon cleared his throat. "How are you faring?"

"I am well," she replied. "And you? Are you faring well?" She closed her eyes, knowing she sounded like a babbling idiot.

He chuckled. "I have no complaints."

"That is good." There. That was a simple response and didn't drag on for too long.

With a glance at her, Greydon revealed, "I discovered something rather interesting today. It appears that my brother wanted to petition Parliament for a divorce."

Enid came to a stop on the path and turned to face him. "Whyever for?"

He cleared his throat. "He claims that the marriage wasn't consummated, but his wife refutes that claim."

"It begs the question, which one is lying?"

"I had that same thought, but Harriet was rather convincing, especially since my brother never missed an opportunity to be with a woman."

Enid furrowed her brows. "So it might have been entirely possible for Lady Charlotte to marry your brother, assuming Parliament granted him the divorce."

"Yes, but Harriet said she convinced Phineas to drop that whole matter of divorce."

"What if Harriet murdered Phineas because he wouldn't drop the divorce?" Enid asked.

Greydon nodded. "I thought of that, as well. However, Harriet claims that she has never been to Phineas' apartment before."

"Do you believe her?"

"I want to believe her, but I still intend to make some inquiries."

Enid gave him a curious look. "How do you intend to do that?"

"My sister-in-law is a beautiful young woman with black hair," he replied. "I have no doubt that someone would have noticed her- or her coach- if she went to that part of Town."

"Oh, I see," Enid murmured as she lowered her gaze to the lapels of his grey jacket. She felt a twinge of jealousy that he found his sister-in-law to be a beautiful woman. Why did that upset her so? She had no claim on him so he could do as he pleased.

Greydon studied her for a moment before asking, "Did I upset you, Enid?"

She brought her gaze back up. "Of course not," she responded. "I was just merely pondering on what you said."

"What did you conclude?"

"About what?" she asked.

His eyes held amusement as he replied, "You said you were pondering on what I said about Harriet."

"I did say that, didn't I?"

"You did."

"Well, I concluded that you were right. Surely someone would have noticed her at the apartment."

"I'm glad that we could come to an agreement about that."

Enid pressed her lips together before saying, "It is a good thing that your sister-in-law is so beautiful that she garners attention."

Greydon's lips quirked into a boyish grin. "You aren't by chance jealous of Harriet?"

"No, no, no…" she started. How many times could she deny it before he would believe her? "I am just merely repeating what you said."

He took a step closer to her. "I want to make something clear, my dear." He leaned closer until their faces were only inches apart. "Every time I look at you, I fall in love with you all over again."

"You love me?" she asked, her heart taking flight.

"I thought it was fairly obvious."

Her eyes roamed over his face until they landed on his lips. She wanted to kiss him, to feel his lips on hers, but was she bold enough to do so?

Greydon lifted his hand and twirled the piece of hair in his finger that had fallen next to her cheek. "May I kiss you?"

"Yes!" she rushed out. As the word left her mouth, she felt her face growing warm at the mortification that she'd responded so quickly and so enthusiastically. She was supposed to be a lady, after all.

With an amused look on his face, he joked, "I can see you are still indecisive."

"A gentleman wouldn't tease me at a time like this," she chided breathlessly as she felt his warm breath on her cheek.

"I thought we had decided that I am no gentleman," he said as he lowered his head.

Just as his lips brushed against hers, Malcolm's irate voice came from next to them. "Unhand my sister, Rushcliffe!" he exclaimed.

In a quick motion, Greydon moved to create more distance between them.

Malcolm's eyes were sparking with anger as he declared, "I have no choice but to challenge you to a duel."

Greydon didn't want to laugh, but it was lunacy on his friend's part to challenge him to a duel. He was a skilled marksman and Malcolm was most assuredly not. Although, he understood where Malcolm's anger was coming from since he had been caught kissing his sister in the gardens with no understanding between them. Not that he hadn't tried for one, but Enid wasn't ready.

With a shake of his head, Greydon said, "I am not going to duel with you."

"Are you and Enid engaged?" Malcolm demanded.

"We are not, but not for a lack of trying on my part," Greydon replied.

Malcolm took a step closer to him, his eyes narrowed. "I cannot let you dishonor my sister so horrendously by kissing her without an understanding in place."

"I can assure you that I meant no disrespect."

"What was your intention, then?" Malcolm asked. "Were you hoping to have a dalliance with my sister?"

Greydon's jaw clenched. "You forget yourself. I would proceed with caution," he said, his voice holding a warning.

"No, it is *you* that forget yourself," Malcolm growled.

Enid stepped in between them and chided, "Are you both quite finished?"

Malcolm scoffed. "Stay out of this, Enid."

"Stay out of this?" Enid repeated. "Surely you can't be serious."

"Rushcliffe went too far and—" Malcolm started.

"I kissed him," Enid declared.

Greydon went to object, for he was fairly certain it had been him that had instigated the kiss, but Enid shot him a look to be quiet.

Malcolm turned his heated glare towards her. "Why would you do such a thing?" he asked. "Do you not care for your reputation?"

Enid gave him a knowing look. "I daresay that my reputation cannot sink any lower."

"Regardless, you cannot go around kissing people," Malcolm said.

"I was not kissing 'people'," Enid drawled, "I was kissing Greydon."

Malcolm's eyes shot back up to him. "You are calling each other by your given names now?"

Placing a hand on her hip, Enid spoke up before Greydon had a chance to reply. "I gave him leave to," she announced.

"What would Father say?" Malcolm asked.

"I don't know because *you* aren't going to tell him," Enid said, her voice unusually firm. "What happened between Greydon and me is between us, not Father."

Malcolm glared at Greydon. "I asked you to watch over Enid, not compromise her."

"I did not compromise Enid," Greydon contended.

"You should do the honorable thing and marry her."

"Happily," Greydon responded.

Enid glanced between them, her lips pursed. "Do I not get a say in this?" she questioned. "After all, you both seem to be planning my future right in front of me."

"I am trying to help you," Malcolm said.

"By forcing Greydon to marry me?" Enid asked in disbelief. "How is that helping me?"

Malcolm sighed as he placed a hand on his sister's shoulder. "I am not forcing him to marry you but I'm giving him a push."

"How is that any different?" Enid shrugged off his touch. "I am not some weak-willed woman that you can boss around."

"I never implied that you were——"

Malcolm's words stopped when Enid turned to face Greydon. "And you," she started, "why would you go along with anything my brother said?"

Greydon went to place his hand on her sleeve but thought better of it. He feared that Malcolm would object profusely and would start up with this whole duel nonsense again. "I want to marry you, Enid. I don't care about the reasoning. I would marry you today, tomorrow, or the day after that."

"I refuse to let my brother dictate our actions," Enid said. "If I marry you, I want it to be on our terms, not his."

"Does that mean you are considering it?" Greydon asked hopefully.

Enid held his gaze as she admitted, "I find that I am not as opposed to the thought as I once was."

Greydon felt his heart take flight at her admission. He was slowly breaking down her barriers, one by one, until he could claim her heart. "I can live with that," he said.

Enid spun back around to face her brother. "You have no right to make demands of us. I am a widow, and I am allowed certain freedoms."

"I am trying to protect you," Malcolm asserted.

"From what?" she asked.

He tossed up his arms. "From yourself!" he exclaimed.

Enid stood her ground, showing no signs of backing down. "Haven't I proven that I can take care of myself?"

"You were forced into a workhouse after you escaped an abusive husband," Malcolm reminded her.

"And I survived," Enid said. "Does that not speak for itself?"

"Enid, you are being entirely unreasonable," Malcolm replied. "You must think of your future; of Marigold's future."

"I am, but I am in control of it. Not you."

Malcolm went to reply, but Enid interjected, "Excuse me, gentlemen, I find that I need to lay down."

As Enid walked away, Malcolm glowered at Greydon as he crossed his arms over his chest. "This is all your fault, you know," he declared.

"I do not contest that," Greydon said.

"What were you thinking kissing my sister?" Malcolm demanded.

"I'm afraid I wasn't thinking and that was the problem."

Malcolm frowned. "Did you mean what you said about having a desire to marry Enid?"

"I did," Greydon replied. "I love her."

Some of Malcolm's anger dissipated at his words. "It is about time that you admitted that and I wish you luck. Enid has had a rough go of it and she still keeps her guard up."

"I am well aware, but her resolve is waning; I am sure of it."

Malcolm uncrossed his arms, dropping them to his sides. "Just be patient with her." He paused and pointed his finger at him. "And no more kissing."

Greydon hoped he could convince Enid to kiss him again, but he didn't dare admit that to Malcolm. When their lips had touched, albeit briefly, he knew he was trying to tell her the depth of how he felt. He felt like he was home in her arms. She was his other half.

Malcolm's voice broke through his musing. "Are you even listening to me, Rushcliffe?"

"I make it a point to listen as little as possible to what you are saying," Greydon joked.

His friend cast his eyes heavenward. "You are nearly impossible to like."

Greydon glanced over his shoulder at the gate in the rear of the gardens. "I think it is time I depart."

As he turned to leave, Malcolm's voice stopped him. "Enid may act tough, but it is just an act. She has a kind heart and deserves a lifetime of happiness. That is what I want for her."

"For once, we are in agreement," Greydon said. "If I can do the impossible and convince Enid to marry me, I will never take her for granted."

"She cares for you; that much I know."

Greydon bobbed his head. "I know," he responded. "She has told me as much but the fear keeps creeping in. Not that I blame her. Her late husband treated her terribly and left scars."

"Everyone has scars. Just some are more obvious than others."

Glancing at the sun setting in the distance, Greydon asked, "Will you inform Enid that I will come call upon her tomorrow?"

"I will, but I daresay that you are making a nuisance of yourself," Malcolm said lightly.

"And Malcolm…" He paused. "If I were you, I would not challenge anyone else to a duel. You would most surely lose."

"That is debatable," Malcolm responded.

"No, it is a fact."

Malcolm puffed out his chest. "I would have you know that I am an excellent shot."

"Maybe for a drunk, blind man," Greydon quipped before he started walking towards the rear of the townhouse. Once he exited through the gate, he headed down the pavement. It wasn't long before he arrived home.

As he stepped through the main door, Davy announced, "Your father wishes to speak to you."

"Lovely," Greydon muttered.

He'd had a long day and the last thing he needed was his father to belittle him or his choices. He sighed. If he were lucky, his father would be so preoccupied with his tasks that he didn't have time for him.

But he was never that lucky.

Greydon stepped into the study and saw his father was sitting on the settee with a drink in his hand.

"Where have you been, Son?" his father demanded.

"I have been seeing to a few things," Greydon replied vaguely.

"Is Lady Enid one of those things?"

Greydon nodded. "She was," he admitted.

His father huffed as he turned his attention to the hearth.

"I do not know why you insist on disobeying me," he said. "Lady Enid would be a terrible choice for your bride."

"We shall have to agree to disagree on this."

"I have taken the liberty of speaking to Lord Forbes on your behalf and we believe an alliance between our families would be beneficial."

Greydon lifted his brow. "What kind of alliance?" he asked skeptically.

His father brought his gaze back to meet Greydon's and replied, "A marriage between you and Lady Alice."

"Lady Alice?" Greydon repeated. "She is hardly out of the schoolroom."

"She may be young, but she is seventeen and is in her first Season. Besides, that was the age your mother was when we got married."

Did his father truly think that he would go along with this madness? He had already decided he would marry Enid or no one else.

His father brought his glass up to his lips. "I know you have some misguided affections for Lady Enid, so you can take her as your mistress."

"No."

His father shrugged. "I do not care if you take Lady Enid as your mistress or not. I just thought it might soften the blow."

With a shake of his head, Greydon said, "No, you misunderstood me. I will not take Lady Enid as a mistress but I intend to make her my wife."

"Not this again!" his father exclaimed. "Your courtship of Lady Enid is improper. She is in no way worthy to be your wife, but Lady Alice is."

Greydon remained calm and collected. No matter what his father said, it wouldn't change his mind about Lady Enid. There was no point in engaging his father on this subject, but he did have a few questions of his own.

He came to sit across from his father. "Did you know that Phineas was planning on divorcing Harriet?"

His father sobered and grew silent. "I did."

"Why would you help push his divorce through Parliament?" Greydon asked. "We both know there was a likelihood that it wouldn't have been granted."

"I know, but it had been over two years and Harriet had not done her duty. She had yet to bear Phineas a son."

"So your plan was to help cast her aside, ruining her in the process?"

"What choice did we have?" his father asked.

Greydon would have liked to say that he was shocked by his father's callousness, but he wasn't. His consistent actions proved the type of person his father was.

His father growled, "Do not look at me like that."

"Like what?"

"As if you are judging me," his father replied. "I am trying to protect our family's legacy."

Greydon leaned forward in his seat. "What would Mother say about your actions?"

His father visibly tensed, and his words grew harsh. "You will leave your mother out of this," he demanded.

"How can I do that?" Greydon asked. "You have done nothing to honor her."

His father jumped up from his seat, spilling his drink onto his hand. "You are out of line, Son."

"I don't think I am."

Placing the glass onto the table, his father removed a handkerchief from his pocket and dried his hand. "You have no idea of what I have sacrificed for this family."

"You intended to help Phineas divorce his wife and are trying to arrange a marriage for me," Greydon said.

"Yes, for the good of the family!"

Rising, Greydon said, "Perhaps it is time that you take a look at the man that you have become since Mother died."

"I know who I am, and I do not need you to preach to me," his father stated before he stormed out of the room.

Greydon stared at the doorway that his father had just departed through and let out a sigh. He didn't think it was possible for his father to change. So why couldn't he just leave well enough alone?

Chapter Seventeen

The following morning, Greydon exited his townhouse and stepped into the waiting coach. He sat across from Mr. Moore and tipped his head at him. "Good morning," he greeted.

Mr. Moore responded in kind before saying, "It would be best if you let me ask the questions when we call on Lady Charlotte."

"Pray tell, why do you say that?" he asked dryly. Why did Mr. Moore insist on being irritating?

"We do not want to frighten the girl."

"The girl?" Greydon repeated. "Lady Charlotte might be a murderer and she is pregnant with my brother's child. She is also seventeen years old. I daresay she is hardly a 'girl' anymore."

"Yes, but she doesn't have any inclination that we consider her a suspect."

Greydon frowned. "You do recall that I am a Bow Street Runner."

"You *were* a Bow Street Runner, but now your priorities have changed," Mr. Moore said. "You are heir to an earldom."

"That doesn't mean I suddenly turned incompetent when it comes to investigating."

"No, but you are distracted."

Greydon's brow lifted. "How exactly am I distracted?"

"I would be blind if I did not notice your attraction to Lady Enid."

"That is neither here nor there," Greydon said, seeing no point in denying it. "I just want to ensure that justice is done for my brother."

"And it will be, but in due time."

"Lady Eugenie doesn't have time," Greydon remarked. "The court of public opinion has already found her guilty."

Mr. Moore nodded. "Yes, but Lady Eugenie will have her day in court. That is all that matters."

Greydon could hear the sincerity in the barrister's voice and he found himself curious as to what kind of man would accept a case where most people had written off the defendant as guilty. "May I ask why you accepted this case?"

"Does it matter why?"

"In the grand scheme of things, no, but I can't help but wonder why," Greydon said. "You have proven yourself to be a competent barrister with your winning record in court. Why would you jeopardize that by representing Lady Eugenie?"

Mr. Moore grew silent. "You and I are not that much different, you know."

"I would say that we are vastly different."

"You may hide behind a gruff exterior, frightening little children along the way—"

"I do not frighten little children."

"That is up for debate," Mr. Moore said with a smirk on his lips, "but I am trying to right a wrong I made long ago."

Greydon cocked his head. "What wrong are you trying to correct?"

"It doesn't matter," Mr. Moore replied, brushing his question aside. "The point being- Matthew's death was not your fault."

"How in the blazes did you know about Matthew?" Greydon demanded.

"You didn't think I would agree to work with you without digging into your past a little, did you?" Mr. Moore questioned.

Greydon had to admit that his opinion of Mr. Moore improved, but he didn't dare admit that out loud. "And what did you discover?" he asked dryly.

"That you are just as broken as I am."

With a shake of his head, Greydon said, "I am not broken- at least, not anymore. I have a purpose now."

"I must assume you are referring to Lady Enid."

"I am."

Mr. Moore turned his gaze towards the window. "I was in love once and it ended very poorly." His words were resigned.

Greydon didn't quite know what to say so he settled on, "I'm sorry."

"I am not against love, mind you, but I just don't believe everyone is fortunate enough to find that one person they simply can't live without." Mr. Moore shifted his gaze towards him, and his eyes shone with sadness. A sadness that could only come from an experience that altered him somehow. "Marriage isn't about simply falling in love once and being done with it. It is about loving someone until the end of your days and growing that love endlessly."

Mr. Moore offered him a weak smile and continued. "I did not mean to preach to you about love. You know it better than I do."

There was something about how Mr. Moore said his words that caused him to pause. "I don't believe that to be true," he remarked.

"I knew it once, but that is in the past. And I would prefer to keep it there." Mr. Moore's words brooked no argument.

Greydon was smart enough to leave well enough alone, especially when it came to matters of the heart. He wouldn't want Mr. Moore to pry into his relationship with Lady Enid. No, it was best if he let the man be.

But he did have one thing that needed to be addressed before they arrived at Lady Charlotte's townhouse. And it was important.

"I do believe that my brother intended to divorce his wife," Greydon revealed. "He even went so far as to draft up a divorce contract for Harriet to sign. She claims she talked him out of it but I have my doubts."

Mr. Moore furrowed his brow. "You are only telling me this now?"

"I just discovered it yesterday," Greydon defended. "Phineas also made promises to Lady Charlotte."

"What kind of promises?"

"He told her that he planned on marrying her," Greydon revealed.

The coach came to a stop, effectively ending their conversation. The door was opened and Greydon followed Mr. Moore out of the coach.

"We are decided, then," Mr. Moore started. "You will let me do the talking."

"You seem to forget that I am a skilled investigator."

"And I argue for a living," Mr. Moore countered.

Greydon knew they would get nowhere if they remained on the pavement so he decided to propose a compromise. "I will allow you to take the lead on this, but I can't promise I won't ask any questions."

Mr. Moore considered him for a moment before bobbing his head. "Very well. I can agree to those terms."

They approached the main door and Mr. Moore knocked. The door opened and the butler greeted them with a wary look. "How may I help you?" he asked.

Mr. Moore removed a calling card from his waistcoat pocket. "I do believe that Lady Charlotte is expecting me."

The butler looked rather uncomfortable as he responded, "Yes, but she was not expecting Lord Rushcliffe."

"I am sure that won't be an issue," Mr. Moore said.

The butler hesitated for a moment before opening the door wide. "Do come in," he encouraged. "I will be just a moment while I go speak to Lady Charlotte."

Greydon stepped into the entry hall and watched as the butler disappeared into the drawing room.

Mr. Moore turned to face him and lowered his voice. "Whatever happens in there, just know that I intend to root out the truth, one way or another."

Before Greydon could reply, the butler stepped back into the entry hall and announced, "Lady Charlotte will see you now."

Greydon followed Mr. Moore into the drawing room and saw Lady Charlotte was standing next to the settee. Her hair was neatly coiffed and she was dressed in a pale pink gown. Which was an odd choice. It seemed much too bright and cheery since her sister was in Newgate on charges of murder.

A smile came to Charlotte's lips as she addressed Mr. Moore. "It is so good to see you, sir," she said.

Mr. Moore bowed. "The pleasure is all mine, my lady," he responded. "Thank you for agreeing to meet with us."

Lady Charlotte's smile disappeared when she turned her attention to Greydon, her expression turning into contempt. "Well, I must admit that Lord Rushcliffe's presence took me by surprise."

Mr. Moore flicked his wrist and said, "Just pretend he isn't even here. I do that all the time."

She giggled. "That is awful of you to say." She lowered herself down onto the settee. "Would you care for some tea?"

"No, thank you," Mr. Moore replied as Greydon followed

suit and sat down on an upholstered armchair. "I came to see how you are faring."

"Thank you," Lady Charlotte said, tilting her chin. "No one has asked how I am doing. Everyone is only asking how Eugenie is doing."

"That is wrong of them," Mr. Moore acknowledged.

A pout came to Lady Charlotte's lips. "I think so, as well. But to answer your question, I am doing as well as can be expected, given the circumstances."

Greydon resisted the urge to roll his eyes at Lady Charlotte's selfish responses. Did she not care that her sister was in Newgate in a misguided attempt to protect her?

Mr. Moore moved to sit on the edge of his seat. "I just need to ask you a few questions, assuming you don't mind."

"I suppose one or two wouldn't hurt," Lady Charlotte said as she moved to lean her back against the settee.

With a glance over his shoulder at Greydon, Mr. Moore asked, "Is it true that the late Lord Rushcliffe promised to marry you?"

Lady Charlotte bobbed her head. "Yes, once he divorced his ghastly wife, he was going to marry me."

"Did he explain that Parliament might not grant his divorce?" Mr. Moore asked.

"Whyever not?" Lady Charlotte asked. "His wife was awful, just awful to him. He was constantly complaining about her."

Greydon couldn't resist saying, "Having a disagreeable wife is not grounds for divorce."

"She also didn't give him a child," Lady Charlotte said. "He needed an heir and she hadn't done her duty."

Mr. Moore spoke up. "Do you know if he spoke to his wife about the divorce?"

"Yes, and she was furious, but Phineas assured me that he wasn't about to back down," Lady Charlotte replied. "Besides, he was used to her bouts of anger, especially when she would show up to his apartment unannounced."

"She has been to his apartment before?" Greydon asked.

"Isn't that what I just said?" Charlotte huffed.

So Harriet had lied to him when she said she had never been to Phineas' apartment. What else was she lying about, he wondered.

Charlotte leaned forward and took a biscuit off the tray. "Lady Rushcliffe even had the audacity to have her lover approach me and bribe me," she revealed. "As if I could be bought off so easily."

"Lord William approached you?" Greydon asked.

"Yes," Charlotte said with annoyance on her features. "Are you even listening to me?"

Greydon kept his voice calm as he replied, "I am. Please proceed."

Charlotte waved her hand in front of her. "He offered me ten thousand pounds to end things with Phineas but I sent him on his way."

Rising, Mr. Moore said, "Thank you, my lady. You have been most helpful."

Charlotte beamed. "You are welcome."

After they departed from the drawing room, Mr. Moore said, "I take it that you gleaned some new information from Lady Charlotte."

"I did," Greydon replied. "Harriet claimed she never went to Phineas' apartment nor did she disclose Lord William's role in all of this."

"It makes you wonder what else she is lying about," Mr. Moore mused.

"Precisely the thought I had."

Enid sat in her bedchamber as she read a book on her settee. She was waiting for Marigold to wake up from her nap so she could take her on a walk through the gardens.

A knock came at the door.

"Enter," she ordered as she placed the book down.

The door opened and her brother stuck his head through the opening. "Are you still angry with me?" he asked.

"Possibly," Enid replied.

He smiled, as he usually did when he tried to disarm her. "I brought you something that might change your mind." He stepped into the room, holding a plate of biscuits. "I had the cook prepare some biscuits for you."

"You aren't playing fair," she remarked. Malcolm knew she had a weakness for biscuits.

Malcolm came and sat down next to her. "Would you care for one?" he asked, holding the plate up.

She reached for one and said, "I am still somewhat angry at you."

"I can work with that," Malcolm responded.

Enid took a bite of the biscuit and savored the delicious taste. "This offering does make me less annoyed at you."

He chuckled. "Then my devious plan worked."

After Enid finished the biscuit, she asked, "How could you have forced me into an arranged marriage with Greydon?"

"I daresay that Greydon had no objections, unlike you." He paused. "Why is that? It is obvious that you care for him."

"I do care for him," she readily admitted, "but that doesn't mean I should marry him."

"Whyever not?"

Enid pressed her lips together. How could she explain to her brother that she was apprehensive about ever marrying again? She'd sworn that she would never be so stupid to ever put herself at the mercy of another man.

Malcolm placed the plate down onto the table. "I know you are scared but that is a good thing."

"Why is that?"

"It means you understand what you have to give up to be with Greydon."

Enid shook her head. "Why am I the one that has to give up everything to be with him?" she asked.

"If you truly love him, it won't seem like such a sacrifice." Malcolm's eyes held compassion as he said, "Your late husband was an awful man. There is no denying that, but that doesn't mean you shouldn't try again with Rushcliffe."

"What of Greydon? His reputation will suffer greatly for marrying me."

Malcolm smirked. "I do not think Rushcliffe cares a whit about that."

"He should."

"But he cares more about you," Malcolm said.

Enid leaned back in her seat as she pondered her brother's words. Everyone was so quick to give her advice on how she should lead her life, but they didn't understand everything that she had gone through to get to where she was today. She was stronger than she was yesterday, there was no denying that, but she was still petrified to make a misstep. She didn't want to lose everything that she had worked so hard to achieve.

Malcolm reached for the plate and extended it towards her. "I know that look. You could use another biscuit."

She laughed. "I could always use another biscuit," she agreed as she reached for one.

As Malcolm lowered the plate to his lap, he said, "I am sorry for trying to force your hand."

"I understand why you did."

Malcolm gave her a chiding look. "Although, you can't just keep kissing Rushcliffe without an understanding."

"It was not planned," she attempted. "It just happened."

"Well, do not let it happen again until you have an understanding between the two of you," her brother said firmly.

Enid knew her brother was only trying to help so she just smiled. "You worry entirely too much about me."

"I have to because you deserve to be happy."

"I am happy."

Malcolm didn't look convinced. "Very well, I shall leave you be." He placed the plate down onto the table. "I will leave the biscuits for you."

"I would appreciate that."

"Just promise me one thing," Malcolm said.

Enid gave him a skeptical look. "What is it?"

"Before you turn down Rushcliffe again, ask yourself what you are fighting for," he advised.

Without a hint of hesitation, she replied, "I am fighting for Marigold."

"And that is noble, but you, my dearest sister, deserve to be loved; to feel the same love you give."

Enid felt her shoulders slump. "You make it sound so easy."

"Loving Rosamond is the easiest thing I have ever done. It is like breathing to me," Malcolm said. "It took some time for me to come to terms with that, but now... I can't live without her."

A part of her wanted to throw caution to the wind and run into Greydon's arms. But a part of her, a very real part of her, couldn't take the chance of rejection again.

Malcolm gave her a knowing look. "Just think on it," he said.

"I can promise to do that, but that is all I can promise at this time."

Rising, Malcolm said, "Furthermore, Mother and I have decided you are not to move out. We want you to stay."

"But Father clearly does not want me here."

"Father doesn't even want *me* here," Malcolm asserted.

"Yes, but you are his heir."

"And you are his daughter."

Enid pressed her lips together. "That means nothing to him," she contested. "Besides, all we do is fight. I am tired of doing so."

Malcolm sighed. "I told Mother I would try to talk some sense into you."

"I appreciate the effort, but this is my life; my future."

"Very well. But tell Mother I tried."

Enid nodded. "I will tell her that you made the most valiant of efforts."

"Thank you, Sister." Malcolm walked over to the door and stopped. "I love you, no matter what you do or where you go."

"I love you, too."

Malcolm exited the room, leaving Enid alone with her thoughts. Which was never a good thing. Perhaps it was time that she went to see if Marigold had woken up from her nap. She exited her bedchamber and walked down the hall to the nursery.

She quietly turned the handle and pushed the door open. As she stepped into the room, she saw her father was sitting on a chair and he was watching Marigold sleep. His eyes held a tenderness to them that she had never witnessed before.

As she went to speak, he held his finger up to his mouth, indicating she should remain silent. He rose and walked past her as he stepped into the hall. She followed him, being mindful to close the door so as not to disturb Marigold.

Enid turned to face her father, giving him an expectant look.

Her father met her gaze and said, "I don't want you to leave."

Nothing could have surprised her more than what her father had just revealed. "Why is that?" she asked. "All we do is fight."

"That we do, but I am hoping to change that," her father said. "Frankly, I cannot stand the thought of not being in Marigold's life."

"Father…" she started.

He put his hand up. "I am not a perfect man, and I know that we are constantly at odds with one another, but I want to be a part of Marigold's life."

"And you shall, but I do think distance would do us both some good."

He winced. "I visit Marigold every day," he admitted. "When she smiles, it is as if I am free to do the same."

Enid was at a loss for words. Her father had never been vulnerable around her before, but that didn't mean they would cease to fight with one another.

Her father stepped forward and placed a hand on her shoulder. "I know I am asking a lot but I hope you will consider staying. I will try to be better."

"What if nothing changes between us?"

He glanced at the nursery door, his eyes filled with anguish. "I don't want to lose Marigold as I have lost you."

"You have not lost me, Father."

Bringing his gaze back, he asked, "Haven't I?" The sincerity in his voice was undeniable, leaving little doubt that he still cared for her.

As she stared at him in utter disbelief, unable to form words, he dropped his hand and took a step back.

"Are we decided?" he asked. "You will remain here with Marigold?" His words were half-hoping, half-demanding.

Enid knew her father was making an effort and the least she could do was meet him halfway. "We will stay for now, but I can't promise more than that."

A rare smile formed on her father's lips. "I will accept that."

"All I want is for Marigold to be surrounded by people that love her," Enid said. "She deserves that."

"I agree, wholeheartedly," he responded. "Now, if you will excuse me, I am needed at the House of Lords."

Her father spun on his heel and walked down the corridor.

Enid stared at his retreating figure and couldn't believe she had agreed to remain at the townhouse with her family. But how could she deny him his request when it was so obvious that he cared for Marigold? That is all that she wanted for her daughter- to be loved.

She went to open the door to the nursery when she saw her mother walking towards her with a bright smile on her face.

"I hear that you have agreed to stay," her mother said. Her eyes shone with happiness.

"Did you speak to Father?"

Her mother bobbed her head. "We spoke briefly on the stairs," she revealed. "I must admit that I am relieved."

Enid furrowed her brow. "I can't quite understand Father's sudden transformation. He hates me, yet he wants me to stay."

"He doesn't hate you."

"His actions suggest otherwise."

Her mother sighed. "Your father is not good at showing his emotions, but he does care for you in his own way."

"I doubt that."

"Regardless, he adores Marigold and visits her every day," her mother said. "Your daughter has brought back your father's smile."

"I just wonder how long it will be before Marigold does something that disappoints Father and he turns on her."

Her mother gave her an understanding look. "Your father is a stubborn man, and I do believe he is determined to not make the same mistakes with Marigold that he did with you."

"That is good."

"If I can give a word of advice," her mother said. "You both have made some mistakes, but true happiness is the ability to move forward with the hope that the future will be better than the past."

With a shake of her head, Enid responded, "It isn't that simple."

"Nothing worth having comes easy. You have to work for the future you desire."

Enid heard some noises coming from within the nursery. "It would appear that Marigold is awake."

Her mother's eyes lit up. "We mustn't make her wait."

"Marigold is thriving here," Enid said as she opened the door.

"Who wouldn't?" her mother asked. "She is loved here, just as you are."

Enid stepped into the room and saw Marigold lying on her bed, babbling away. When she stepped closer, Marigold smiled, filling her heart with joy.

Her mother brushed past her and went to pick up Marigold. "Oh, my sweet child," she cooed, lifting Marigold into her arms.

Enid had made a lot of mistakes in the past but they had all led her to right here. And that wasn't such a terrible place to be.

Chapter Eighteen

Greydon exited his coach in front of Lord William's familial townhouse. It was a three-level whitewashed building with an iron fence surrounding the exterior.

He approached the main door and used the knocker to make his presence known. The door promptly opened and a short, balding man greeted him. "Good afternoon," he said. "How may I help you, sir?"

Greydon removed a calling card from his waistcoat pocket and extended it towards the butler. "I would like to speak to Lord William."

The butler accepted the card and nodded. "I shall see if he is available, my lord."

"It wasn't a request," Greydon said firmly. He knew he was being rude but he didn't have time for games. He needed to speak to Lord William and he wouldn't be brushed aside.

The butler didn't appear to be surprised by his gruff response. He just opened the door wide to allow him entry.

Greydon stepped into the entry hall and waited as the butler closed the door behind him.

"Wait here," the butler ordered before he started walking down the hall.

As he admired the tapestries that hung on the wall, a familiar voice came from one of the rooms. "What a pleasant surprise. I haven't seen you in ages."

Greydon turned his head and saw Lord William's older brother, Lord Kendal, standing in the doorway. Though they had once been good friends when they attended Oxford, time had drifted them apart.

"Good evening, Kendal," Greydon acknowledged.

Lord Kendal gave him a curious look. "Are you here to see me?"

"I am not," he replied. "I need to speak to your brother."

All humor was stripped away from Lord Kendal's expression. "What did he do now?" he asked, his words dripping with criticism.

"I just have to ask him a few questions."

Lord Kendal approached him, stopping a short distance away. "What is so urgent?" he asked. "Did you not just bury your brother?"

"I did, but there are a few things that are unresolved that I need to take care of," he replied, his words intentionally vague.

"I suppose you will not tell me what those things are."

"I will not."

Lord Kendal smiled, but it didn't quite reach his eyes. "You always were a man who preferred intrigue." He gestured towards a room just off the entry hall. "Come have a drink with me while we wait for my louse of a brother."

Greydon knew that one drink would do no harm so he tipped his head in acknowledgement. "I would be honored."

He followed Lord Kendal into a room that had yellow-papered walls and ornate woodwork that ran the length of the room. Furniture of all types and sizes filled the small, rectangular-shaped room, making it rather cluttered.

Lord Kendal walked over to the drink cart in the corner and picked up the decanter. "I do apologize about the furniture but I haven't had the heart to remove any of it since my mother died."

"My condolences for your loss," Greydon murmured.

Lord Kendal's eyes roamed the room with pride. "My mother loved collecting antiques, much to the chagrin of my father," he said. "He indulged my mother entirely too much."

"My father was the same with my mother, although my mother preferred shopping along Bond Street."

"Ah, yes," Lord Kendal said as he poured two drinks. "Bond Street was a popular destination of my mother's, as well."

Greydon chuckled. "I do believe our mothers would have liked each other very much."

Lord Kendal walked over and extended him a drink. "That they would have." He paused. "My father and mother passed away much too soon."

"As did my mother."

Glancing down at the drink in his hand, Lord Kendal said, "I was not prepared to assume his title and all the responsibility that came with it. I wish I had listened more and learned by his hand." He sighed. "Nor was I prepared to deal with my brother and his wayward behavior."

Not knowing what to say, Greydon took a sip of his drink and turned his head towards the doorway, half-hoping to see Lord William.

Lord Kendal continued. "How did you handle Phineas' behavior?"

"I must admit that his behavior drove a wedge between us," Greydon replied. "We were estranged when Phineas died."

"That is awful, but I understand why that was the case. The only reason why I still support William is because I promised my mother on her deathbed to always watch out for him," Lord Kendal revealed. "I'm trying to keep our family together but I feel as if I am failing."

"I am sure you are doing better than you realize."

Lord Kendal grinned. "Since when were you the optimistic one?"

"I suppose I have changed over the years."

"I never understood how much my father carried on his shoulders until I was forced to take the reins," Lord Kendal said. "I know I have no right to complain, but it is a terrible burden to carry. Between voting in the House of Lords and running our estate, I have time for little else, much less a wife and family."

Greydon took a sip of his drink as he pondered Lord Kendal's words. He knew his father lived and breathed his work, but perhaps he hadn't understood the toll it had taken upon him personally.

Before he could respond, Lord William staggered into the room with his cravat hanging around his neck. His hair was tousled and his eyes were bloodshot.

"Stanhope said you wanted to see me," Lord William said in a booming voice.

Lord Kendal looked unimpressed by his brother's haggard appearance. "You have been drinking."

"But of course I have," Lord William responded. "What else am I supposed to do with my life?"

Placing his drink down onto the tray, Lord Kendal said, "You could finish your studies at Oxford and do something with your life."

"For what purpose?" Lord William burped. "I am perfectly content the way I am."

"You are wasting your life," Lord Kendal asserted.

Lord William brought a hand up to his chest. "I disagree, and I would prefer it if you kept your voice down. You are shouting."

"No, *you* are the one shouting," Lord Kendal remarked.

"Am I?" Lord William asked, looking baffled by the thought. "I suppose I am."

Lord Kendal shook his head. "You are an utter drain on my finances."

In a soft voice, Lord William replied, "Father didn't seem to have any complaints. Why do you have so many?"

"You are whispering and I can barely hear you," Lord Kendal said.

Lord William cleared his throat. "Good, perhaps you will stop nagging me."

Lord Kendal stiffened. "We shall continue this conversation when you are sober," he stated. "Until then, Lord Rushcliffe has a few questions that he wants to ask you."

"Do you mind if I lay down?" Lord William asked as he walked over to a camelback settee. "I had an exhausting night last night."

"I do mind, actually," Greydon said.

Lord William either didn't hear him or chose to ignore him because he went to lay down on the settee. He reached for a decorative pillow and positioned it under his head. "Go ahead and ask your questions," he muttered with his eyes closed.

Lord Kendal tossed his hands up. "He is all yours," he remarked before he departed from the room.

Greydon walked closer to the settee and said, "You lied to me about knowing Lady Charlotte. Why was that?"

"Did I?" Lord William asked, unconcerned. "Well, I suppose I didn't think it was your business to know who Phineas spent his time with. Every man has a right to take a secret or two to the grave with him."

As much as he wanted to press Lord William on that issue, he knew his next question was much more important. "Did you approach Lady Charlotte and try to bribe her to stay away from Phineas?"

"What's it to you anyways?" Lord William asked.

"Indulge me."

Lord William shifted his head on the pillow, his eyes

remaining closed. "I don't think I will," he replied. "Phineas is gone. You should just let him rest in peace."

"I'm trying to do just that." He paused. "I am going to ask again- did you approach Lady Charlotte and try to bribe her?"

Silence.

And it was followed by a slight snore.

Good heavens! Had Lord William truly fallen asleep so quickly? Greydon refused to be dismissed so easily. He tossed his drink into Lord William's face.

Lord William shot up in his seat. "What do you think you are doing?" he exclaimed.

"I thought it was fairly obvious," Greydon said. "I want you to answer my question and I won't ask nicely again."

Reaching into his pocket, Lord William removed a white handkerchief and wiped his face. "This is not very becoming of you."

"I care little of what you think about me."

Lord William gave him an exasperated look. "Not that it is any of your business but Harriet asked me to kindly encourage Lady Charlotte to stay away from Phineas."

"By bribing her?"

"Why not?" Lord William asked with a shrug of his shoulders. "But the dumb chit claimed she loved him and refused to leave him be."

"Did you threaten her?"

Lord William narrowed his eyes. "I do not threaten ladies, and I resent the question. When she wouldn't take the money, I told Harriet that I did all that I could."

"How did she take the news?"

"She was angry, but what else could she do?" Lord William replied.

Greydon placed his empty glass down onto a table. "Have you been to Phineas' apartment before?"

"I would go, quite frequently, in fact. It was the one place that my brother wouldn't find me and nag me about wasting my life."

"Did Harriet ever go with you?"

Lord William looked at him as if he were mad. "Why would Harriet ever sully herself by going to that apartment?"

"I was told that she visited the apartment before."

"Whoever told you that is lying," Lord William said. "Harriet is too much of a lady to ever go anywhere near that apartment."

Greydon eyed him curiously. "Were you aware that Phineas knew about your liaison with Harriet?"

"What are you talking about? What liaison?" Lord William asked in a less than convincing voice. Did he take him for a fool?

"I am not interested in the nature of your relationship with Harriet, assuming you both use discretion," Greydon said. "I am just trying to discern the truth."

Lord William rose from the settee. "What truth?" he asked. "Truth is subjective."

"Not to me. There is only one truth, and I intend to get to the bottom of it."

Walking over to the drink cart, Lord William poured himself a generous helping of brandy. He picked up the glass and took a sip. Finally, he spoke. "If you must know, Phineas was not pleased with my relationship with his wife."

"That is hardly a surprise," Greydon mocked.

Lord William harrumphed. "I did not intend to start a relationship with Harriet," he revealed. "It just happened."

"I daresay you allowed it to happen."

"I am not blind. Harriet is a beautiful young woman and Phineas just neglected her needs. What would you have me do?"

Greydon shook his head. "It is generally frowned upon to seduce your friend's wife."

"Regardless, everything was going well until Phineas asked

Harriet for a divorce," Lord William said. "I couldn't be with a woman when her husband was petitioning for divorce. Just think of the scandal it could cause for me."

"How noble of you," Greydon remarked dryly.

"I ended things with her, right then and there, but Harriet refused to accept that. She pleaded with me to stay and she promised she would convince Phineas not to proceed with the divorce."

"Did she say how she was going to do that?"

"I didn't ask, and she didn't say, but I assumed she would just reason with him," Lord William replied.

Greydon's mind was racing. Would Harriet have been so desperate to keep Lord William as her lover that she would murder Phineas to keep him from divorcing her? It was definitely a possibility that he needed to explore.

Lord William tossed back the rest of his drink. As he placed the glass down, he asked, "Is this inquisition over?"

"You may go."

Lord William dropped into a flamboyant bow. "Thank you, my lord," he mocked.

The silence was deafening as Enid sat at the dining table with her father and mother. Her father, to his credit, had not insulted her once. But he wasn't talking to her either. She wasn't sure which side of her father she preferred.

She wanted to believe that her father was willing to change, but she had her doubts. She could see the hostility in his eyes when he looked at her, but that all melted away when he looked at Marigold. She wanted to do what was best for her child, but could she endure the tongue lashings from her father that would undoubtably come?

As a footman removed her plate, Osborne stepped into the

dining room and announced, "Pardon the interruption, but Lord Rushcliffe has asked for a moment of Lady Enid's time. He said it was of the utmost importance."

Her father flicked his wrist. "Send him away. We are eating dinner."

"Wait," Enid said as she placed her white linen napkin onto the table. "I wish to speak to him."

"We are eating dinner as a family," her father stated with annoyance in his voice.

Were they, Enid wondered. After all, her father had hardly said a word to her all evening. "We are almost done anyways," she pressed. "I will only be a moment."

Her father opened his mouth to no doubt object but his mother spoke first. "Let her go, George," she encouraged.

"She is ruining our pleasant dinner," her father muttered.

Her mother smiled. "It is Enid's loss if she does not get dessert."

"Regardless, I asked her to stay away from Lord Rushcliffe," her father said.

Enid pushed back her chair and rose. "And I believe I told you my thoughts on the matter."

Her father pursed his lips. "Yes, you did, quite passionately, if I might add," he remarked. "I would be remiss if I did not tell you that a woman should not be led by emotion alone."

"Lord Rushcliffe is my friend," Enid said.

"I daresay that he is more than that to you."

Enid went to protest but her father put his hand up, stilling her words. "Go, but inform Lord Rushcliffe that we shall turn him away the next time he arrives during our supper."

With a grateful glance at her mother, Enid walked swiftly out of the dining room and into the entry hall. She smoothed back her chignon, hoping she looked halfway presentable for Greydon.

She stepped into the drawing room and saw Greydon near

LAURA BEERS

the window, looking out. He was dressed in a rich green jacket, tan trousers and his top hat was in his hands. A maid sat in the corner, engrossed in her needlework.

"Good evening," she greeted.

Greydon turned towards her and smiled. "Thank you for agreeing to meet with me."

"It was no bother."

"I do apologize for interrupting your dinner, but I wanted to speak to you about what I discovered."

Enid took a step closer to him. "What did you learn?"

"Lady Rushcliffe had means and motive for killing Phineas," he replied. "She wanted to continue her liaison with Lord William, but he was unwilling to do so if Phineas moved forward with the divorce."

"You think Lady Rushcliffe killed her husband to stop him from doing so?"

"It is entirely probable."

Enid furrowed her brow. "That seems rather vengeful."

"I have known people that have killed for less," Greydon said. "There is a darkness to people that I do not discount, but I do not need to preach to you about what great lengths people will go to get what they want."

Enid knew Greydon spoke true. The world could be a cruel place, especially to people that did not have an income to support themselves. "I have seen some awful things, but I must have hope, for my daughter's sake."

Greydon took a step closer to her, but still maintained a proper distance. "What about for your sake?"

"Marigold is all that matters."

"So you give up on your future?"

"I do not see it that way."

Greydon's eyes held compassion. "You are a good mother- there is no denying that- but you have a right to be happy, as well."

"I am happy."

268

"Are you?" he asked. "Because your eyes tell a different story."

Enid lowered her gaze, afraid of what Greydon could see in them. "As long as Marigold is happy, then I am happy."

"Happiness should not be conditional, my dear," Greydon said. "I have learned that the hard way. For too long, I thought happiness would come with every arrest I made and every wrong I made right. But I was wrong. Happiness is a choice, and it is one that you must make every day."

"That is easier said than done."

"I know." Greydon grew silent. "I had a good friend that I failed, and he died as a result of my pigheadedness."

Bringing her gaze back up, she saw the pain that was lurking in Greydon's eyes, but she knew there must be more to the story. He was a good man, and she didn't think he was capable of failing anyone. "May I ask what happened?" she asked.

Greydon winced slightly as he shared, "Matthew and I went to a tavern in the unsavory part of Town. We thought it would be an adventure." He huffed, as if he could hardly believe his words. "But we were fools and got drunk. As we were leaving the tavern, a group of ruffians came out from an alleyway and demanded our coin purses. I refused, of course, and started fighting with the men."

He continued. "The ruffians suddenly ran off and I thought we had won. When I turned back towards Matthew, he was on the ground with a knife sticking out of his side. I rushed to him but it was too late."

Greydon's eyes grew moist. "Had I just given the men my coin purse then Matthew would still be alive."

Enid closed the distance between them and placed a hand on his arm. "You don't know that. If you hadn't fought back, you might have been killed as well."

"I wish it was me that died that night," Greydon admitted.

Hearing the sadness in Greydon's voice was her undoing

and she wrapped her arms around him. "You did nothing wrong," she rushed to assure him. "You were just at the wrong place at the wrong time."

"That is why I became a Bow Street Runner," Greydon shared as he embraced her. "I wasn't strong enough then, but I am strong enough now."

Enid looked up at him. "You are the strongest person that I know."

"I disagree," Greydon said. "Your strength surpasses my own."

"I am not strong. I have far too many scars to remind me of my past."

Greydon's eyes crinkled around the edges. "Do not be ashamed of those scars. It is proof that you are stronger than whatever tried to hurt you."

"I can say the same to you."

His eyes dimmed. "You give me far too much credit."

"I daresay that you are not giving yourself enough," Enid said. "Matthew's death was not your fault."

"I want to believe you, but I have held on to this anger for so long."

Enid nodded. "I understand that. Perhaps it is time we both let go of the anger that has come from our sordid pasts."

"I am willing to try, if you are. But it is only because of your strength that I am able to do so."

"Now it is you that is giving me too much credit."

Greydon's eyes held her transfixed as he said, "If only you knew how much these little moments with you matter to me. I am in half-agony, half-hope that you will understand how much you mean to me."

The maid cleared her throat and Greydon went to drop his arms, but Enid stopped him. She didn't want to let him go, not yet. In his arms, she felt safe, protected.

As she held Greydon's gaze, Enid addressed the maid. "You are dismissed."

"But, my lady..." the maid started to protest.

"Leave us," she ordered.

The maid rose from her chair and walked swiftly from the room.

Enid grinned. "There are some advantages to being a widow," she said.

Greydon returned her smile. "You do realize that your mother and possibly your father will be arriving soon."

"Time is short, then. We must take advantage of our time together."

His eyes dropped to her lips, but instead of kissing her like she had hoped, he released her and took a step back. "I should be going."

Enid tried to hide her disappointment by saying, "So soon?" She wasn't ready for him to leave. Not yet. His presence always seemed to lift her spirits and it was as if her soul craved to be near him.

"Yes, it would be for the best if I departed at once," Greydon said, his words sounding entirely unconvincing.

"Greydon..." she started but was interrupted by her father storming into the room. His eyes latched on to Greydon and they narrowed slightly.

"What is the meaning of dismissing the maid?" he demanded.

Enid tilted her chin. "I sent her away."

Her father shifted his gaze towards her. "Do you intend to throw propriety out the window as well?"

Greydon spoke up. "If anyone is to blame, it is I."

"I somehow doubt that," her father muttered. "I think it would be best if you said your goodbyes to my daughter and retire for the evening."

"As you wish." Greydon turned towards her and bowed. "Goodnight, my lady."

She dropped into a curtsy. "Goodnight, Lord Rushcliffe," she responded. "Allow me to walk you to the door."

Her father shook his head. "I will do so."

Enid didn't wish to fight with her father, at least not in front of Greydon, so she conceded. "Very well."

She watched their retreating figures and then heard the main door open and close. No surprise to her, her father stormed back into the room with pursed lips. "You cannot be alone with a gentleman. Do you not care a whit for your reputation or Lord Rushcliffe's?"

"I care greatly for Lord Rushcliffe's reputation."

"Then prove it," her father responded harshly.

Her mother appeared in the doorway with a frown on her face. "George, we talked about this," she said firmly.

Some of the anger dissipated from her father's expression, but not much. "I just wanted Enid to know——"

Her mother cut him off. "You made your point, did you not?"

"I did," her father reluctantly agreed.

"Now say something nice to Enid."

Her father looked displeased by his wife's request. In a forced voice, he said, "You look well, Enid."

Her mother nodded in approval. "That wasn't so hard. Was it?" She shifted her gaze to Enid. "What do you say to your father?"

Enid resisted the urge to roll her eyes but rather she said, "Thank you, Father."

Her mother smiled victoriously as she glanced between them. "That is how you two can communicate without fighting. Isn't it wonderful?"

"I suppose so," her father replied. "Shall we adjourn to dinner and finish our dessert?"

Her mother accepted her father's arm and asked, "Will you be joining us, Enid?"

"I think I will go spend some time with Marigold before she retires for bed."

"You'd best hurry, then," her mother encouraged.

Enid followed them out into the entry hall before she headed up the stairs. She always treasured every moment she had with Marigold. Her daughter was the reason why she had never given up, even when the odds were stacked against her, but she was beginning to realize that Greydon was right. It was time to let go of the anger of her past and embrace the future. Her future. A future that included Greydon.

Chapter Nineteen

Greydon walked along the uneven pavement as the morning sun was low in the sky. His plain brown, ill-fitting jacket and matching trousers were scratchy against his skin, but he had more important matters that he had to deal with.

He had received word from one of his informants that he had some information that he would find interesting. But he would only meet him at The Shifty Bandit tavern in an unsavory part of Town at dawn.

As he stopped in front of The Shifty Bandit tavern, the door was thrown open and a man was thrown out, landing in a heap in front of him.

"Don't you come back, you hear?" the man shouted before slamming the door closed.

Greydon went to assist the man in rising but he yanked back his arm. "Leave me be, Bloke," he ordered, his voice slurring.

Rather than fight with the man, he sidestepped him and headed into the tavern. He opened the door and was greeted by a short man with a round belly.

"How can I help ye?" he asked.

"I am meeting someone here," Greydon said, his eyes

roaming over the few patrons in the hall. His eyes landed on a shadowed figure in the corner and he knew he had found his man.

The barkeep put his hand up. "If ye want to stay in here, ye got to order something to drink. We ain't a tea shop."

"Bring me a pint of ale." Greydon brushed past the man and headed towards the corner.

His informant didn't stand but instead remained in the shadows, sipping his drink.

Greydon pulled out a chair and tipped his head. "Wilson," he greeted. "What do you have for me?"

Wilson smiled, revealing missing teeth. "What? No pleasantries?"

"Why did you bring me out here?" Greydon asked.

"I didn't dare go to your townhouse," Wilson replied. "It is far too posh for the likes of me."

The barkeep placed a drink in front of him. "Will there be anything else?"

"Fetch me another drink since my friend is buying," Wilson said.

Greydon reached into his jacket pocket and removed a few coins. He placed them on the table and the barkeep snatched them up.

"I will return shortly," the barkeep said.

Once the man had stepped away, Greydon pushed his drink towards Wilson. "You can have mine as well."

Wilson chuckled. "Is this watered-down ale not to your satisfaction, my lord?"

"We both know it is not."

Reaching for his drink, Wilson brought it up to his lips. "I didn't bring you here to chat, though. I have the information you requested."

Now Wilson had his attention. "What did you discover?" Greydon asked.

"On the morning your brother was murdered, his wife went to visit him at the apartment," Wilson shared.

"How can you be certain?"

"A shopkeeper informed me that a beautiful woman with black hair arrived in a crested carriage, bearing your coat of arms, and she parked in front of his store until half past the hour," Wilson revealed.

Greydon leaned closer. "Did he say anything else?"

"The only thing else that he noticed was that the lady seemed agitated when she left the building," Wilson responded.

"Did the shopkeeper happen to notice anyone else approach or depart from the building?" Greydon asked.

"No, but it wasn't long after that he heard screaming from your brother's apartment," Wilson said. "And he was one of the first people up to see Lady Eugenie standing in front of the late Lord Rushcliffe's body."

"Why didn't he tell the coroner this?"

Wilson shrugged. "No one asked him, especially since Lady Eugenie had blood on her hands. It seemed to be a rather open and shut case to me." He paused. "Is it?"

"It is rather complicated, I'm afraid."

Wilson let out a burp and brought a hand up to his mouth. "It sounds like it, but it is not my problem."

Greydon removed a few gold coins from his pocket and slid them across the table to Wilson. "I will need the shop-keeper's name."

"I assumed as much," Wilson said as he retrieved the coins. "It is a Mr. Jacob Rose and he has a flower shop next to the building that housed your brother's apartment."

"You did good, Wilson."

Reaching for the pint, Wilson said, "I thought you would be pleased with what I uncovered."

Greydon shoved back his chair and rose. "I will be in touch."

"Will you?" Wilson asked. "I have heard rumors that you no longer work as a Bow Street Runner."

"I have one more case I must solve before I hang up my uniform."

Wilson held the drink up. "I wish you luck, then."

Greydon departed from the tavern, and his mind was racing. Harriet had lied to him about never being at his brother's apartment and she was there on the morning of the murder. Would this be enough evidence to halt the criminal proceedings against Lady Eugenie and have Sir David open up the investigation again?

There was only one way to find out. He needed to speak to Sir David about this right away. He hailed a hackney and ordered the driver to take him to Sir David's home.

He didn't have tangible proof that Lady Eugenie was innocent but he had reasonable doubt that she could be the killer. Now he just had to convince Sir David of that.

The hackney came to a stop in front of a brownstone building and he stepped onto the pavement. He approached the main door and knocked.

And waited.

He knocked again.

Finally, the door was opened, and a lanky butler stared back at him. "May I help you, sir?"

"I need to speak to Sir David at once," Greydon informed him.

The butler looked displeased by his request. "I'm afraid that Sir David is unavailable to take callers at this time."

Greydon removed a calling card from his jacket pocket and extended it towards the butler. "Will you see if he will make an exception?"

The butler glanced down at the card before saying, "Yes, my lord." He opened the door wide. "Would you care to wait in the entry hall?"

"Thank you," Greydon said as he stepped inside.

After closing the door, the butler crossed the entry hall and disappeared down a corridor. It was sometime later that the clipping of the butler's shoes could be heard on the marble floor.

The butler met his gaze and said, "Sir David will see you."

Greydon followed the butler down the corridor and walked into a room in the rear of the townhouse. Sir David was sitting behind his desk and he had an annoyed look on his face.

"What in the blazes are you about, Rushcliffe?" Sir David asked. "Do you know what hour it is?"

"I do, but I needed to speak to you. I assure you that the matter is most urgent."

Sir David pressed his lips together as he leaned back in his seat. "Very well," he replied. "What is it?"

"I have taken it upon myself to investigate my brother's murder—"

Sir David cut him off. "You have wasted your time, then," he said. "Lady Eugenie confessed to the murder last night."

Greydon's brow shot up. "That is impossible."

"I don't know why you are acting so surprised, considering she was caught red-handed," Sir David stated. "Her guilty plea was the only obvious choice for her."

"But, sir, she is not guilty of this crime," Greydon asserted.

"Then why would she confess?"

"I cannot speak for her, but I have found some rather interesting information pertaining to the case."

Sir David gave him a bored look. "Pray tell, what did you discover?" he asked dryly.

"My brother's wife, Lady Rushcliffe, visited his apartment on the morning of the murder," Greydon replied. "She left shortly before Lady Eugenie started screaming for help."

"Are you implying that Lady Rushcliffe had something to do with her husband's murder?" Sir David asked.

"I am merely saying that it is worth looking into. Phineas

was in the process of trying to divorce her, giving her a motive."

Sir David moved to sit on the edge of his seat. "You are out of line, and I should have you arrested for interfering in a criminal case. You are no longer a Bow Street Runner and have no authority here."

"I am trying to ensure my brother's murderer is brought to justice."

"And she is," Sir David declared. "I understand your infatuation with this case, but it ends here."

"Sir, if I may——"

Sir David put his hand up. "You may not," he said. "It is only because of professional courtesy that I am just going to pretend this conversation never happened."

Greydon ran a hand through his hair as he tried to quell his growing irritation at being dismissed so readily. "I know how it seems, but if you would just give me a chance to prove it," he said through gritted teeth.

"Rushcliffe," Sir David sighed, "you are wrong about this one, and it pains me to tell you this. Just go home and grieve your brother properly."

"I am not wrong."

"Regardless of what you believe to be true, Lady Eugenie will be hung for the murder of your brother."

"The wrong person is condemned."

Sir David abruptly rose and shouted, "Do not tell me how to do my job! Do you know the pressure on me to deliver your brother's murderer?"

"I don't doubt that you are under pressure, but——"

"Good day," Sir David said, dismissing him.

Greydon knew there was no point in staying here and arguing with Sir David. The coroner would not yield, and he was wasting his time. If he wanted to prove that Lady Eugenie was innocent, he would have to do it himself.

He spun on his heel and departed from the room. After he

stepped outside, Greydon knew it was time to speak to Harriet again and present her with the information that he had. With any luck, she would confess. But it rarely was that easy.

Greydon found himself walking towards Mayfair to see Enid. He was never one to work with another, but he found he valued her opinion. She might have some insight on why Lady Eugenie confessed to a murder that she did not commit.

Enid held Marigold in her arms as she strolled around the gardens. It was a beautiful day and not a cloud was in sight. The sound of Marigold babbling in her arms filled her with contentment. She didn't think she would ever tire of that noise.

A red-tailed bird landed on a bush in front of them, drawing Marigold's attention. Enid inched forward towards the bird as she tried to avoid startling it. When she was a short distance away, she stopped and Marigold squealed in amusement, causing the bird to take flight.

The nursemaid stepped forward and pointed towards one of the paths. "You have a visitor, my lady," she informed her.

Enid turned her head and saw that Greydon was approaching them with a smile on his face. Dear heavens, he was handsome!

Greydon stopped in front of them and bowed. "Good morning, Enid."

She returned his smile. "Good morning, Greydon."

His eyes shifted towards Marigold. "Hello, dear," he greeted with kindness in his voice.

In response, Marigold snuggled up against her mother, resting her head on Enid's shoulder.

"It would appear that Marigold has turned rather shy," Enid shared.

"No bother," Greydon said. "I shall win her over, just as I did with you."

Enid gave him an amused look. "You did not win me over."

"Haven't I?'

The way Greydon was looking at her caused her cheeks to grow warm. She didn't want him to know how deeply he affected her so she turned her attention towards Marigold. "We are on a walk around the gardens."

Drats. Why had she said something so stupid? Of course they were on a walk through the gardens. What else would they be doing there?

Greydon nodded. "It is a fine day to take a stroll."

"That it is," she readily agreed.

Marigold brought her head back up and smiled at Greydon. Then, to Enid's surprise, she put her arms out towards him.

In response, Greydon asked, "May I hold Marigold?"

"You may," Enid said, secretly pleased by his request. She stepped closer to Greydon and extended Marigold to him.

Greydon held Marigold awkwardly in his arms, not in a way that was unsafe, but it didn't appear as if he were comfortable with holding a child.

Enid laughed at his discomfort. "Have you ever held a child before?"

With a sheepish smile, Greydon asked, "Is it so obvious?"

"You just need to relax."

"But what if I drop Marigold?" he asked, the worry etched on his features.

"You won't, I promise."

Greydon shifted Marigold in his arms and he visibly relaxed. Marigold tried to place a hand in his mouth, but he reached up and caught her hand. "Let's keep our hands to ourselves," he chided lightly.

Enid felt her heart take flight at the sight of Greydon

holding Marigold so tenderly. She didn't think it was possible, but she found that she loved him even more.

"My mother would have loved Marigold," Greydon said. "She loved babies and would have loved nothing more than having a myriad of them."

"A myriad seems like a lot of children," Enid joked. "I can't imagine loving another child as much as I love Marigold."

Greydon ran his finger over Marigold's cheek. "My mother never treated me like the spare. She just loved me, unconditionally."

"It sounds like you had a good mother."

"That I did," Greydon responded. "She was the best of women. When she died, I thought that I would never recover from the loss. But time has helped ease my grief."

Enid nodded. "Time has a way of showing us what really matters."

"That it does," Greydon responded. "I was fortunate to have my mother in my life as long as I did."

"I feel the same way about my mother."

Marigold started babbling in Greydon's arms and he chuckled. "It would appear that Marigold has something that she wants to say."

"She always has something she wants to say," Enid said. "She is quite vocal, but I wouldn't change it for the world."

The nursemaid stepped forward and announced, "It is time for Miss Marigold's breakfast."

Greydon handed Marigold off to Marie's waiting arms.

As the nursemaid walked off towards the townhouse, Greydon said, "You have a beautiful daughter."

"I think so, but I am biased."

"It is all right to be biased when it is your own."

Enid put her hand out towards the path and asked, "Shall we take a stroll in the gardens?"

"I would like nothing more," Greydon replied as he offered his arm.

She placed her hand on his arm and allowed him to start leading her down the path. A silence came over them, but it was a comfortable silence, one that only forms when two people are content with one another.

Greydon glanced over at her. "How are you faring today?"

"I am well," she replied. "I am not sure if I told you but my father is trying to make an effort to be civil with me."

"That is a good thing. Is it not?"

"It is, but it is proving to be rather difficult for my father," Enid replied. "We have been at odds for so long."

"It doesn't mean he isn't capable of change."

Enid bobbed her head. "If you'd said that a few days ago, I would have disagreed with you, but now..." Her voice trailed off. "He is afraid of me leaving and taking Marigold with me."

"Where would you go?" Greydon asked.

With a slight shrug of her shoulders, Enid replied, "I have enough funds to buy a cottage and live my days in the countryside."

Greydon came to a stop on the path and turned towards her, his boots grinding on the gravel. "Is that what you want?"

Enid blew out a puff of air. "Quite frankly, I don't know what I want, but I just want Marigold to be surrounded by people that love her."

"Isn't that what you have now?"

"It is, but I grow tired of my father criticizing every choice I make."

Greydon gave her a knowing look. "There is another solution; an obvious one, if you ask me," he said. "You could always marry me."

"But what of your reputation?" Enid asked.

"What of it?"

Enid bit her lower lip. "It would suffer if you married me."

"Have I not proven to you that I care more about you than my silly reputation?"

"It isn't silly—"

He spoke over her. "It is to me," he said. "I love you more with every breath that I take."

"The truth is that you are the reason I believe in love, but I am terrified to try again," Enid admitted.

Greydon's face softened. "I will wait for you, then. This is not a passing whim for me. I want you as my wife and I will take you as you are. For when I look at you, I see a lot of things: my best friend, my soulmate, my confidant."

How could Enid explain what she was feeling? She wanted to throw herself into his arms, to love him, wholly and unconditionally, but the fear crept in. It always did. It was always the fear that paralyzed her. She knew what she wanted to do, but she was unable to do so, despite everything she had ever wanted was right in front of her.

"You aren't ready, and that is all right," Greydon said. "I just want to be able to tell you that I love you, and often."

Enid's voice was soft as she admitted, "I have no objections."

"Then we are in agreement."

"I suppose we are."

Greydon offered her a boyish smile. "I like it when we agree on something."

"I wouldn't get used to it," she responded cheekily.

The amusement on his face faded as he said, "I wish we could continue as we are but I'm afraid I am the bearer of bad news."

"Which is?"

Greydon hesitated. "Sir David informed me that Lady Eugenie confessed to the murder of my brother."

Enid gasped. "Why would she do such a thing?"

"I don't know, but I was hoping you would tell me," Greydon replied.

"She must be trying to protect her sister in her own way. We must go speak to her at once!" Enid exclaimed as she started to walk towards the townhouse.

Greydon easily caught up to her and placed a hand on her sleeve, turning her to face him. "There is no point. By now, she is in the wing where they keep the condemned."

"We can't let her do this," Enid declared.

"I know, but the only way we can help her is to have the real murderer confess, and quickly," Greydon said.

"Do you know who killed your brother?" she asked him with wide eyes.

"I suspect it was my sister-in-law, Harriet," Greydon replied, "but now I have to prove it. The difficult part is that Sir David has threatened me with arrest if I continue to investigate the case."

"Doesn't he care that Lady Eugenie is innocent?"

"He doesn't care who is convicted as long as someone is held accountable for the crime."

"That is awful, and not at all right."

Greydon dropped his arm to his side. "I never said it was right, but coroners tend to only care about their own political careers. Truth is just inconvenient to them."

With a shake of her head, Enid said, "I refuse to accept that. I won't let Lady Eugenie die without a fight."

"I agree, wholeheartedly." Greydon glanced up at the sky. "I have things I need to see to first, but I'm hoping to formulate a plan that will catch a killer."

"You will."

Greydon brought his gaze down to meet hers. "You seem to have a lot of faith in me. I hope it is not misplaced."

"I know it isn't." Feeling bold, Enid went on her tiptoes and pressed her lips against his. "If anyone can figure this out, you can."

He stared at her, open wonder and amazement on his face, as if he couldn't quite believe her bold behavior. But she didn't care. She did not regret the kiss, not one bit. She had wanted to kiss him for far too long. If anything, it was past due.

Greydon cleared his throat as he offered his arm. "May I escort you back inside?" he asked in a hoarse voice.

As Enid placed her hand on his sleeve, she knew that Greydon would find a way to fix this. He always found a way. That was just one of the many reasons why she loved him.

Chapter Twenty

Greydon exited the hackney and stepped onto the pavement in front of White's. He adjusted the top hat on his head and approached the main door, which was promptly opened by a liveried servant.

As he headed inside, his eyes roamed over the room until he saw Mr. Moore sitting in the corner. His shoulders were slumped and his eyes were fixated on the drink in his hand. This did not bode well for him if Mr. Moore was in an inebriated state.

He approached the table and asked, "May I sit down?"

"Do what you want," came Mr. Moore's gruff response. He didn't even bother to look up.

Greydon pulled out a chair and sat down. "Are you drunk?"

"No, but I wish I was." Mr. Moore tightened his hold on the glass. "It might help this gnawing guilt that I am feeling."

"Why are you feeling guilty?"

Mr. Moore brought his gaze up. "It is my fault that Lady Eugenie confessed to the murder. I pressured her to have her sister testify, hoping to create doubt in the jury's mind, but I underestimated her determination to protect her sister."

"That was a mistake."

"Having her sister testify was the only way for the jury to sympathize with her," Mr. Moore said. "I was trying to save her life, and in doing so, I had her condemned."

"You were trying to help her."

Mr. Moore huffed. "Yes, but look where she is now," he demanded. "She is in the condemned area of Newgate."

"I think I might have a solution."

Bringing the glass up to his lips, Mr. Moore said, "I don't think that is possible. Besides, I heard that Sir David forbade you to continue looking into this case."

"He did, but I am not one to follow his orders."

"He could have you arrested."

It was Greydon's turn to let out a huff. "Do you think he would really arrest me?" he asked. "Just think of the scandal that it would create for him."

Mr. Moore lowered his glass back to the table. "It doesn't matter now. We have lost and Lady Eugenie will be killed soon enough."

"You just intend to give up?"

"She made her choice and we must accept that," Mr. Moore replied.

Greydon leaned forward and lowered his voice. "I suspect that Harriet killed her husband and we can't let her get away with it."

Mr. Moore looked uninterested. "Do you have any proof?"

"Harriet was at my brother's apartment the morning of the murder and she departed shortly before Lady Eugenie discovered the body."

"That doesn't mean she killed him."

"She also had motive," Greydon pressed. "She didn't want him to proceed with the divorce so she could keep Lord William as her lover. He threatened to leave her if Phineas pressed the issue."

Mr. Moore pushed his drink away. "That does create doubt, but that doesn't prove she murdered her husband."

"That is why I need her to confess."

"It has been my experience that people don't usually confess to murders that they commit," Mr. Moore said. "The consequences are dire."

Before he could reply, Lord Roswell Westlake and Mr. Westcott came to a stop next to him and pulled out chairs.

"Are we too late?" Lord Roswell asked as he sat down.

"You are right on time," Greydon replied. "Thank you for coming."

Mr. Moore gave him a baffled look. "What are these men doing here?" he asked.

"I needed men that I could trust; ones that Sir David couldn't dismiss as unimportant or untrustworthy," Greydon replied.

Lord Roswell smirked. "I am rather important."

"Only in your mind," Mr. Westcott muttered.

A server came and placed drinks down in the center of the table before he departed.

As Mr. Westcott reached for a glass, he asked, "What exactly are we doing here? Your note was rather vague."

Greydon grew somber. "We are going to catch a killer."

"Please say that your plan is better than just knocking on the door and hoping the murderer will allow us entry," Mr. Westcott mocked.

"That plan worked once before, did it not?" Greydon asked.

"You were lucky," Mr. Westcott said.

Greydon gave him a pointed look. "I don't rely on luck. I understood the odds and I acted accordingly."

Lord Roswell glanced at one of the drinks but didn't make a move to take one. "Perhaps you should start from the beginning."

Greydon knew his plan revolved around these gentlemen's

involvement so he needed to convince them to go along with what he was proposing. "Lady Eugenie just confessed to killing my brother, but we do not believe she was the murderer."

"Then why did she confess?" Mr. Westcott asked. "Innocent people tend not to admit to something they didn't do."

Mr. Moore spoke up. "I played a hand in that. She is very protective of her younger sister and I tried to get her sister to testify in her trial. I wanted to cast doubt in the jury's mind of her guilt."

"By implying Lady Charlotte had something to do with the murder?" Lord Roswell asked.

"That was the idea, but Lady Eugenie refused," Mr. Moore replied. "The next thing I am told is that she confessed, leaving no need for a trial."

Lord Roswell furrowed his brow. "Is it possible that Lady Charlotte did play a hand in Phineas' murder?"

"My brother promised to marry her once his divorce was granted," Greydon explained.

"Yes, but it is nearly impossible for members of Parliament to grant a divorce," Lord Roswell said. "It almost seems like an empty promise."

"True, but Harriet was seen leaving my brother's apartment not long before Lady Eugenie discovered the body," Greydon shared. "And it goes without saying that she did not want Phineas to go forth with the divorce proceedings. It would ruin her."

"Do you think Lady Rushcliffe is capable of murder?" Mr. Westcott asked.

"Everyone is capable of murder, given the right circumstance," Greydon replied. "Harriet did not want to give up the life that she had grown accustomed to and decided to take matters into her own hands."

Lord Roswell frowned. "Do you have any tangible proof, other than she was seen leaving his apartment?"

"No, but people have killed for a lot less," Greydon said.

"I do not dispute that, but Lady Rushcliffe could have a reasonable explanation for visiting her husband's apartment," Lord Roswell said.

"Yet Harriet was rather adamant that she had never visited that apartment."

"That is odd."

"Furthermore, her explanations always seemed too convenient," Greydon expressed. "She claims that she had convinced Phineas to stop the divorce proceedings, despite him knowing she was having an affair."

"It sounds as if she were the one that benefited the most from his death." Mr. Westcott hesitated before saying, "Other than you, of course. Upon his death, you became your father's heir."

Greydon put his hand up. "This is not the life that I envisioned for myself. I would much rather have my brother alive."

Mr. Westcott nodded. "I believe you."

"Good," Greydon said. "That will save us a considerable amount of time."

"But why do you need us?" Mr. Westcott asked.

"I need you to witness Harriet's confession so we can exonerate Lady Eugenie," Greydon explained.

Mr. Westcott's brow shot up. "And you expect Lady Rushcliffe to just confess to the murder with us there?"

"I am still working through the particulars," Greydon admitted. "But I will have a plan in place soon enough."

Mr. Moore interjected, "I hate to be a naysayer, but what if Lady Rushcliffe doesn't confess?"

"Then we are out of options and Lady Eugenie will die for a murder she didn't commit," Greydon responded.

"How do you know she didn't commit the murder and she is just playing you for a fool?" Lord Roswell asked.

Greydon shifted his gaze towards Lord Roswell. "I was once where you are now, doubting Lady Eugenie's intentions, but I could see the truth in her eyes. Her whole intention was to protect her sister, who she suspects murdered my brother."

"Why would she suspect that?" Lord Roswell questioned.

"Lady Eugenie went to Phineas' apartment to retrieve her sister and try to convince my brother to stop his dalliance with her," Greydon shared. "But, when she arrived, he had a knife sticking out of his chest."

Mr. Westcott looked unsure. "Have you told the coroner of your suspicions?"

"I did, but he has dismissed them," Greydon stated. "His main concern is closing this case with as little fanfare as possible."

"That doesn't surprise me, especially since Sir David has political aspirations," Lord Roswell acknowledged.

"Precisely," Greydon said. "Besides, he has ordered me off this case."

"Why am I not surprised that you didn't listen to him?" Lord Roswell joked.

"All I care about is that justice is done for my brother," Greydon said.

Mr. Moore gave him a smug look. "Are you sure this isn't about you trying to win Lady Enid's favor?"

"It may have started about that, but it has evolved over time," Greydon replied. "I love Lady Enid, but I am not doing this for her. I am doing this because it is the right thing to do."

Lord Roswell bobbed his head. "I am not surprised in the least," he remarked. "It was evident that you held her in high regard when we saved her from her mad husband."

"Was I that obvious?" Greydon asked.

"Just to me," Lord Roswell replied.

Mr. Westcott gave him an amused look. "You will have to ignore my friend since he is a hopeless romantic."

"I am not," Lord Roswell responded. "I just want to believe that love trumps all."

Mr. Moore scoffed. "Love is a shackle, and I will not fall prey to the parson's mousetrap," he declared.

"You will feel differently when you meet the right woman," Lord Roswell pressed.

"The right woman?" Mr. Moore asked. "Is there even such a thing?"

Lord Roswell grew quiet. "There is," he said, his voice full of anguish. "If you are lucky enough to find your match, you must never let her go."

"I don't have time to look for a wife," Mr. Moore shared. "My time is better spent working as a barrister."

"I don't usually agree with my friend, but he is right," Mr. Westcott said.

Lord Roswell bobbed his head. "It is true," he responded. "Tristan never sides with me. It is rather annoying."

"That is because you are hardly ever right," Mr. Westcott bantered back.

Mr. Moore took a sip of his drink before asking, "Can we focus on what is most important right now?"

Greydon interjected, "While you were all discussing love and whatnot, I came up with a plan."

"Is it a good one?" Lord Roswell asked.

With a slight shrug of his shoulders, Greydon replied, "It won't get anyone killed."

"Now where is the fun in that?" Lord Roswell joked.

Greydon leaned forward in his seat and lowered his voice. "All right. Listen carefully. We have one shot at this."

***

Enid came to an abrupt stop in the doorway when she saw her father was sitting at the head of the table with the morning newssheets in his hands. Where was her mother, she wondered. She glanced over her shoulder, hoping she would materialize out of thin air. But she was not so lucky. The hall remained empty and her mother was nowhere to be seen.

Did she dare eat breakfast with her father or should she just request a tray be sent to her bedchamber? She knew they both were making an effort to be civil to one another, but most of their encounters were awkward at best. Her father would offer up the vaguest of compliments in an attempt to appease his wife, but Enid knew they weren't sincere.

While she debated upon what she intended to do, her father's voice broke through the silence. "You may as well come in," he said, peeking over the top of the newssheets at her. "Your mother has a headache this morning and will not be joining us."

"Oh," Enid murmured, not knowing what else to say. To leave now would make her look petty. She had no choice but to have breakfast with her father.

Enid walked over to the chair and waited as the footman pulled it out. Once she was seated, a plate of food promptly appeared in front of her.

All she had to do was eat and she could leave. She didn't even need to engage her father in conversation. There was no shame in just eating in silence. She hoped that her father felt the same.

But she was wrong.

Her father folded the newssheets back and said, "Lady Eugenie confessed to murdering the late Lord Rushcliffe."

"I am aware." What else could she possibly say on that matter?

"Her sentencing is imminent, but she most likely will hang for her crime." He placed the newssheets down onto the table. "You are lucky you did not have the same fate as her."

"Why would I?"

Her father looked at her like she was a simpleton. "You killed your husband."

"That is not entirely true," Enid responded. "I was one of

the people that took a shot at him, but I do not know who actually killed him. You must understand that John was trying to kill me, and we had no choice but to shoot him first."

"Who else took a shot?"

Enid pressed her lips together. "It is of little consequence."

Not satisfied with her response, he asked, "How exactly was it that you avoided a trial again?"

"Lord Rushcliffe saw to that," Enid replied vaguely.

Her father watched her for a moment before saying, "It just makes me wonder how he was able to circumvent a trial for you."

"Does it truly matter?"

"I suppose not, but I am relieved to hear that you weren't alone that night you confronted John."

Enid reached for her cup of tea and took a sip. She had no intention of confiding in her father about how Greydon worked as a Bow Street Runner or who else was involved that fateful night. Some things were best left in the past.

Her father frowned. "Do you intend to marry Lord Rushcliffe?"

The question caught her by surprise. It shouldn't have, but it did. Her father had always spoken his mind so why did she think this would be any different? "I don't know," she replied honestly. "He has asked, multiple times, in fact, but I have turned him down each time."

"Why is that? If he is foolish enough to want you as a wife, why wouldn't you accept his offer of marriage?"

"Because I'm unsure if I ever wish to marry again."

"But you are a woman."

It was Enid's turn to frown. "Thank you for noticing," she mocked.

"What I mean is that your options are limited," her father said. "Why would you turn down the opportunity to be a countess one day?"

"I care little about titles."

"Then what do you care about?"

Enid didn't want to have this conversation with her father. He wouldn't understand her reasonings, and if he did, she had no doubt that he would mock them.

Picking up her fork, she said, "Perhaps we should just focus on breakfast and avoid idle chitchat."

Her father eyed her curiously. "You love him."

"Was that a question?"

"No, it was an observation," he replied. "If you love Lord Rushcliffe, why won't you marry him?"

Enid shifted in her seat to face her father. "Because, Father," she started dryly, "as you have so kindly pointed out, I am a ruined woman. Why would I want to bring that shame to Lord Rushcliffe and his family?"

"You are ruined," he hesitated, "but I think you should marry him."

Fearing she'd misheard him, she asked, "Pardon?"

"Lord Rushcliffe is a smart man and I have no doubt that he knows what he is getting himself into by taking you as a wife."

"I won't do that to him."

"You would give up on a chance for a love match?"

Enid grew quiet. "I thought I had a love match before, and I was wrong. I can't make the same mistake again. I won't do it. Lord Rushcliffe is better off without me."

"I have a feeling that Lord Rushcliffe doesn't agree with you."

She shook her head. "No, he says he doesn't care about his reputation."

"I believe him. Do you?"

"I don't know."

"A man's reputation is not as fragile as a woman's, and it can be restored over time."

Enid pushed the food on her plate around with her fork.

"What if Lord Rushcliffe grows tired of having me as a wife? Will he grow to resent me?"

Her father sighed. "I know you have endured more obstacles than most, but that doesn't mean you give up on love."

"I have Marigold to think about now. I can't just do whatever I want, no matter what my heart dictates."

"Yes, but Marigold needs a father."

Enid placed her fork down as the image of Greydon holding Marigold in the gardens came to her mind. He seemed so unsure, but he was still protective of her child at the same time. He would make a brilliant father, but was he prepared for the responsibility of raising another man's child?

"You are smiling," her father pointed out.

"Am I?" Enid asked as she schooled her features.

Her father gave her a knowing look. "I daresay you agree with me."

"That is impossible," Enid joked. "We haven't agreed with one another in years."

To her surprise, her father chuckled. "That we haven't, but I am hoping that will change in the future."

Enid felt herself relax around her father. Perhaps they were on a path of reconciliation? Or was she being entirely too optimistic and misjudged the situation completely? She never knew with her father.

"In a world full of uncertainties, shouldn't you try to live life to the fullest?" her father asked.

"It isn't that simple."

"No, it isn't," her father said, "but Leonardo Da Vinci once said- 'Life without love, is no life at all.'"

"Should I just ignore everything that Lord Rushcliffe has to give up to be with me?"

Her father's face softened. "I suspect that he doesn't think it is much of a sacrifice," he replied. "My question to you is- what are you willing to give up to have a chance at happiness?"

"I am happy," she rushed to reply. "Marigold makes me happy."

"I don't dispute that, but you deserve to carve out your own future."

Enid lowered her gaze to her plate as she tried to come up with another argument about why she couldn't be with Greydon, but her mind was blank. She wanted to be with him. She wanted to love him. But it was her own fears that were stopping her.

Her father leaned forward and said, "I know you are scared, but what is your heart telling you to do?"

She brought her gaze back up to meet his. "My heart beats only for him."

"Then you must do something about that."

"And if I am wrong?"

His eyes held mirth as he replied, "You already got rid of one husband, why not another?"

Her mouth dropped before a slight giggle emerged. "That is awful of you to say."

"But it made you laugh."

"That it did," Enid agreed.

Her brother's voice came from the doorway. "Did I hear laughter in here?" Malcolm asked. The confusion was written on his face.

Her father leaned back in his seat and the usual gruff look came to his face. "You must have been hearing things."

Walking further into the room, Malcolm said, "Mother sent me down to ensure you two were both on your best behavior."

"That wasn't necessary," her father remarked. "You are wasting your time."

Malcolm sat down next to Enid. "Dare I ask what you both were discussing?"

"The weather," came her father's quick reply.

"The weather?" Malcolm repeated.

Enid smiled. "Yes, we were discussing the weather," she answered, exchanging an amused look with her father.

Malcolm glanced between them with disbelief on his features. "Surely you do not think I am so gullible as to believe that?"

"I do," her father said as he brought the newssheets back up.

"Thank you, Father," Malcolm responded.

A footman placed a plate of food in front of Malcolm as he draped the white linen napkin onto his lap. "What will occupy your time today?" he asked as he directed his attention towards his sister.

"I intend to take Marigold on a stroll through the gardens after I finish breakfast," Enid replied.

"May Rosamond and I join you?"

Enid nodded. "I would enjoy that."

"Good," Malcolm said with a decisive bob of his head. "Let's eat before our food gets cold unless you would like to continue your conversation on the weather."

Her father lowered the newssheets in his hand. "I do believe I made my point on the weather."

"That point being?" Malcolm prodded.

"The weather can be unpredictable, so do not plan for gloom; focus on the good days ahead," her father replied.

Enid knew what her father was trying to tell her and she appreciated him more because of it. He wanted to keep their conversation private. His words rang true. She shouldn't plan for bad things to happen because they would assuredly come. She should focus on what made her happy, and that was Greydon.

He filled the holes in her heart, making it whole once more.

Rising, Enid said, "I should go collect my hat." She stepped closer to her father and kissed him on the cheek. "Thank you, Father."

He smiled, a warm smile that she hadn't seen in quite some time. "You are welcome, Child."

Enid took a step back, ignoring Malcolm's bemused look. "I will strive to heed your advice," she said before she departed from the room.

Her father had surprised her by his show of compassion, and she hoped this meant that they could start over, putting their past behind them.

Chapter Twenty-One

The trap had been set and now Greydon had to ensure his plan went off without a hitch. If not, Lady Eugenie was as good as dead. He needed to get a confession, one way or another.

A knock came at the door.

It was time to catch a killer.

Greydon crossed Phineas' apartment and opened the door, revealing Harriet. He put his hand out and encouraged, "Please come in."

With a rigid back, she stepped into the apartment and said, "I do not know why you insisted on us meeting at Phineas' apartment or that I come alone."

"It will all make sense soon enough." He closed the door and asked, "If memory serves me correctly, you have never been here before?"

"That is correct," Harriet snapped. "Why would I lower myself to visiting my husband's apartment? This is where he brought his whores."

"If you would like to become familiar with the apartment—"

She gave him a defiant look. "Why would I wish to do

that?" she asked, speaking over him. "This place means nothing to me."

"It was where your husband died, after all."

"He shouldn't have been here in the first place."

Greydon put his hand up. "I will not dispute that, but you must have some questions about how Phineas died."

"Sir David told me everything that I needed to know." Harriet's eyes roamed over the apartment, her eyes guarded. "Nothing in this place is worth saving. The furniture is rather tacky, if you ask me."

"I do not think my brother came here for the furniture."

"No, he most assuredly did not," Harriet muttered.

A knock came at the door.

"Right on time," Greydon said as he went to open the door.

On the other side of the threshold was Lady Charlotte. She was dressed in a pale yellow gown and a straw hat sat slightly askew on her head.

He opened the door wide. "Do come in," he said. "We have been waiting for you."

"We?" Lady Charlotte asked with a baffled look.

Harriet's shrill voice met his ears. "What is *she* doing here?" she demanded.

As he closed the door, he replied, "I see you are acquainted with Lady Charlotte already. That should save us a considerable amount of time."

Lady Charlotte stood back as if she were trying to disappear into the papered walls. "You said the matter was urgent."

"It is," Greydon said. "I needed to speak to both of you. I assure you that it is of the utmost importance."

"What could be so important that you needed both of us here?" Lady Charlotte asked.

Greydon held his arms out. "I take it that you are familiar with Phineas' apartment."

Harriet scoffed. "Of course she is," she declared. "She was Phineas' favorite whore after all."

Lady Charlotte tensed. "I am not a whore."

"No, pray tell, what are you?" Harriet asked. "You sleep with another woman's husband. What did you get out of it?"

"He promised to marry me," Lady Charlotte replied.

"I hate to be the bearer of bad news, but he was never going to divorce me," Harriet said. "You were just a passing fancy."

"You are wrong."

"I can see why it was so easy for my husband to seduce you," Harriet mocked. "You are so incredibly naive that it is painful to even speak to you."

Lady Charlotte tilted her chin. "At least he wanted to spend time with me."

Harriet narrowed her eyes. "You know not what you are speaking of."

"Don't I?" Lady Charlotte asked. "He told me that you were a terrible excuse for a human being and he regretted marrying you."

"How dare you!" Harriet exclaimed. "You have no right to speak to me that way."

Greydon knew it was time to intercede before things got out of hand. "I just have a few questions and then you two can leave."

Harriet crossed her arms over her chest. "Why should I answer your questions?" she asked.

"Because if you don't, I will cut your allowance," Greydon replied.

"You wouldn't dare do something so despicable. You are too honorable," Harriet said.

Greydon walked over to the table where the tea service sat. "How long were you poisoning my brother with arsenic?"

Harriet blinked. "I beg your pardon?"

"It is a really simple question," he replied. "How long were you poisoning him?"

Dropping her arms to her sides, she said in a less than convincing voice, "I was not poisoning your brother."

Greydon picked up the teacup and held it up. "The interesting thing about arsenic is that it is odorless and tasteless but there are some physical signs on the body that show up." He placed the cup down onto the tray. "Did you know that?"

"Why would that matter to me?" Harriet asked.

"I had the good sense to speak to your housekeeper before I came here and she informed me that you insisted on serving Phineas his tea every morning," Greydon said. "Which would be the perfect time to poison him."

"I did no such thing!" Harriet asserted.

Greydon shrugged. "It doesn't quite matter though, now does it?" he asked. "The arsenic would have eventually killed him, but he was killed by a knife into the chest."

"Then why does it matter?" Harriet asked.

"I can't help but wonder if the arsenic wasn't working as quickly as you were hoping for and you decided to take matters into your own hands," Greydon said.

Harriet pressed her lips together. "That is preposterous! Besides, I haven't even been to this apartment before."

"I think we both know that isn't true. I have someone willing to testify that they saw you exit the building on the morning of the murder."

"He would be lying," Harriet declared.

Greydon gave her a knowing look. "You didn't want that divorce and I suspect that Phineas had no intention of dropping the matter. When Phineas got an idea in his head, he could never quite seem to think about anything else."

"I knew I just had to wait out his whore," Harriet said with a snide glance at Lady Charlotte. "It was only a matter of time before he would lose interest and move on to another one."

Lady Charlotte stomped her foot. "Phineas loved me!" she stated.

"Phineas only loved himself," Harriet responded. "He was incapable of loving another."

"You are wrong," Lady Charlotte said.

Harriet turned towards Lady Charlotte. "He told me that you were pregnant and he was ecstatic. But when you lost the baby, I knew he would move on from you, without another thought."

Lady Charlotte brought a hand to her stomach. "He told you that?"

"He told me all about you," Harriet replied. "Nothing brought him more joy than hurting me."

Greydon spoke up. "When did you tell Phineas that you lost the baby?"

Lady Charlotte lowered her gaze. "A few days before he was murdered," she admitted. "He started growing distant after that, but it was only because he was trying to sort out his emotions."

"Phineas didn't care about you," Harriet said. "He never did. He only pretended to do so to get you into bed."

Lady Charlotte's jaw clenched. "At least I didn't poison him."

Harriet tossed her hands up in the air. "Fine. I will admit that I added a little arsenic to his tea every morning, but it doesn't matter. I didn't kill him. Lady Eugenie did."

"Then why did you come to his apartment the morning of his murder?" Greydon asked.

With hesitation in her voice, Harriet replied, "He didn't come home that night and I needed to speak to him about the divorce."

Greydon nodded. "Was Lady Charlotte here when you arrived?"

Harriet glanced at Lady Charlotte before she replied, "She was not. Phineas was alone."

"Interesting," Greydon muttered. "My brother was not one to be discreet with his indiscretions. So it makes me wonder if you are telling the truth."

"Why would I lie about such a thing?" Harriet asked.

Greydon gave her a pointed look. "You have been lying this entire time. Why should I believe anything you say?"

"My mind is just a little muddled with the facts, considering my husband just died," Harriet said.

"You wanted your husband dead," Greydon pressed. "You knew the only way to end the divorce proceedings was to kill him."

Harriet's face grew hard. "You are right, but I didn't kill him."

"I know," Greydon said. "Lady Charlotte did."

Lady Charlotte's mouth dropped. "How could you even suggest such a thing?"

"I figured it out when I realized that no one saw Lady Charlotte leave the morning of the murder, leaving me to believe you were here when Harriet arrived and you heard them argue," Greydon replied. "If I had to guess, I would say that Phineas said some rather hurtful things about you."

Tears came into Lady Charlotte's eyes. "Phineas told Harriet that he was done with me and that I meant nothing to him."

"I believe that," Greydon said. "It made you angry enough to kill him."

Lady Charlotte shook her head vehemently. "No, I didn't kill him. I loved him!"

"You waited until he got back into bed and then you shoved a knife into his heart," Greydon said, his voice rising. "After you killed him, you washed off your hands in the water basin and cleaned yourself up."

Greydon continued. "That is why your sister confessed to the murder because she knew you killed Phineas."

Lady Charlotte's face grew pale. "I... uh..." Her voice

stopped and her panicked eyes started darting towards Harriet.

"But you didn't act alone, did you?" Greydon turned his attention to Harriet. "You wanted Phineas dead... no, you needed him dead. So you convinced Lady Charlotte to kill your husband."

"That is preposterous!" Harriet declared.

"You waited until Lady Charlotte shoved a dagger into his chest before you returned to your coach."

"Why would I do such a thing?" Harriet asked, her breathing becoming labored.

"Because you needed to burn those divorce papers in the hearth," Greydon replied. "You wanted to burn all the evidence of what Phineas intended to do."

Harriet lifted her brow. "Your accusation is baseless and ludicrous. I had nothing to do with Phineas' murder."

"That is what you wanted everyone to believe," he said. "You just wanted to play the part of the grieving widow, but that is far from true."

Harriet huffed. "I had no choice in marrying Phineas and he made my life miserable. Why would I mourn his loss? I am glad that he is dead, but I did not kill him."

"You may not have shoved the knife into his chest, but you are just as guilty as Lady Charlotte," Greydon stated. "You manipulated her into doing your will."

As Harriet walked over to the door, she said, "I am done with this interrogation. I am leaving."

"By all means, but you will be arrested once you step outside of that door," Greydon shared. He hoped that Harriet didn't call his bluff because no one was outside to stop her from leaving.

Harriet stopped and turned around to face him. "You have no proof. Furthermore, Lady Eugenie was found over Phineas' body and she confessed to his murder. It is over."

"Is it?" Greydon asked. "If I was able to piece this together, don't you think Sir David will as well?"

"Sir David only cares that he caught the killer," Harriet responded.

"Not when I tell him my suspicions. I am confident that he will open the case again."

Lady Charlotte reached into the reticle that was around her wrist and pulled out a muff pistol. "You think you are so smart," she said as she pointed the pistol at him. "But if you die, no one else will discover the truth."

Harriet turned towards Lady Charlotte. "What are you doing?" she asked. "He has no proof. He is just making this up as he goes along."

"No, he knows too much," Lady Charlotte protested. "We can't let him leave."

"If you shoot me, people will hear the pistol discharging and they will come to investigate," Greydon said.

"We will hide in the wall, just as I did when Harriet arrived unexpectedly." Lady Charlotte walked over to a cabinet along the far wall and pulled it open, revealing a hidden compartment. "After I killed Phineas, I waited in here until everyone cleared out."

"That is why no one saw you leave that day," Greydon mused.

"It was," Lady Charlotte confirmed.

With a flick of her wrist, Harriet said, "Just shoot him so we can be done with this."

Greydon put his hands up. "I wouldn't kill me just yet."

"And why is that?" Lady Charlotte asked in an uninterested tone.

"Because I am not alone," Greydon replied.

Lady Charlotte's eyes scanned the apartment. "I see no one else."

"They are hiding."

Harriet stepped closer to Lady Charlotte and seethed, "He is clearly lying. Shoot him."

Lady Charlotte took aim at him, her eyes showing no sign of hesitation. "I'm sorry it had to be this way, but you couldn't leave well enough alone."

"Before you shoot me," Greydon started, "why did you kill Phineas?"

"After everything I did for him, all that I gave up for him, he just cast me aside after I lost the baby. He used me and I refused to let him get away with it," Lady Charlotte said. "When Harriet approached me about getting my revenge, I knew I had no choice. Phineas deserved to die. Just as you do."

Greydon still had a question that remained unanswered. "Where did you get the dirk dagger?" he asked.

"It was my father's," Lady Charlotte replied.

Greydon held her gaze, unflinchingly. It all made sense now. "Eugenie must have recognized the dagger and knew you killed Phineas," he said. "Are you truly that cruel to let your sister hang for your crime?"

Lady Charlotte's eyes sparked with anger. "She should have minded her own business," she grumbled. "It was her own fault that she arrived when she did."

"She was trying to protect you."

"No, she was trying to control me," Lady Charlotte declared. "But I know my mind."

"Do you?" Greydon questioned. "Lady Rushcliffe used you, and you have failed to see it."

"That is not true," Lady Charlotte responded. "We both wanted your brother dead."

Harriet interjected, "I have had enough of Lord Rushcliffe." She turned towards Lady Charlotte. "Shoot him."

Lady Charlotte nodded. "My pleasure."

As she pulled the trigger, the sound of multiple pistols discharging could be heard before he felt a searing pain in his chest.

With Marigold in her lap, Enid sat in an upholstered armchair as she read a book. She had just turned to the last page when Malcolm stormed into the room, his eyes frantic.

"Here you are," he said. "I have been looking for you everywhere."

Hearing the panic in his voice, she asked, "What is wrong?"

Malcolm hesitated before revealing, "Greydon has been shot."

Enid could feel the blood drain from her face. "Is he dead?"

"No, but I just received word from Roswell," he replied. "The doctor is tending to Greydon now at his townhouse."

Rising, Enid said, "I must go to him."

"I assumed as much and the coach is waiting out front," Malcolm responded. "I will escort you for propriety's sake."

As she handed off Marigold to the nursemaid, she stated, "I care little about propriety right now."

"I know, but please appease me."

Enid knew her brother was just trying to help her but she cared about little else right now. She needed to ensure that Greydon was all right. She couldn't even stomach the thought that he wasn't. She didn't want to imagine a world where Greydon wasn't in it. He meant so much to her that a life without him wasn't a life worth living.

She brushed past her brother and headed towards the main door. The butler opened the door and she stepped into the waiting coach. Once Malcolm sat across from her, the footman closed the door and the coach jerked forward.

It wasn't far to Greydon's townhouse but every moment that went by was excruciating. Never had she known such fear. Everything seemed so inconsequential compared to this.

Malcolm's voice broke through the silence. "It will be all right."

Enid nodded slowly, knowing her brother was just trying to provide comfort in his own way. But nothing would be all right if Greydon died.

What a fool she had been. She thought she was protecting herself by keeping him at arm's length, but she should have kept him close. That is where she wanted him to be from now on.

The coach came to a stop in front of Greydon's townhouse and Malcolm opened the door, not bothering to wait for the footman. He stepped out onto the pavement and extended his hand to assist her out of the coach.

With quick steps, they approached the townhouse and Malcolm pounded on the door.

The door promptly opened and the butler asked, "How may I help you?"

Malcolm opened his mouth to speak but Enid didn't have time for pleasantries. "Where is he?" she asked.

"Where is 'who', Miss?" the butler asked.

"Lord Rushcliffe," she replied. "I need to see him at once."

The butler must have sensed her urgency because he opened the door wide. "Do come in," he encouraged.

After she stepped inside, she heard loud laughter coming from a room off the entryway. Who was laughing at a time like this, she wondered.

The sound of Greydon's voice drifted out of the room and she rushed towards it. She knew she was being rude to not wait for an introduction but she didn't care. Nothing else mattered to her but seeing Greydon.

She stepped into the room and saw Greydon sitting down on the settee, a smile on his face. He was conversing with Lord Roswell, Mr. Westcott and Mr. Moore.

"Greydon," she said.

Greydon turned towards her and surprise registered on his face. He quickly rose and walked over to her. "What are you doing here?" he asked.

"I heard you were shot," Enid replied.

"I was, but the doctor removed the bullet and stitched me up," Greydon said.

Now that Enid was standing in front of Greydon, knowing that he was all right, her emotions rushed to the surface. Tears filled her eyes as she admitted, "I was so scared."

Greydon moved to stand in front of her. "It is going to take more than a bullet to stop me," he teased.

"You shouldn't joke at a time like this," she chided.

"I'm sorry, but other than a sore shoulder, I will be fine."

Tears spilled over and started running down her cheeks. "I am so relieved to hear that," she said.

Malcolm stepped closer and interjected, "We are going to give you a minute to speak privately, but I will be in the entry hall if you need me."

Enid barely acknowledged her brother's words since she was so focused on Greydon. She had so much she needed to tell him, and she knew it was time. He completed her in a way that she'd never thought possible.

Once her brother and Greydon's friends left the room, Greydon opened his arms up and she stepped into them. She laid her head against his chest and his heartbeat soothed her soul. He was her future; she was sure of it.

After a long moment, Greydon released her but remained close. For that, she was most grateful. "I am happy that you are here with me."

"I am, too," Enid said. "I have never known such a fear as the thought of losing you."

Greydon's eyes held compassion. "You will never lose me, Enid. You must know that."

"What if you are shot again?"

"That is highly unlikely because I no longer work as a Bow

Street Runner," Greydon replied. "I am hanging up my uniform."

"Is that what you want to do?"

"It is," he replied. "I need to start helping my father run our estate and ensuring it remains profitable."

Enid bobbed her head. "I think that is wise."

"But I do have a problem," he said.

"What is that?"

Greydon reached for her gloved hand and replied, "I find that I am still wifeless."

"That is a problem," she agreed.

"It is, and I am hoping you will reconsider my offer of becoming my wife," Greydon said, his eyes searching hers. "I love you, and I always will."

Enid wanted to throw her arms around him and say yes, but there were a few things that needed to be said between them.

"I love you, too, but I want you to be sure," she said. "I don't want you to wake up one day and regret marrying me."

"That is impossible. I started falling in love with you from the moment I saw you, and I care little about my social standing."

"You say that now, but—"

He leaned forward and pressed his lips to hers. As he leaned back, he said, "That is my new favorite way to silence you."

"I have no complaints," she said.

Greydon took his hand and cupped her right cheek. "I am nothing special, of this I am sure, but my love for you is correct and perfect. I want all of you, forever, every day. You and me... every day."

"If you are sure," she said.

"I have never been so sure of anything in my life."

Knowing she couldn't deny him any longer, she said, "Then yes, I will marry you. A hundred thousand times, yes."

Greydon's face broke out into a boyish grin. "Had I known getting shot would have brought us together, I would have gotten shot much sooner."

Enid realized that she didn't even know the circumstances about how he was shot. She had been so distracted by making sure that Greydon was all right. "How did you manage to get shot?"

"Lady Charlotte shot me," he replied, "but only after she confessed to Phineas' murder."

"She killed him?"

Greydon nodded. "Yes, but Harriet played a hand in his murder, too. She manipulated Lady Charlotte into doing it."

"Please say they aren't going to get away with murder."

Greydon sobered. "Unfortunately, Lady Charlotte was killed after she shot me, but Harriet is at Newgate. She was arrested for attempted murder since she had been poisoning Phineas with arsenic," he revealed. "Lord Roswell, Mr. Moore and Mr. Westcott were hiding in Phineas' apartment and over-heard their confessions. They came out of hiding just as Lady Charlotte pointed her pistol at me and they all discharged their weapons at her."

"Does this mean Lady Eugenie will be released soon?"

"Yes, Sir David has to process the paperwork, which is something that he is not thrilled about, but he couldn't justify keeping Lady Eugenie in Newgate any longer."

Enid smiled. "Thank you for what you did for Lady Eugenie."

"I am pleased for Lady Eugenie, but this started all because of you and your belief in your friend," Greydon said. "If you hadn't pushed for me to investigate this case, the wrong person would have been punished for Phineas' murder."

"Well, I thank you for believing in me."

Greydon leaned closer to her until their faces were just inches apart. "No matter what happens to us in the future, every day we are together is the greatest day of my life. I will always love you."

Enid could feel his warm breath on her lips and she could stand it no longer. She went to her tiptoes and kissed him. His lips parted and he kissed her back, mouth warm and firm against hers. It was a moment that she never wanted to end. For it felt as if her soul had just taken its first breath.

A deep clearing of a throat came from next to them and they jumped apart.

Malcolm was standing a short distance back with a disapproving look on his face. "I said you two could talk, not kiss."

"Do not be such a prude, Brother," Enid chided.

Her brother frowned. "Dare I hope that you two are engaged or do I need to challenge Greydon to a duel... again?"

Enid exchanged a look with Greydon before saying, "We are to be married."

Malcolm's expression slipped slightly. "That is a relief. I didn't really want a reason to shoot Greydon."

Greydon chuckled. "I was not worried since I have seen you shoot."

"When is to be the wedding?" Malcolm asked. "Please say that you are not eloping again."

Enid shook her head. "I want to do it right this time and post the banns, assuming Greydon has no objections."

"Just tell me when and where and I will be there, my love," Greydon said.

Enid laughed. "I do hope you will always be this agreeable in our marriage."

"I wouldn't count on it," he joked.

Malcolm gestured towards the doorway. "Shall we depart and tell our parents the good news?" he asked. "I have no doubt they will be elated."

"I suppose that would be for the best," Enid acknowledged.

Greydon reached for her hand. "I shall call upon you later today."

"Promise?" Enid asked.

"Nothing will be able to stop me."

Enid stepped closer to Greydon and pressed her lips against his.

"Enid!" Malcolm shouted. "Show some restraint."

She broke the kiss and gave her brother an unrepentant smile. "I'm afraid I am incapable of doing so."

Malcolm sighed. "This is going to be a long three weeks, isn't it?"

As Enid met Greydon's amused gaze, she finally found a world where she belonged. She was home. With him. Always.

Epilogue

One month later...

With quick steps, Enid walked down the hall towards the nursery. She was dressed in a silver ballgown with a net overlay and her hair was neatly coiffed. She was ready for the ball, but she seemed to have misplaced her husband. If they didn't hurry, they would be late to the ball that was being held in their honor.

She stopped outside of the nursery door and listened. No noise was coming from within. Perhaps Greydon wasn't in there. But where else could he be?

Enid slowly turned the handle and opened the door. She saw Greydon had fallen asleep in the rocking chair with Marigold in his arms. It was a tender memory that she knew she would treasure, but she had to wake Greydon up.

She placed a hand on his sleeve and his eyes opened. "I fell asleep again," he whispered.

"We must hurry or we will be late for the ball," she said, matching his low tone.

Greydon nodded his understanding before he rose with

Marigold in his arms. He gently placed the sleeping child in her bed.

They exited the nursery and Greydon closed the door behind him. "I did not mean to fall asleep."

Enid smiled. "You never do," she replied as they started walking down the hall. "You spoil Marigold by rocking her to sleep."

"She deserves to be spoiled, especially since we will be leaving on our wedding tour tomorrow."

Her smile dimmed. "I do hope she will be all right."

"I have no doubt she will be spoiled terribly by her grandparents," Greydon said.

"You are right, of course, but Marigold and I have never been apart."

Greydon reached for her hand and said in a flirtatious tone, "I promise that we will find ways to occupy ourselves."

"You are incorrigible," she chided lightly.

They descended the stairs and headed towards the ballroom. They had just arrived at the doors when her mother's exasperated voice came from behind them.

"There you two are," she said, coming to a stop in front of them. "The whole townhouse has been in a frenzy as they searched for you two."

"Greydon fell asleep in the nursery again," Enid revealed.

"I should have suspected," her mother said, "but it is nearly time for you two to have your first dance."

"We are ready," Enid assured her.

Her mother bobbed her head in approval. "Good," she said. "Wait here, and do not move until those doors open."

After her mother disappeared into the ballroom, Greydon turned to face her and perused the length of her. His eyes shone with approval. "You are looking especially lovely this evening, my love."

"You are looking quite dapper yourself."

Greydon leaned forward and kissed her. As he leaned back, he said, "You deserve to be kissed, and often."

"I agree, wholeheartedly." She paused. "Thank you for agreeing to stay at my parents' townhouse until after we return from our wedding tour."

"You do not need to thank me. It is what is best for Marigold."

"It is, but I know it can't be easy on you."

Greydon chuckled. "Just wait until you live with my father," he joked. "He wasn't exactly keen on our marriage."

"But he has never made me feel unwelcome."

"I am glad to hear that because I threatened to ride far away with you and never come back if he was rude to you," he said.

Enid could hear them being announced in the ballroom and the footmen promptly opened the doors.

Greydon offered his arm. "Are you ready for this?"

"I am," she replied as she accepted his arm.

As he led her into the center of the ballroom, Enid's eyes roamed over all the guests that were in attendance. She had never seen the ballroom so full and people were craning their necks to get a good look at them. No one was glaring at them, but they all appeared to be happy to be there.

"This is a *crush*," Enid said under her breath.

"It is," Greydon agreed. "Your mother mentioned that everyone had accepted their invitations. I just hadn't realized she had invited so many people."

"Neither did I."

Greydon gave her an amused look. "You seem disappointed."

"I just find the *ton* to be entirely too fickle," Enid remarked. "After word got out that you exonerated Lady Eugenie and you brought the murderers to justice, you have been London's golden boy."

"Yes, but everyone knows that you played a part in that, as well."

"I am not used to people looking at me without scorn in their eyes," Enid admitted.

"Well, you best get used to it," Greydon encouraged. "The *ton* is fascinated with you and what you helped accomplish."

They came to a stop in the center of the room and the orchestra started up. Greydon placed his hand on her waist and brought their hands up. Once they started dancing the waltz, Enid felt herself relax in her husband's arms.

This past week had been a dream. She never thought she could be so happy. Quite frankly, she never thought she deserved to be this happy. But Greydon had changed her life, for the better. She never wanted to go back to a life without him in it.

The music came to an end and Greydon dropped his arms. "Now is the part that I dread," he grumbled.

"Which is?"

"Engaging in dull conversation," Greydon said.

"I promise that you will survive."

"Just barely."

"You poor lord. What a burden you must bear," she joked.

"Finally, someone recognizes my plight."

Enid laughed. "Perhaps you can lead us to someone that won't be as dull," she said as she placed her hand on his sleeve.

"My pleasure."

They had just exited the dance floor when she saw Lady Esther standing by the table with a flute of champagne in her hand. She looked utterly miserable.

Enid slipped her hand off Greydon's arm and said, "Excuse me for a moment."

"You are leaving me?" he asked.

"I need to go speak to Lady Esther," she said, glancing at her friend.

Greydon followed her gaze and watched Esther for a moment. "She doesn't appear happy, does she?"

"No, she doesn't," Enid agreed.

"You should go to her, but I will remain close."

Enid walked over to her friend and Esther didn't seem to notice her approach. "Esther," she said.

Esther gasped as she placed a hand on her chest. "My apologies. I'm afraid I was woolgathering."

"Whatever is the matter?"

"Nothing," Esther attempted.

Enid gave her friend a knowing look. "Something is bothering you."

Esther winced as she admitted, "My stepmother wants to marry me off to Lord Warley. They have already begun the negotiations."

"But Lord Warley is—"

"So old," Esther interjected. "He is older than my father."

"What are you going to do?"

Esther sighed. "I don't know, but I can't marry Lord Warley."

"You can always refuse to marry him."

"If I do so, I am ruined. No one will want me."

"There are worse things than being ruined."

"I am beginning to believe that," Esther said before taking a sip of her champagne. "I just never thought I would be placed in this situation. I had hoped that I would be able to marry for love."

Enid met Greydon's gaze from a short distance away and said, "It is a wonderful thing to marry the man of your dreams."

"You are most fortunate," Esther acknowledged.

"That I am," Enid agreed.

Esther let out an unladylike groan. "My stepmother is looking for me. If you will excuse me, I need to hide from her," she said before disappearing into the crowd.

In the next moment, Greydon came to stand next to Enid. "Is everything all right?"

"Esther's stepmother is forcing her into an arranged marriage," she revealed.

"That is awful, but not uncommon in our circles."

"I know, but I wish there was a way to help her."

Greydon reached for her hand and said, "Perhaps a walk through the gardens will give you an idea."

"You want us to leave our guests?" The thought alarmed and excited her.

"Just for a moment."

Enid knew she couldn't deny Greydon his simple request, not after all the concessions he had made for the ball. "But we must hurry."

As they walked onto the veranda, Greydon asked, "Are you happy?"

"Blissfully so."

"I am happy to hear that," Greydon said, turning to face her. "I never thought I could be so content."

"That pleases me to hear."

Greydon leaned closer and whispered against her lips, "I love you, my viscountess."

With her heart pounding, she tried to think of the words to express her utter joy and just how much she was in love with him. But his kiss banished the need for words, and she reveled in being in his arms, knowing that all her dreams had finally come true.

The End

Coming soon...

Feigning an attachment was the easy part, but falling in love was not part of the plan.

Lady Esther Harrington finds herself in a terrible predicament when she is being forced into an arranged marriage. Out of options- and hope- she tries to escape and meets a man that is sympathetic to her plight. In desperation, they hatch a plan to solve her problem. They will form an attachment with one another for the Season, knowing it comes at a great risk to them both.

Mr. Samuel Moore never anticipated the heartache that would come when he saw his long-lost love on the arm of another. That is the only thing that could explain why he agreed to pretend to pursue Lady Esther, but he quickly realizes that she is the perfect distraction.

As Esther and Samuel's friendship takes hold, they are drawn to one another and the lines between what is pretend and what is real begin to blur. Their plan quickly spirals out of control, but neither one of them expected to fall in love. With so much at stake, can they trust their hearts to know what is truly best for them?

About the Author

Laura Beers is an award-winning author. She attended Brigham Young University, earning a Bachelor of Science degree in Construction Management. She can't sing, doesn't dance and loves naps.

Laura lives in Utah with her husband, three kids, and her dysfunctional dog. When not writing regency romance, she loves waterskiing, hiking, and drinking Dr Pepper.

You can connect with Laura on Facebook, Instagram, or on her site at www.authorlaurabeers.com.

Printed in the USA
CPSIA information can be obtained
at www.ICGtesting.com
LVHW012007260124
769864LV00004B/925